Praise for *Yesterday's Weather:*

"[Enright's] sentences have rhythm and snap. . . . Enright is getting better and better. . . . The best pieces in this collection are as intense and evocative as poems. They should be savored like poems, slowly, a few at a time." —*San Francisco Chronicle*

"Many of these thirty-one stories are like one-person plays. . . . It's good to have so many stories in one collection. There's room for voices to echo, ghosts to flit in the corners and characters to change shapes and roles." —*Los Angeles Times*

"Eulogizing the illustrious James Joyce at his funeral in 1941, a British dignitary noted that Ireland would continue to enjoy lasting revenge over England by producing literary masterpieces. Anne Enright joins a long line of Irish writers who prove that prediction accurate." —*Star Tribune* (Minneapolis)

"Enright, who does much well, is at her best at exploring the human condition, focusing on small moments to illustrate larger complications. . . . And Enright has a gift for the unexpected bon mot, summarizing a character and situation with enviable brevity." —*The Denver Post*

"A collection of thirty-one little gems . . . Enright observes and records the messiness of life in minute detail. She understands how we fight against the messiness and then miss it when it is gone." —*The Plain Dealer*

"Dazzling triumphs of love . . . breathtaking detail . . . Enright has been rightfully praised for her imaginative and stylistic powers. . . . one of the most distinctive and necessary authors writing today." —*Library Journal* (starred review)

"A remarkable, stirring collection that is often dizzyingly good. . . . Enright is a singular talent, and has been since the beginning of her career. . . . Haunting moments of beauty and grace in lives of turmoil and emotional uncertainty—this is the fundamental nature of human life itself, rarely chronicled quite so well or so honestly." —*The Vancouver Sun*

"[Enright's] deft sentences often contain a simplicity that is bonded by an amalgamation of irony, honesty, and humor. In many respects, she is a terrific method actor, climbing under the skins of characters from all walks of life and all sets of circumstance, and bringing them voice."   —*The Providence Journal*

"Thrilling . . . Enright is a master of the short story . . . a writer at the top of her craft."   —*The Chronicle Herald* (Canada)

"As a writer of short stories, [Enright] always found her stride. . . . These candid tales of compromised marriages and mid-life miscarriages . . . leap from the page. As always her style is intimate, humorous, and to the point."   —*The Independent* (UK)

"Shockingly beautiful and painfully funny."   —*The Observer* (UK)

"Beguiling . . . We are privy to the innermost thoughts and, at times, the darkest dreams of middle-class Irish people of all ages, as they struggle with infidelity, guilt, resignation, illness, and death."
—*Bookforum*

"When the Irish writer Anne Enright is at her best . . . she yanks her readers almost violently into a story. . . . Only her countryman John McGahern could accomplish so much so briefly."
—*The Virginia Quarterly Review*

"Mesmerizing language . . . a beguiling collection . . . these stories spill over with warmth, wisdom, earthiness and an exceptional vision. Another tour de force from a writer whose voice and perspective mark her as one of the cherishable talents of our era."
—*Kirkus Reviews* (starred review)

"A fascinating slide show of one very gifted writer's development. . . . The stories in *Yesterday's Weather* . . . contain whole worlds inhabited by complex, contradictory characters. . . . sensuous, energetic, in-your-face prose that retains the intelligence and gleam of the British literary tradition."   —*The Boston Globe*

"Anne Enright is a fantastic novelist. . . . [her stories] are all jam-packed with insights; they are saucy, hard-edged, gritty, provoking and full of unexpected gusts of vulnerability and intimacy. . . . A blend of tart wit, cadence, and vigorous scrutiny . . . Enright [is] a pleasure to read."   —*Globe and Mail* (Canada)

"A powerful writer going free-range and operating outside the demands of a novel. . . . She is a confident writer, letting stories unfold at their own speed. . . . "Caravan" . . . is just the sort of cutting, generous, surprising story that Raymond Carver might have written, had he been an Irishwoman."   —*The Washington Post*

"Enright's talent lies in her ability to tweak an ordinary situation and create something that is at once unique and universal."
—*Publishers Weekly*

"Nervy, unsparing . . . Her depiction of the humdrum satisfactions of married life, the tensions in old friendships, the childhood rivalry that will not die, are pitch-perfect . . . Enright completely inhabits these characters."   —*O, the Oprah Magazine*

"We're all the richer for [*Yesterday's Weather*]. . . . Enright [has a] mastery of the opening sentence."   —*The Gazette* (Montreal)

"Perfect pitch . . . When she ventures into the grungier side of life, Enright can even sound like Raymond Carver . . . [though] Enright feels closer to Joyce than Carver."   —*America Magazine*

"Particularly impressive is Enright's ability to inhabit the fug of repetitive tasks, and fleeting moments of clarity, rage, and ambivalence that accompany the roles of mother, wife, and daughter. She excels at capturing instances of both pure love and unadulterated irritation, often within one sentence."   —*The Toronto Star*

Yesterday's Weather

ANNE ENRIGHT

Grove Press
New York

For Theo and Eileen Dombrowski

These stories first appeared in *First Fictions: Introduction 10*, published in 1989 by Faber and Faber, *The Portable Virgin*, published in 1991 by Secker & Warburg, and *Taking Pictures*, published in 2008 by Jonathan Cape

Printed in the United States of America

ISBN-13: 978-0-8021-4432-4

Grove Press
an imprint of Grove/Atlantic, Inc.
841 Broadway
New York, NY 10003

Distributed by Publishers Group West

www.groveatlantic.com

09 10 11 12   10 9 8 7 6 5 4 3 2 1

CONTENTS

INTRODUCTION

This collection brings together stories written over the course of nineteen years. It includes all of *Taking Pictures* (Cape 2008), much of *The Portable Virgin* (Secker 1991), and two stories from Faber's *First Fictions: Introduction 10,* which was my first outing into print in 1989.

The stories are presented here in reverse chronological order, partly, it has to be said, for the comic effect. I may be the only one who is laughing, but it is a great and private joke to see myself getting younger – shedding pounds and wrinkles, gaining in innocence and affectation – as the pages turn. The stories have been very lightly edited, not because I did not want to rewrite them, but because I found that I could not. It is impossible to inhabit a former self. You can not be the writer you were in 1989, nor, in a funny way, would you want to be. Still, there is much to regret – the fact that the creative moment is not one that can be repeated, is both a wonderful and a melancholy one. The path your words make as you herd them across the page is the only viable route, after all.

Working on the stories, I was surprised by the pity I felt for my younger self – so assured and so miserable at the same time. The best kind of misery, of course – spiky, artistic, fullhearted – but still, it does make you blunder around a bit.

The irony is that so much of my early work is spent discussing the woes of middle age. I got most of them wrong. I didn't imagine the many insults to your vanity that age brings, nor could I foresee the sense of urgency you get as the years go by, like typing faster before you hit the end of the page. No, I thought the most terrible thing about middle age would be marriage, in all its loneliness and hypocrisy. And I suppose marriage can be both of these things, but I have also discovered that these kinds of emotion are beside the point: the whole business has been been one of unexpected happiness, for me. Worst of all, the women in my early stories have children and say that the experience has not changed them. How wrong can you be?

It is interesting, but only in a sociological way, to see the sympathy two of my narrators have for men who have just lost their virginity. It is odd, but only to me, to read of the bitterness that exists between female friends, when my own girlfriends are so generous and important to me. These stories are not written by the person who has lived my life and made the best of it, they are written by people I might have been but decided against. They are written by women who take a different turn in the road. They are the shed skins of the snake.

None of this matters – my life, and how it is reflected or distorted in the stories here. I discovered, when I started to look at them again, that I had forgotten the content of some of these pieces. What I remembered, with great clarity, was their shape. I knew whereabouts on the page the thing shifted; I remembered the moment it stumbled or lurched toward an ending. I could turn it around in my head – almost in three dimensions. The stories played like music for me; the way music can give you a sense of space.

What I seem to be saying – a little to my own surprise – is that the person may change, but the writer endures. The writer wants a thing to be well made, because a well-made thing is a gift. This gift is presented not just to the reader, but also to the future – in my case, to an old woman called Anne Enright, who will read this too, with a bit of luck, and laugh.

A. E.
Bray, 2008

YESTERDAY'S WEATHER

Until the Girl Died

The girl died.

Well, what was that to me? The girl died. And it was nothing to do with us, with either of us. She died the stupid way
that people do – in a car crash, in Italy. Where, presumably,
she was driving on the wrong side of the road.

Silly twit.

If the girl had not died then she would not have mattered
in the slightest. She would have been a lapse; my husband is
prone to lapses – less often of late, but yes, once every couple
of years he does lapse, after the office party say, or travelling
on business. I don't think he visits prostitutes – I mean, some
men do, some men must. Or quite a lot of men must, actually
– but my husband doesn't. And I know, I know, I would say
that, but . . .

I've thought about this a lot over the years; things catch my
eye in articles, in magazines. I have wondered, What makes
them go and what makes them stay, what do they want, men?
It's the great mystery, isn't it? What men 'want.' And the
damage they might do to get it.

The things you read in the papers.

'Oh, sure they're all the same.' Isn't that what your mother
used to say? 'They're all the same.'

But they're not. They have their reasons and they have their
limits. They have hearts, too. And I can say, without a shadow
of a doubt, that my husband is not the kind of man to buy sex
in the street. He likes intimacy. That is what he craves. My
husband is the kind of man who will always look you in the
eye. He loves women – even older ones. He loves to talk to
them, and make them feel good, and he loves to kiss them, and
be a little dangerous; he loves the melancholy of all that, it
makes him feel so young. And he also loves me.

He is not a bastard, that is what I am saying. I am saying that he is a fantastic man. My husband is a fantastic man. And until the girl died, beetling along in her little Renault Clio on the wrong side of a road in Tuscany, until the girl died, that was enough for me. To be married to a fantastic man who loved me, and was prone, once in a long while, to a little lapse and a lot of Catholic guilt about it. Oh, the bloody bunch of flowers and the new coat in Richard Alan's sale. Isn't it worth it? I used to say. Isn't it bloody worth it for a trip to Brown Thomas's and a long weekend with the kids, all of us together in Ballybunion, walking the winter beach, a couple of bottles of wine and more conjugal antics than is decent at our age, with my wonderful husband, home again after his little lapse; some overambitious young one who will Shortly. Be. Fired. Thank you darling and, no, I know you will never do it again.

But actually I hated it. It was like living on a page of some horrible Sunday newspaper. Horrible people. Horrible people with their horrible sex lives and their horrible money.

No.

He works hard, my husband. And I have always been a great asset to him. And we are ordinary people. And I am proud of that too.

Ke . . . I can't say his name. Isn't that funny?

It is quite an ordinary name, I say it fifteen times a day. Mind you, he never calls me anything back. Isn't that the way of it? What do men call their wives. 'Em . . .' Like every woman on the planet was christened Emily.

'Em . . . is that shirt clean?'

The girl was called – listen to this – Samantha.

Not that I knew this at the time. Not that I knew anything at the time.

And she was only called 'Samantha' because she died. If it hadn't been for the car crash she would have been, and always remained, that young one in IT, or even that slapper over in IT. O'Connell Street might be full of slappers, but if one of them slaps off, pissed, in her mini skirt and high heels, and gets herself run over, then she's – what? – she's a fine young woman, who liked to wear white.

4

I'm sorry.

But.

The poor child, who thought it was a laugh to sleep with my husband – and it is a laugh, God knows I have laughed enough myself – the poor child, who thought it was a laugh to sleep with the father of my three children, did something worse than all that. She went and died on him too. She went and died on us all.

Of course, I didn't have a clue.

He came home – when I think about it, it must have been the day he'd heard the news – and he sat in the sofa, and for the first time since his mother's funeral, I saw him cry. The children saw him cry. I had no idea what he was crying for. I felt like calling an ambulance. Then I put two and two together and realised he must be lapsing again, he must be mid-lapse. And I panicked.

I know that. I did panic. And it's not like me. He lifted his head to speak to me and I said,

'I don't want to know.' That was all. 'I don't want to know.' And I said it really fast, like I was talking off the record, here. Like what was happening was not actually happening. Or he'd better make bloody sure it wasn't happening because I wasn't having the mess of it all over my beautiful, hard-won house. And he pushed his face around to clear away the tears – not hot tears, not outraged, grief-stricken tears, just that leaky, worn-out water you find on your face sometimes, when you are sick or defeated – he wiped the tears away and then he just sat.

My fantastic man.

The first time it happened, at a guess, was when the children were small. I was up to my tonsils in nappies and mayhem, falling asleep before my head hit the pillow, fat as a fool. Anyway. They feel 'excluded', fathers; isn't that what the articles say? They have the weight of the world on their shoulders, and after a while – I'm convinced of this – they start to resent you, maybe even to hate you. Then, one day, they love you madly again and you realise – slowly, you realise – that they have been up to something. They've had a fright. They've come running back home.

Which is nice, too. In a way.

Oh, what the hell.

The first time it happened, my father was in having some tests, actually, and I was far too busy to shout at my husband, or go through his pockets, or sniff at his clothes before I put them in the washing machine. I had more important things on my mind. In the end, everything went so well, Daddy didn't even have to have chemo – after which, I was too relieved to double back and start shouting at my husband, or sniffing at his clothes. It was over by then, and besides, I had learned something about myself. I'd learned that I was not that sort of woman – the sniffing sort, the type to rage and scream. And that was an odd kind of feeling, I must say. Because I grew up with the same dreams as every other girl, but when the chips were down . . . When the chips were down, I kept my head held high.

What was I supposed to do?

One part of me thought he deserved a holiday, to be honest; that if I had the chance I might take one myself. Another part of me thought, 'Someone must die.' I really thought I might kill someone for this. I might kill her. Or I might kill him. Or I might leave them to it and kill myself. Well, that's no use, is it? This stupidity, this *incontinence* of my husband's was too small to bother about. And it was too large to leave us all standing; all still alive.

But maybe it was in my head, from that time. In both our heads. The idea that someone must die.

So what are we looking at? Two or three more, over the course of the years? A scattering of 'accidents', and then, one day, this, whatever it is. A man crying on the sofa. Grief.

It was half past five. The children were watching telly before tea. I cleared them out of there – my daughter, the apple of her father's eye, welling up a bit herself at the tragic look of him, with his coat thrown beside him and his briefcase still in the other hand.

Kids bury that sort of stuff very deep. I thought it would be better if she talked about it, but when I asked her, a week later, about her father crying on the sofa she just looked at me, like I had landed in from outer space.

'What sofa?' she said. 'Which sofa?'

That's Shauna for you, who is nine. There's no point talking to her brothers about it, they've already gone into the grunting phase.

And then I think, Why not? Why not talk to your sons about things? Why not rear men who can speak?

Because there's my husband, collapsed against the oatmeal-coloured linen mix, staring mortality in the face. And what else? His own smallness. Looking as though he had killed her himself, although he had not killed her, he had not even loved her. Thinking (as I imagine) about some beautiful part of her, mangled by the door or bonnet, and turning already to clay.

And there is no one he can talk to about this. No one at all.

Men don't have friends like that – guys you might ring and say, 'Take him out for a drink. Talk it over. Sort him out.' No. The only friend he has is me.

And he can't tell me, because I really do not want to know.

All this in hindsight, of course. At the time, I looked at him and I thought that our marriage was finished, or that he was finished. I was looking at extended sick leave and then what? My husband crying on the sofa was forty-nine years old. And if you think forty-nine is a tough station, try fifty-five.

I was looking at a long future with a man who had forgotten what he was for.

So when he pushes the tears off his face with his hand, and when he lifts his face to tell me all about it, there is only one thing I can say to him, and that is:

'I don't want to know.'

How did we get through the next week? Normally, at a guess. That's how we did it. We got through the week in a completely normal way. While I waited for some hint or clue. The back page of the paper that he stares at too hard and too long. And then, on Tuesday morning, I come in from the school run and he's still there, in his dark suit, putting on his funeral tie.

'Who's dead?'

'Some girl,' he says.

'What girl? Someone's daughter?' He doesn't answer. He brushes his shoulders off in the mirror.

He says, 'We only get them trained and they're gone.'

'Well, I'm sure she didn't mean to.'

Round and round goes the funeral tie, down through the knot. Pull it tight, ease it a little loose again. Kiss the wife goodbye.

'You don't want me to show?' I say, because I am raging now. I know what has happened, now. I want to twist the knife.

'No,' he says. 'She was only in the door.'

'You sure?'

'No, no.' Pick up your briefcase, pull your phone off the charger, check for your keys.

'Home for tea?' I say.

'What is it?'

'I thought I'd grill a bit of salmon.'

Forget where your good coat is kept, open one door of the wardrobe, the other door of the wardrobe, look to your wife who says, 'It's under the stairs.'

Look your wife in the eye as she says this, reach out to touch her neck and hair.

Say, 'Thanks,' then off you go.

Oh, I know what you are thanking me for.

The front door clicks shut on my husband in his funeral tie and I wander downstairs to tidy away the breakfast things and make my usual cup of coffee. I fill the kettle and plug it in. I take out my mug and put it on the counter. And then, before the water is boiled, I have the recycling bin spilt all over the floor, and I'm going through the old newspapers for death notices.

Samantha 'Sammy' MacHale, tragically, abroad. Easy. I get out the phone book and look that up too.

The church is in Walkinstown, so that's her family off the Cromwellsfort Road. She might have lived at home still, at twenty-four – the price of everything these days. I could go there now, if I wanted to. I could drive there in my little car. I wonder do her parents know what she got up to? I have a shameful desire to tell them – so sharp, I have to stand still until it subsides.

I am not that kind of person.

No.

I make my cup of coffee and I calm down.

Still, I wonder what she looked like. What school did she go to; do they have pictures in the corridors, of former girls in a row, the class of – what year would she be? – the class of 1998.

So young.

Who could be that young?

All the time I am loading the dishwasher and pulling out the hoover and doing my morning round, the funeral is happening in my head. But I am not going to jump in the car and hack my way across town to Walkinstown. I am not that kind of person. I am not going to panic at the last minute and show up at the cemetery to check the faces at the grave and pick up a few words here and there, about what a fine girl she was, 'irrepressible', 'full of fun'. Bloody right she was full of fun.

Or not. Maybe she was shy, unassuming. Easily impressed. She might have been a quiet kind of girl. A girl who was anxious to please.

No.

I am not going to find this out, or anything else. Because that would be obscene. I am not going to show up like a ghost at the wedding – what's the opposite of that? – like a flesh and blood wife, at this last dance with the dead.

We had the salmon when he came home. Potatoes. A bit of asparagus.

'Lovely,' says my husband. 'Delicious.' Then he gets up afterwards and makes himself a sausage sandwich, cold from the fridge. Butter, mayonnaise, the lot.

And I say, 'Why don't you stick some lard in there, while you're at it?'

This is the last real thing I say to him, for a long while. *Where's the gas bill gone when will you be home would you pick up Shauna from her ballet?* We could do this for ever. After a few weeks of it, my husband gets a nervous cough: he wonders if it could be lung cancer. His toe is numb, isn't that a sign of MS? And I just say, 'Get it checked out.' Because the girl is dead. So let's not bother with the fuss and foother of getting back together. Let's not do all that again. Not this time. This time let us mourn.

I am too proud. I know that. And in my pride I watched him – my fantastic, stupid man – lurch around in his life. And I did not offer him a helping hand.

Where's the key to the shed when will you be home would you buy a pack of plastic blades for the Flymo?

The girl was with us, all this time. Dead or alive. She was standing at the bus stop on the corner, she was sitting in our living room watching *Big Brother,* she was being buried, night after night, on the evening news.

I think that milk's gone off when will you be home I really don't want the children having TV sets in their rooms.

After a month of this, I looked at my husband and saw that he was old. It did not happen overnight; it happened over thirty nights or so. My husband shaking hands with death. And what else? Thinking about it. Thinking it wouldn't be so bad to be dead, after all. Like she was.

Whenever I woke in the night, he was awake too. Once I heard him crying again; this time in the shower. He thought the noise of the water would cover it. I listened to him snuffling and choking in the spray and I realised it was time to put my pride away. It was time to call him back home.

On Saturday, after the supermarket run, I put on my good coat and my leather gloves. And a hat, even – my funeral hat. And when my husband said, 'Where are you off to?' – because God knows I never go anywhere without drawing a map – I said, 'I'm going to visit a grave.'

I had a beautiful bunch of white lilies, all wrapped up in cellophane. I picked them off the kitchen counter and walked past him – I cradled the lilies against my shoulder and I walked past my husband, who was now old – and I did not look back, as I went out the door.

She did not matter to him, I know that. I know she did not

matter. So I went to the cemetery and sought out her grave. I wandered through the headstones until I found her, and I put the lilies on the ground under which she lay, and I told her that she mattered. Then I went home and said to my husband. Then I went home and said to Kevin:

'Let's do something for Easter, what do you think. Something nice. Where would you like to go?'

Yesterday's Weather

Hazel didn't want to eat outside – the amount of suncream you had to put on a baby and the way he kept shaking the little hat off his head. Also there were flies, and her sister-in-law Margaret didn't have a steriliser – why should she? – so Hazel would be boiling bottles and cups and spoons to beat the band. Then John would mooch up to her at the cooker and tell her to calm down – so not only would she have to do all the work, she would also have to apologise for doing all the work when she should be having a good time, sitting outside and watching blue-bottles put their shitty feet on the teat of the baby's bottle while everyone else got drunk in the sun.

She remembered a man in the hotel foyer, very tall, he handled his baby like a newborn lamb; setting it down on its stomach to swim its way across the carpet. And Hazel had, briefly, wanted to be married to him instead.

Now she grabbed a bowl of potato salad with the arm that held the baby and a party pack of crisps with the other, hoofed the sliding door open and stepped over the chrome lip on to the garden step. The baby buried his face in her shoulder and wiped his nose on her T-shirt. He had a summer cold, so Hazel's navy top was criss-crossed with what looked like slug trails. There was something utterly depressing about being covered in snot. It was just not something she had ever anticipated. She would go and change but the baby would not be put down and John, when she looked for him, was playing rounders with his niece and nephews under the apple trees. He saw her and waved. She put down the bowl and the crisps on the garden table, and shielded the baby's head against the hard ball.

The baby's skin, under the downy hair, breathed a sweat so fine it was lost as soon as she lifted her hand. Women don't even know they miss this until they get it, this smoothness, seeing as men were so abrasive or – what were they like? She tried to remember the comfort of John's belly with the hair stroked all one way, or the shocking silk of his dick, even, bobbing up under her hand, but he was so lumbering and large, these days, and it was always too long since he had shaved.

'Grrrr . . .' said Margaret, beside her, rummaging a bag of crisps from out of the party pack. This is what happens when you have kids, Hazel thought, you eat all their food – while Margaret's children, as far as she could see, ate nothing at all. They ate nothing whatsoever. Even so, everyone was fat.

'Come and eat,' Margaret shouted down the garden, while Hazel turned the baby away from the sudden noise.

'Boys! Steffie! Please! Come and eat.'

Her voice was solid in the air, you could almost feel it hitting the side of the baby's head. But her children ignored her – John too. He had lost his manners since coming home. He pretended his sister did not exist, or only barely existed.

'How's the job coming?' she might say and he'd say,'. . . Fine,' like, *What a stupid question.*

It made Hazel panic, slightly. Though he was not like that with her. At least, not yet. And he lavished affection on his sister's three little children, he threw them up in the air, and he caught them, coming down. Still, Hazel found it hard to get her breath; she felt as though the baby was still inside her, pushing up against her lungs, making everything tight.

But the baby was not inside her. The baby was in her arms.

'Come and eat!' shouted Margaret again. 'Come on!'

Still, no one found it necessary to hear. Hazel would shout herself, but that would definitely make the baby cry. She stood by the white wrought-iron table, set with salads and fizzy orange and cut ham, and she watched this perfect picture of a family at play, while beside her Margaret said, 'God between me and prawn-flavoured Skips,' ripping open one of the crinkly packets and diving in.

The ball thumped past Hazel's foot. John looked up the length of the garden at her.

'Hey!' he called.

'What?'

'The ball.'

'Sorry?'

'The ball!'

It seemed to Hazel that she could not hear him, even though his words were quite clear to her. Or that she could not be heard, even though she was saying nothing at all. She found herself walking down the garden, and she did not know why until she was standing in front of him, with the baby thrust out at arms' length.

'Take him,' she said.

'What?'

'Take the baby.'

'What?'

'Take the fucking baby!'

The baby dangled between them, so shocked that when John fumbled it into his arms, the sound of wailing was a relief – at least it turned the volume in her head back on. But Hazel was already walking back up to the ball. She picked it up and slung it low towards the apple trees.

'Now. There's your ball.' Then she turned to go inside.

John's father was at the sliding door; his stick clutched high against his chest, as he managed his way down the small step. He looked at her and smiled so sweetly that Hazel knew he had just witnessed the scene on the lawn. Also that he forgave her. And this was so unbearable to her – that a complete stranger should be able to forgive her most intimate dealings in this way – that Hazel swung past the tiny old man as she went inside, nearly pushing him against the glass.

John found her hunkered on the floor in the living room searching through the nappy bag. She looked up. He was not carrying the baby.

'Where's the baby?' she said.

'What's wrong with you?' he said.

'I have to change my top. What did you do with the baby?'

'What's wrong with your top?'

Snots. Hazel could not bring herself to say the word; it would make her cry, and then they would both laugh.

But there was no clean T-shirt in the bag. They were staying in a hotel, because Hazel had thought it would be easier to get the baby asleep away from all the noise. But there was always a teething ring left in the cool of the mini-bar, or a vital plastic spoon in the hotel sink, and so of course there was no T-shirt in the bag. And anyway, John would not let her bring the baby back to the hotel for a nap.

'He's fine. He's fine,' he kept saying as the baby became ever more cranky and bewildered; screaming in terror if she tried to put him down.

'Why should he be unhappy?' she wanted to say. 'He has had so few days in this world. Why should the unhappiness start here?'

Instead she kept her head down, and rummaged for nothing in the nappy bag.

'Go and get the baby,' she said.

'He's with Margaret, he's fine.'

Hazel had a sudden image of the baby choking on a prawn-flavoured Skip – but she couldn't say this, of course, because if she said this, then she would sound like a snob. It seemed that, ever since they had arrived in Clonmel, there was a reason not to say every single thought that came into her head.

'I hate this,' she said, eventually, sinking back from the bag.

'What?'

'All of it.'

'Hazel,' he said. 'We are just having a good time. This is what people do when they have a good time.'

And she would have cried then, for being such a wrong-headed, miserable bitch, were it not for a quiet thought that crossed her mind. She looked up at him.

'No, you're not,' she said.

'What?'

'You are not having a good time.'

'Sure,' he said. 'Right. Whatever you say,' and turned to go.

Margaret hadn't, in fact, asked the baby to suck a prawn-flavoured Skip. She had transformed the baby into a gurgling stranger, sitting on the brink of her knee and getting its hands clapped. The baby's brown eyes were dark with delight, and his mouth was fizzing with smiles and spit. At least it was, until he heard Hazel's voice, when he turned, and remembered who his mother was, and started to howl.

'Well, don't say you didn't like it,' said Hazel, taking him on to her shoulder, feeling betrayed.

'Sorry,' said Margaret, 'I was dying to have a go.'

'Oh, any time,' said Hazel, archly. 'You can keep him if you like,' listening already to her housewife's camp.

Why not? She sat down at the table and threw a white baby cloth over the worst of the slug trails on her chest and lifted her face to the weak Easter sun.

'How's the new house?' said Margaret.

'Oh, I don't know,' said Hazel. 'You can't get anything done.'

'Five years,' said Margaret. 'Five years I have been trying to get carpet for the back bedrooms.'

'I know what you mean.'

'I mean, five years I've been trying to get to the shop to look at the carpet books to start thinking about carpet for the back bedrooms.'

'What did you used to have?' said Hazel, then realised she shouldn't ask this, because it was John's parents' house, and talking about the old carpet was talking about his dead mother, and God knows what else.

'I mean, did you have lino or boards, or what?'

'I couldn't look at them,' said Margaret. 'I got down on my hands and knees and I got – you know – a claw hammer, and I prised them up.'

Hazel looked at the laughing children running after John, who was also laughing.

'The dirt,' said Margaret.

'John!' said Hazel. 'Tea-time. Now please.' Then she said to her sister-in-law, 'A friend of mine found amazing stuff on the Internet. Stripes and picture rugs, and I don't know what else.'

'Really,' said Margaret, and started to butter a round of bread.

★ ★ ★

John's father turned to them, and either shook his fist, or just lifted his hand – he had such a bad tremor, it was hard to tell. And this was another thing that Hazel could not figure out: what part of him was affected by the Parkinson's, or was it Parkinson's at all? Was his speech funny? Truth be told, she never understood a word he said.

'Hffash en silla?'

'Well, they're kids, Daddy,' said Margaret without a blink – so maybe it was just her, after all. They watched him for a while, poking at the flower bed with his stick.

'He used to love his sweet pea along that wall,' Margaret said, like the man was already dead.

Hazel said nothing.

'Will you take a bite to eat, Daddy, pet?' but he ignored her, like all the rest.

Hazel had a sudden pang for her little garden in Lucan. The seeded grass was sprouting, and the tulips were about to bloom. She had planted the bulbs the week they got the keys: kneeling on the front path, seven months pregnant, digging with the little shovel from the fire-irons; a straight line from the gate to the door of fat, red tulips, the type you get in a park – 'a bit municipal,' as her mother had said, squinting at the pack – that were now flaming red at the tips, like little cups of green fire.

'That's what I love about this place,' she said. 'This wonderful stretch of garden.'

'Yes,' said Margaret, carefully.

'John. Divorce! Now,' shouted Hazel, and he finally brought the laughing children to the tableside.

The baby didn't cry when she shouted. That was something she hadn't known, that the baby didn't actually mind shouting. Or maybe he just didn't mind her shouting.

Still, it was an advance.

'Who wants ham?' Hazel said to the kids; loading it on to the bread, helping out.

'I don't like ham,' said Stephanie, who was nearly four.

'No?'

'No, I don't like it.'

'I don't like ham.' They were all saying it now, the big brother and the little brother. 'I don't like ham.' It was all a bit intense, Hazel thought, and accusatory.

'I think you are confusing me with someone who gives a fuck,' she said – changing at the last moment, of course, to, 'Someone who cares whether, or not, you like ham.'

John gave her a quick glance. The child, Stephanie, gazed at her with blank and sophisticated eyes.

'Maybe a little bit of ham?' said Hazel.

'I don't think so,' said Stephanie.

'Right.'

John picked an apple out of the pile on the table.

'A is for?' he said, holding it high.

'Answer,' said Stephanie. 'A is for A-A-Answer,' and the children laughed, even though they didn't quite know what the joke was. They laughed on and on, and then they laughed at the sound of their own laughter, for a little while more.

'How do you spell "wrong"?' said Kenneth, the eldest.

'W-R-O-N-G,' said Hazel.

'W is for Wrong,' he said. 'W is for Wrong Answer,' and they were off again; this amazing, endless, senseless sound – and this time the baby joined in, too.

He was asleep before they reached the hotel. The weather had changed and they carried him through a wind-whipped car park that did not even make him stir. Nor did he wake up in the room, when Hazel prised him out of the car seat – so she lay him on the bed as he was, profoundly asleep, in a dirty nappy and milk-encrusted babygro.

'He'll wake up in a minute,' she said. 'He needs a feed.' But he still didn't wake up: not for his feed, not when John went down to the bar for drinks. He slept through the remains of a film on the telly and another round of drinks, and he slept through the sound of his parents screaming at each other from either side of the bed where he lay. It blew up from nowhere.

'And you can tell your fucking sister that I don't want her fucking house.'

'No one says you want it.'

'Jesus, sometimes I think you're just pretending to be thick and sometimes I think you actually are thick. You can't talk about the carpets without her thinking what you'd put down on the floors if you got her out of there when the old man died.'

'Oh, you are,' he said, with his voice quite trembly. 'Oh, you really are . . .'

'You fucking bet I am.'

'No, well done. Well done.'

'Oh, shut up.'

'Carpet, is it? I thought you were talking about my father.'

'Whatever.'

'I thought you were talking about my father, there, for a minute.'

'Well, I am not talking about your father. That is exactly what I am not talking about. You are the one who is talking about your father. Actually. Or not talking about him. Or whatever passes in your fucking family for talking.'

'You are such an uppity cunt, you know that?'

'Yes, I am.Yes, I fucking am. And I don't want your fat sister's fat house.'

'Well, actually, it's not her house.'

'Actually, if you don't mind, I don't want to talk about whose house it is. We can get our own house.'

'We have our own house.'

'A proper fucking house!!!'

Hazel was so angry she thought she might pop something, or have some style of a prolapse; her body, after the baby, being a much less reliable place. Meanwhile, the reason they needed a house in the first place slept on. His blissful flesh rose and fell. His mouth smiled.

The baby slept like he knew just what he was doing. The baby slept like he was eating sleep; his front stiff with old food and his back soft with shit. He slept through the roaring and the thrown hairbrush, and the storming of his father off to the residents' bar. He slept through the return of his father twenty seconds later to say something very level and very telling, and the double-fisted assault as his mother pushed him back out to the corridor crying that he could sleep in the fucking bar. He slept through his mother's anguished weeping, the roar of the taps, and the sad slosh and drip of her body shifting in the bath. It was, in fact, only when Hazel had fallen asleep, crawling for a moment in under the covers, that the baby decided to wake up and scream. Maybe it was the silence that woke him. Mind you, his screaming sounded the same as every other night's screaming, she thought, so it was impossible to know how much he had been damaged by it all; by the total collapse of the love that made him. Could anger hurt him, when he had never heard it before?

Hazel plugged his roars with the bottle that was still floating, forgotten, in the hotel kettle. She undid the poppers on his babygro, as he sucked, and extracted him from it, one limb at a time. She reached between his soft legs to undo the poppers of his vest, which had a wet brown stain across the back, and she rolled the vest carefully under itself to keep the shit on the inside. When the vest was finally off, she pushed two baby wipes down into the nappy to stop the leak. All of this while the baby sat in her naked lap, with her left hand propping up the bottle and his eyes on hers.

The baby was huge. Maybe it was because she had no clothes on, but he seemed twice as big as the last time she had him in her arms. Hazel felt like she kept losing this baby, and getting someone new. She thought that she would fall in love with the baby if only it would stay still, just for a minute, but the baby never did stay still. Sometimes it seemed like it was all around her, as though there was nothing in her world except the baby, but every time she looked straight at the baby, or tried to look straight at the baby . . . whatever it was, just wasn't there.

She was looking at him now.

But she still clung to it, whatever it was. She still hoped and hung on. Was this enough? Was this the way you loved a baby?

The line of milk pulsed and bubbled as it sank down into the teat, and the baby started to suck air. Hazel pulled the empty bottle out with a pop and set him on her shoulder, holding him with her forearms now, because she thought there might be shit on her hands.

The baby was full, his belly taut. She would get some wind out of him, and then clean up. Meanwhile, the feel of his bare skin against her own made Hazel vague with pleasure. She brushed her cheek against his fine hair, and the baby belched fantastically down the skin of her back.

'Oh! so clever,' she said, dipping and turning around. 'Oh! so clever,' dipping and turning back again. She did it a few more times, just to get the weight and poise of it, with the fat baby against her fat chest, and her crossed hands dangling beneath his bum. Dip and turn, dip and turn. The baby's cheek a millimetre away from her own cheek – a hair's breadth, that is what that was called. A hair's breath.

Outside, the wind had picked up.

Rock a bye baby, she sang in a whisper, On the tree top.

She was nearly out of wipes. She did not have the courage to put him in a slippery bath. She would dunk a hotel towel in the sink and use that, no matter who had to pick it up, or use it afterwards. God, this baby business brought you very low, she thought, and turned with a smile to the opening door.

They were shattered when they got home.

John drove as though the road could feel his tyres; the tyres could feel the road. The whole world seemed as tender as they were. At Monasterevin, he reached his hand to touch her cheek, and she held it there with the flat of her own hand while, in the back of the car, the baby still slept.

When they pulled into the driveway, Hazel saw that her tulips had been blown down – at least, the ones that had opened first. She wondered if the storm had hit here too, and how strong was that wind anyway – was it a usual sort of wind? What would she be able to grow, here? She tried to think of a number she could ring, or a site online, but there was nowhere she could find out what she needed to know. It was all about tomorrow: warm fronts, cold snaps, showers expected. No one ever stopped to describe yesterday's weather.

WIFE

There was a new woman behind the counter in the newsagent's and it took Noel a while to realise that her throat had been slit. The scar was still a little livid, and Noel wondered who had done it to her. It was quite a horseshoe, bigger than you got from something medical, he thought. With a scar like that, you'd have to be careful about throwing your head back, in case the damn thing fell off.

'And a packet of Maltesers, thanks.'

He wanted to see her do it. Idiot that he was, he wanted to make a little joke and make her laugh in a big, decadent, fifties way – a woman with a scarlet mouth, her face flung high, stubbing out a cigarette. *You are a card.*

'Four euros, ten cent,' said the woman with the scar, and Noel handed her a five.

Of course there was no scarlet lipstick; the woman was a faded sort of creature in a blue-check nylon coat. Still, she made him feel quite jaunty. Noel did not know how many times he had seen her – he only went in there for the weekend papers, or sometimes for a pint of milk if they ran out, and maybe a packet of Maltesers for his wife. Besides, the girls behind the counter changed all the time, he didn't even see the good-looking ones any more – which was sad, but there you go. And he was halfway back to the house before he realised that the good-looking girls didn't see *him* any more: he had it the wrong way around.

But the woman with the scar saw him. She was alert to where people's eyes went and where they stayed, and even though she didn't look at you when she handed over your change, still she was noticing every bit of you. Noel couldn't tell what age she might be – he never could, with women – even her wrinkles sat lightly on her face, like they hadn't the energy to cut into the skin. Who would bother trying to murder her? Someone she had bored into a frenzy. Or a stranger in an alleyway. Christ, it didn't bear thinking about. Then again, maybe she had put the scar there all by herself. Maybe, in some sudden surge of strength, she had done it herself.

Noel threw the Maltesers across the kitchen to his wife, who said, 'God, I love you.' Then he went into the sitting room, and sat for a while reading the papers.

'Your mother rang,' his wife said – or shouted – from the next room.

'What? When?'

'When you were out.'

'Well, thanks for telling me,' he said. And was ignored.

He went back to his paper but it was spoiled, slightly, and he folded it and let it drop to the ground beside the leg of the chair.

'I wish you'd tell me these things,' he called out.

'What?'

'I wish you'd tell me when I get a call to the house.'

'Jesus, Noel, I was hardly keeping it from you. You're only in the door.'

She had come out into the hall and was looking in at him.

'Are you all right?

'What?'

Ten years ago he might have pointed out that just because she failed to pass on a phone message did not mean that he was suffering from some larger emotion. But that was ten years ago. These days, he didn't bother. So things were looking up, then. 'Course I'm all right.'

And he went into the hall to phone his mother.

His mother wanted to talk about the upstairs tap. The upstairs tap had been dripping for decades, but now she was a widow Noel's mother wanted something to fuss about. As if it was his father's fault – the drip – and she could finally get it fixed, now that he was out of her way.

'I don't know,' said Noel. 'Forty euros' call-out, anyway – or used to be when I last got someone – which is a long time ago.'

'Forty euros!'

His mother was on the new phone with the walk-around handset, which sort of cut out when she wasn't speaking, so you couldn't read the silences any more. What did she want?

'Someone could do it. I could do it. It's just a washer, probably.'

'No, no,' she said. 'That's not what I meant at all.'

But he bribed the youngest into the car and went over there, anyway, with his wrench beside him on the front seat. His daughter in the back was making up a song, and laughing through the words which, when he listened in to them, were all about 'poo'. Noel looked at her in the mirror.

'Would you ever?' he said.

The night before she had broken the last, pink string that held one of her bottom teeth, and her gum had surged with blood. Now she was laughing through the fresh gap, singing:

'And in that poo there was a plop,

A rare plop, a poo-poo plop.'

'Ah, stop it,' said Noel. But she didn't stop, so he switched on the sports news and listened to that instead.

She ran up to the door and rang the bell to her granny's, while Noel followed up the path, testing the weight of the wrench by swinging it into the cup of his left hand.

'I told you not to,' said his mother after she had kissed and cooed over her grandchild. 'I told you I'd get a man in. That's what I wanted. I wanted someone in.'

'Not to worry,' said Noel.

She smiled at him as he passed. His wife said it was like a romance, the pair of them these days. And maybe there was something in it. Since his father died, they were on the phone a lot more. They talked about things Noel would not usually talk about – not just about skirting boards and damp, but gardening, and people's lives, and who said what to whom.

'What's that?' he said, looking up from under the wash-hand basin.

'The Dempseys up the road. I said he's off the sauce. Those poor girls, what they put up with.'

'Did I ever tell you I had a thing with the middle one? The blondie little one.'

'The one you liked?'

'How did you know I liked her?'

He came out from under the white ceramic. Both of them felt it – something clear and possible in the air between them – because, let's face it, she had been talking about the neighbours for years.

'Ah now,' said his mother. 'Sure I know everything.'

And she went back downstairs to make a cup of tea, leaving the ghost of the girl who lived up the road with him. The amazing fact, if you ever got your hand down there, that girls actually sweat. It only happened once, and briefly. But it was quite a shock.

Not as much of a shock now, though, as the realisation that the girl in question could not have been more than eleven years old. Too young for him, even at fourteen. What calculation had gone into all of that, he wondered? What style of a little shit was he, in those days?

Downstairs, his daughter was parked in front of the cartoons, sucking her hair.

'Out of your mouth,' he said.

She looked over at him – his beautiful daughter – with her skirt up and one leg thrown over the arm of the chair. The leg was covered in bruises, and the streel of hair cut across her cheek.

'Have you been to the toilet?' he said, as his mother came in behind him with the tea on a tray.

He could barely sit to drink it, sitting between daughter and mother – his agitation was so sudden and fierce. Noel bundled his daughter into the car and drove at speed with the wrench on the seat beside him and the match turned up high. The child wanted an ice cream – he had promised, she said, if she went to her gran's; he had *promised*. So he pulled in at the local shop and sat, holding the wheel, thinking about the woman with the second grin, inside there in her blue coat behind the till.

'You go in,' he said finally. 'Go on, give her this. Give the lady this.'

He handed the outraged child a fiver and, with a loud show of reluctance, she opened the car door.

Noel did not know what he was looking for. Or avoiding. He sat there trying to figure it out. He did not want to kill the woman with the scar, or kiss her, but he did want to do something, if possible to a woman, and he felt that it was all her fault.

'Are you happy now?' said his daughter, still sulky despite the Magnum in her hand.

'Put your seat belt on,' he said, but she was too busy with the ice cream. He pulled out into the traffic anyway – he did not want to go home, but home was the only place there was to go. He knew what he was looking for – as he let his daughter in under the arm that put the key in the door. He was looking for the kind of pain he could bury himself in.

'Are you back already?'

'That's us,' he said. And he looked at his wife.

CARAVAN

The clothes hissed as she wrung them out and a little fizz of bubbles sprang out of the weave.

'I thought we were supposed to be doing well?' she said.

'What?'

Michelle was bent over the shower tray. Dec was just behind her, standing at the cooker.

'I thought we were doing well?'

'We're not doing well,' he said. 'We're doing all right.'

'Hah!' she said. If he stooped to get a saucepan out from under the sink, their backsides would collide through the bathroom door. The van, she called it. Le tin can. The kids were messing on the bunk-bed, and the wall above Michelle's head buckled where they kicked. If you could call it a wall. It was more like a piece of wallpaper, gone hard.

'Stop that!' she said.

'They're back,' said Dec, looking out through the back window.

'Stop it now!' said Michelle. She had to remember not to shout. 'Or I won't pick up the hamster when we get home.'

Complete silence. A car door clunked a foot away from the sink, and you could hear the neighbours – two sweet little girls and their perfect parents – climbing the wooden steps on to the deck outside their own mobile home.

Michelle straightened up and her back put out a fiery twinge. Oh, yes. A good, old-fashioned sort of pain, that. The campsite washing machines were a disaster so she was reduced to Wipp Express and the plastic box she had brought for the kids' toys. She dangled the shower head into the box and threw the twists of clothes on top of it, to stop it writhing around when she turned on the water. She watched the cloth relax, and lift, and start to float, then she bent over again to knead and swirl and wring the clothes out for a second time. It was actually quite pleasant, as work went; tending to your family when they weren't there to annoy you; loving them up, in the shape of their clothes. She threw the twists into the sink: Emmet's blue cotton shorts, Katy's kitten T-shirt with the diamanté crown, worn to a flitter; Dec's heavyweight T-shirt that he wore because she liked it, though, as he said, all T-shirts looked the same to him. Finally there was her own crinkle skirt, a cheap cotton thing that looked exactly like what it was. Time to move on, she thought. Time to look like people who were doing 'all right'. Not to mention 'well'.

'Emmet! Katy!' said Dec. 'Your pals are here.'

You could feel the rustle and the suck of air as the kids debunked. They were, as she craned out of the bathroom, already standing stock-still at the front door. The two perfect girls were on the threshold, in matching pink capri pants and light-up trainers.

Stand-off.

'Would you like to go out and play?' she said.

Katy turned to check with her mother, but Emmet didn't need the distraction. He stared at the girls some more. Then he said, in a large sort of way, 'I had half a doughnut in the car.'

The girls thought about this. And were impressed.

'Did you go somewhere nice?' said Michelle.

'We went under the bridge,' said the bigger girl.

'Lovely.' And all four of them were gone. She would have given a sigh of relief, as her mother used to do, but Michelle could not let go. She was not used to it. She tracked the sound of their voices up and down the path outside, as she lumped the clothes back into the plastic box. Katy was shy and Emmet was only three: they had never been out on their own before and any silence would bring her out to check where they were gone. Much better to actually go out there and pretend to do something, or really do something, as now, chasing the little patches of sunlight along the wooden rail of the deck to hang the clothes in, because the site they had been given was in the shade.

On the sunny side of the little road, a woman was sitting outside her mobile home with a glass of rosé in her hand. She let the other hand dangle over the arm of her white plastic chair, and turned her face up to the sun. Bliss. Not a child in sight. She had six at least, maybe more – two of them slept in the car. It was Dec who finally twigged it.

'His, hers and theirs,' he said one evening, watching them all at dinner. Which made them both pause, and look again.

'She's in good nick,' said Michelle.

'Do you think?'

Most people on the campsite had two. Most people, like them, were doing 'all right'. They probably weren't doing 'well' – the women hadn't lost the baby weight, and the men's legs looked a bit self-conscious in shorts – but even 'all right' cost a fucking fortune.

They were in the Vendée, which was Co. Louth, basically. Flat. It was the least French place in the whole of France, she thought, with scutty little houses and no style. The campsite pool was crammed and there was bingo every second night, but it was great for the kids, as everyone said. It was great for the kids.

'Emmet! Katy!'

They were already nowhere to be seen. Michelle hurried up the path between the two rows of mobiles, and tried not to shout for them.

'Emmet! Now!'

She went right to the end, and then ran back again.

'Declan! Declan!'

He came out on to the deck.

'What?'

'Where are the kids?'

He stood there for a moment, listening. Then he said, 'They're in the hedge.'

It started to rain.

By the time she had hustled the kids inside Michelle had forgotten all about the clothes, and she ran out again, pulling them off the wooden railing and stumbling down the steps to get at the few things on the line. They sat in a heap in the shower tray, wetter than before, while she sorted out Katy who was screaming crying because she wasn't allowed go into the perfect girls' mobile.

'There is one rule,' said Michelle. 'There one rule. What is the rule? I have to be able to see you. I haveto beableto seeyou.'

Dec said he would take them to the pool. The crying stopped.

'In the rain?' said Michelle.

'Why not?'

When she found the swimming bag, the togs were damp and smelly from the day before and the towels sticky with salt. Also wet.

'It doesn't matter,' said Dec, over and over, as she wrestled the kids into the stinking things. 'It doesn't matter.'

She watched them go down the path, her children: their straight and pliable backs, the exquisite waddle of their beautiful bums, as they walked with their daddy through the warm rain. The smell, she thought, would get knocked out by the chlorine.

While they were off at the pool, Michelle took the clothes out of the shower tray and wrung them out again, and hung them around the mobile. She put the towels across the pelmets and small things on the rungs of the bunk ladder. The adult stuff, she put on clothes hangers, and she suspended these from the plastic curtain wire that ran across the front door. The place looked like a second-hand clothes shop, after the Flood.

The kids came back from the pool barking and raving with hunger, so she stuffed them full of ham before they were even out of their togs. They ate it from the packet, dancing and jigging around the open fridge door.

'I thought we were going to eat out?' said Dec.

'Listen,' she hissed with sudden rage. Then put her hand over her face and went into their bedroom. There was no-where to stand in there, so she sat on the bed.

'Will you dress them?' she said, quietly through the wall.

And he did.

It was past bedtime when they finally got to the crêperie and the kids were beyond themselves. Impossible. It was like talking to a pair of junkies.

'I don't want a proper crêpe! I don't want a proper crêpe, I just want ice cream!' Dec suddenly white around the mouth, saying, 'Do you want to go home? Do you want to go home right now?'

Of course, the ice cream just jizzed them right up again, and it was ten o'clock before they were finished bouncing off the walls. They had to be caught and forcibly stripped and put in their pyjamas, one kicking leg at a time, and it was nearly eleven before they had stopped writhing around in their sheets, like souls in torment.

Peace. Dec opened the fridge.

'Do you know how much this beer cost?'

'No.'

'Have a guess.'

'Just open it, would you?'

'How much?' he said, holding up a bottle of Leffe.

'I don't know,' said Michelle.

'Guess!'

'Oh dear God give me patience,' said Michelle.

'One euro forty-nine. For a bottle of Belgian beer. One euro forty-nine!' and, now that she was duly impressed, he cracked the top off and poured her a glass.

'We should have brought Scrabble,' she said.

After the second beer they went to bed and had sex, in utter silence; staying so close and tight for the first while, Michelle thought she might shout if he drew back an inch. But she didn't shout and, when they were finished, the children were still asleep.

'Christ,' she said. 'What did you say your name was again? Christ.' Then she dragged herself off the bed and into the living room. It was odd being naked in this little space – everything was too near, the ceiling was very low, and there was a ghost sitting at the table as she walked past to the bathroom. At least that was what she called it at the time, though she was sitting on the toilet before she thought to wonder at the fact of it. A ghost. And when she got up, it was gone.

The next day there was patchy sunshine in the morning, so Michelle draped a few things outside, and packed up the still-wet swimming gear, and they headed for the beach.

'I don't like the beach,' said Emmet. 'I don't like the beach!'

The beach was beautiful. The kids ran down the slope of it, shedding clothes, and could not stand still for the suncream.

Michelle didn't get into her own togs. She wondered if she ever would again. She sat on the edge of the dunes and pulled back her skirt to let the sun get at her legs.

'The thing is,' she said to Dec. 'From here, right? They look OK. The way the fat falls down, I can't actually see it. From where I'm looking, is what I am saying, everything looks OK.'

'So it's not that you're fat,' said Dec. 'It's just that your eyes are in the wrong place.'

'Well, exactly.'

'Come on. Have a swim.'

'Oh, I don't know.'

'Come on. It'll do you good.'

'In a minute.'

She sat on the sand watching the shapes of her children, black against the glittering sea; Dec running down to the wave's edge for buckets of water to throw on them, making them run and scream. It was all so delicious: the squirm of Katy's shoulders away from the flung water, the heavy splash of it on the sand; it was all so like a picture of a family having fun that Michelle found herself thinking about the caravan ghost – the way it was like a picture too; flat-looking, almost a bit creased. A woman. Young or old, it was hard to tell. But really horrible. Seething. She was sitting on the banquette behind the little table, and Michelle got the strong impression that she couldn't leave – that she was just stuck.

There was no trace of her when they got back from the beach. They had been chased off by the rain and the clothes left out that morning were wet again. Michelle picked them up and draped them back on pelmets and hangers, and in the middle of lunch she got up to hang some stuff from the spokes of the big umbrella outside. Nothing had dried, inside or out. She gathered yesterday's clothes and threw them into the plastic box under the shower.

While she was rubbing and wringing, Michelle thought maybe it was this that brought the ghost on. She was a handwash ghost – some woman who had wrung out clothes all her life, and moved them round from place to place, and failed to get them dry. But Michelle didn't mind the work, as work goes. There was something else about this woman: the set of her face; there was some other wreckage in her that Michelle did not yet recognise.

The kids were rattling around the place; pulling the cushions off the banquette, unscrewing the plastic catch on the bathroom door. Kids got in everywhere. How many of them had been through this one mobile, over the years? Every inch of it had been touched and pawed and used. Michelle made room for the new wet clothes beside yesterday's damp clothes, and rigged another few hangers in the shower. Across the way, the woman with six children and a good pair of legs was packing up, in the rain.

The perfect girls arrived. They sat outside under the umbrella and the kids played with them, quite formally, like ladies having tea. Michelle brought out some white French peaches, and she kissed the hard, round foreheads of both her children, whose soft skin still smelt of the sea. The perfect girls looked at her as she did this, in a polite sort of way. Perhaps they were not much kissed. Maybe that was her problem – too much kissing – maybe that was the thing Michelle was doing wrong. Ten minutes later the perfect girls were still perfect, while her own two were drenched in peach juice and once again, she had to find something clean and strip them down.

Around four o'clock, the sky began to clear and Michelle took the least wet clothes outside. She put them in the sunny spots, and the wetter things in the shade. She wondered if she was doing this the wrong way around – did she want a few dry clothes, or a lot of damp ones? How many days were left anyway? She had to use her fingers to count. She stood in front of the kids' wardrobe, touching shorts and dresses, saying, 'Wednesday, Thursday . . .' and then starting over again.

The ghost, she decided, was a woman who had actually died in the mobile. Some stiffening kind of death. She died rigid, sitting on that banquette, playing solitaire. Michelle was bizarrely convinced of this. She could feel the sandy slither of the cards on the table, as she set them down.

'How old are these yokes, would you say?'

Dec considered it. 'Ten years? I dunno. Twelve?'

That was it. She died playing cards while her children slept, within hands' reach, in the room next door.

Knock knock.

Michelle tapped on the thin little wall.

Knock knock.

On the sunny side of the little road, the adulterers, with all their brood, drove off for the last time. Michelle was over there in a flash, stealing the bit of sunshine they had left behind. She spent the next while ferrying the rest of the stuff over, checking the sky, turning Emmet's shorts like a slice of toast under the grill. She thought, as she did all this, of the next family that would come here, and the one after that; the fattening wives and the steadfast husbands and all the beautiful children; the thousands of beautiful children, growing in the rain. It was a while before she noticed that she couldn't hear her own pair, hadn't in fact heard them for some time. She looked down the little road, and she started to run.

She must have just missed them, because when she came around the block, she saw the two perfect girls peering under their mobile. Emmet's sandalled feet were sticking out from under there, quite still. Michelle stopped. The world stopped. The ghost turned in the window of their own mobile, and looked out through a glaze of reflected sky.

And then his little feet moved. Of course they did. When she hurried closer, Michelle saw that both her children were in under there, wriggling on their bellies in the dirt.

'Jesus Christ!'

The girls' father put his head, briefly, out of the door.

'It's a pussy!' said Emmet. And it could have been the stupid word, or the dirt of the clothes she would have to change and wash again, but, the next thing she knew, she was pulling Katy out backwards by one leg, and Emmet was wriggling further into the gloom, and she was hissing at him to get out of there immediately, get out of there now.

The two perfect girls were not so much mortified by the scene as saddened, and their father came out, to grin and reassure. And she probably hadn't, as she said to Dec later, used the word 'fuck' to her child, as in 'get the fuck out of there', but Katy was roaring crying that her knee was scraped, and Michelle, after swiping at her son a couple of times, had to stand up and turn the other way, until he decided to crawl out on his own. Which he did not, of course, because she was so cross. Michelle stood, and looked up, and wished that she was a different kind of mother – if there was a different kind of mother – while Katy cranked up the wails.

'Shut up!' she said, wrenching the top of the child's arm like a woman you might see on the side of the street. Then, just to achieve the full crescendo, she strode away from them both until they came, howling and screaming, after.

Her gorgeous children. Her pride and joy.

Three days later they were out of there. The plastic box was filled with toys, the wet laundry was rotting cheerfully somewhere in a bag; they sat in the car, ripe in their unwashed clothes, and headed north.

Half a mile down the road, Katy said, 'That was the most absolutely fantastic holiday I have ever had.'

'Was it?' said Michelle.

'Yes.'

'What did you like about it?'

'Best?'

'All right, best.'

'I liked our little house best.'

'Right.'

'Did you like our little house?'

'Well, I suppose I did.'

Dec glanced over and gave a small smile. Michelle was still light-headed from cleaning it before they hit the road. Something drove her to wipe every inch of it, as she backed out of the damn thing. There was a sort of madness to it, throwing the cloth, finally, into the rubbish outside the front door. She had used the same cloth for the kitchen counter and the toilet bowl, and she wondered, suddenly, if she had done it the right way round. She wondered what was in the boot and what was in the roof box – had they left anything behind? Did she have the correct number of children in the back seat, and were they bringing an extra corpse with them, all the way home?

THE CRUISE

In the spring of that last year, Kate's parents took a notion and went on a cruise. Seven days out of Miami to the eastern Caribbean: Puerto Rico, Haiti, Turks and Caicos, St Thomas. Watching them go through the departure gate at Dublin airport – her mother in a powder-blue tracksuit and her father in white running shoes – Kate realised that they would die. It was the tracksuit that did it.

She hoped her father would wear a hat in the sun. But not his usual hat, the one that said 'Clondalkin Tyre Remoulds' across the front. He wasn't even a mechanic. Her father was an insurance agent, long retired, and Kate hoped that he would buy himself a decent hat somewhere in the Caribbean, and wear that instead.

'The place is full of shops,' she said, looking at the brochure. 'I don't mean the Caribbean, I mean the boat is full of shops. Sure where would you be going?' she said. 'Look!'

Her father looked – he was a man who avoided shops at all costs. But it wasn't just shops: the boat had an ice rink, and a climbing wall, and some kind of perpetual-motion wave on the top deck, where you could surf the night away.

'Sure where would you be going?' said Kate again, thinking there were probably card clubs and bingo and places to get your hair done, too.

'Yes. Even the drink is free,' said her mother, and she gave a little laugh. 'Apparently it comes out of a tap.'

Kate knew her mother would not drink too much, or probably would not drink too much. At worst she'd have something pink with an umbrella in it. Her mother had always loved the sun – just the sun shining was glamour enough for her. And her father loved to romance her, once in a long

47

while: he would take her hand in a stolid sort of way, and move her across some hotel dance floor.

They would have a great time. It was a great thing for them to do. Though, it had to be said, they were very out of sorts on the airport road. Kate had to pull over on the hard shoulder to check that her father's pills were buried in a bag in the boot; half the country tearing past.

'Who needs tablets?' Kate shouted at her mother over the noise of the traffic, 'when we can just get him run over by an articulated truck?' She felt immediately guilty. Though it cheered her up too.

'In! Get in, you eejit. And put your seat belt on!'

So she got them there. She managed the suitcases, and the see-through bags for their toiletries, and the old supermarket bag her father had brought for his slippers and for the in-flight stockings he would wear on the plane – and they walked through the departure gates, and were gone.

They sent a few e-cards, painfully picked out on a keyboard in the ship's Internet café. *'St Maarten beautiful! Hope all well!'* One evening, an image of her mother's face appeared – or could he be dreaming it? – on the site where Kate's youngest, Jimmy, spent his time; sending goofy messages to other nine-year-olds in front of their slowly uploading webcams.

'It's Granny!' he said.

'What?'

Kate crossed to the living room to look, and there indeed was her mother's face in a corner of the screen, straining upwards, blue and silent.

'Oh my goodness,' she said, as the image faltered and froze.

It looked like something out of a science-fiction film. A message from another star, sent many years before.

Then, just as soon as they were gone, they were home. Kate looked at the calendar to check, but it seemed that a week on a cruise liner had the same number of days and nights in it as a week in her kitchen, after all.

She caught up with them the evening they flew in. The tan made them look younger but – maybe it was the jet lag – she could tell they were tired. They talked dutifully about the islands – the size of the spiders, the palm trees, a manta ray they had seen from the harbour wall in a place called Labadee – but they seemed slightly disappointed with the world, now that seeing it was so easy. Her mother was very taken by the warmth and the endless beauty of the sea, though there wasn't much time for a swim, she said, when they went on shore. Besides, the ship had jacuzzis and what have you. The big excitement was the ship.

'Amazing,' said her father.

They didn't feel sick at all, said her mother, apart from once, on the second day. It was huge. It was like being in a shopping centre, only you knew you were moving, somehow, you could just sense it.

Then you got off, said her father, and the ground set solid. 'The thump of it,' he said. 'Under your feet.'

'Did you get a hat?' Kate asked him, unaccountably jealous. 'I did not.'

'I told you to get yourself a hat.'

'Sure I have a hat,' he said.

But they stopped talking about the ship, and asked instead about the family, children and grandchildren; who was where, this week – Kevin, Kate's brother, was in Maryland on business, coming back via New York.

'You might have flown up to meet him, for a day or two. Seen Manhattan,' said Kate, knowing, as she said it, that such a thing was beyond them. They had had their adventure. They would never leave the country again.

'You forgot all about the sea,' her mother said, wistfully. The middle of the boat was hollow.

'Like a spaceship,' she said. 'Oh, it was huge.' It was the size of two football pitches, said her father, set end to end.

'And four storeys high,' said her mother, with every type of restaurant and bar; Thai, Mexican – a lot of it very spicy, so they steered clear.

'Hard to sleep,' said her father.

Yes, it was funny how hard it was to sleep. You would think it would rock you, like a baby. And sometimes, even with the size of the thing, you'd hear a booming in the metal walls.

'Very far away,' her father said.

The air conditioning was perfect, but there the two of them were – wide awake. She got up out of bed one night with an urge to see the water, walked for miles, past the nightclub and shut-up restaurants, looking for the right lift, the one that went all the way to the top. And when she got out into the fresh air, she said, the stars were so beautiful, you could almost see the sky turn. Then the black sea, and the waves breaking in a white V, everything moving and shifting, miles and miles below.

'Lovely,' said Kate.

They stopped talking about it for a while – by midsummer, you might have thought the cruise altogether forgotten – but when autumn came and the cold crept in, it started up again. Even more amazing, this time around. The Cruise! The Cruise! It was a dream, endlessly retold: from the miniature fittings in the bathroom to the other couples they met over dinner. There was a pair from Limerick called the Feenys who owned a furniture showroom, 'four thousand square feet of it!' There was a mixed race couple, 'from Belfast, of all places'. Most famous of all were the Carters from Yorkshire. There was nothing Kate did not know about the Carters from Yorkshire. She knew about their daughter's second round of fertility treatment, and she knew about their taste in Tanqueray gin. Mr Carter had had his veins stripped. Mrs Carter played golf. They set up Texas Hold'em in the Silver Lounge and begged a jar of dried pasta from the steward, for chips.

Mrs Carter said the hairdresser was only paid five pounds an hour. Mr Carter said there was a body in the freezer – there always was on the big ships – and the purser said it would be two, by the time they made it back home.

At which point her mother would pause, out of respect for the anonymous dead.

Kate imagined a retired advertising executive stiffening as the boat ploughed on; his lips covered with frost, his back pushed and dropped by the sea, in a discreet compartment between the breakfast rashers and a hundred ready-made pavlovas, while the five different swimming pools swelled and rolled counter to the waves.

One day, when her father was really quite sick, Kate idly scanned a letter on her parents' hall table. It was one of those round-robin things people send at Christmas. *'Imagine our consternation,'* she read, *'when we discovered that the paw prints on the living-room carpet, were actually those of a badger!!'* There were three family photos printed on the second page, *'Freezing our **ses off in Cromer,'* *'Grandparents at last!'* and *'Call that a dog?'*. It was signed *'Lewis and Sally (Carter)'*. They looked happy, Kate thought, as she chucked the thing back down. They looked like another world.

Now, whenever they wanted to say how much he had changed, people said how well Kate's father had looked when he came back from the cruise. It was the last fixed point they had for him. He was in bed a lot of the time – quite cranky, if the truth be told – and Kate's mother was at a loss. There was no more talk about the Carters, or the green flash at sunset, or the marshmallows they floated on your coffee in the bar on Deck Fourteen. But sometime later, Kate found another letter with a Yorkshire postmark and, when she asked, her mother said, 'I wanted to tell them about your dad.'

Kate was so cross she had to turn away.

'I wish you wouldn't, Mammy,' she said.

'Darling,' said her mother, 'I am seventy-two years of age.' Though what that proved, she didn't presume to say.

When it came to it, her father did not have an easy death, though the ward sister said that she had seen a lot worse. 'I know that's not much comfort to you.' But they were all outraged by the end – not that there was anyone to blame – it was just so outrageous: watching the tide of their father's death wash over him and recede, wave after wave of it, until, by the end, they didn't know if they wanted him to stay, or to go.

And when he did go, finally, they couldn't believe that either. They looked around at each other, brothers and sisters – real to each other for the first time. There was something very honest about the days that followed. The funeral went well, the graveside prayers were almost bearable, and they managed their mother between them. She was the great worry, of course. They kept wishing their mother would cry, but she didn't. Grief had made her astonishing. Kate's mother wore a suit of dove grey, with a blue scarf at the neck, and she looked like Bacall might have done at the death of Bogart: untouchable. She hugged and shook hands with neighbours and friends, and not one of them made a dent in her. It wasn't a good sign. Kate was on the other side of the crowd, inviting people back and organising lifts, when she finally heard the noise they had all been hoping for since – well, since her father had gone into decline. It was the sound of weeping. She pushed through to her mother and found her, collapsed and sobbing, in a strange man's arms.

'There, there, now,' said the man, stroking her blonde-grey hair. 'There, there.'

He was dressed in a safari jacket the colour of sand; his neck was thick and red, and his eyes were an uncertain blue. Beside him, a tiny woman in a trenchcoat picked up her mother's hand and stroked it.

'There, there,' said the woman, joining in. 'There, there, Marjorie. There, there.'

From behind her mother's heaving shoulders the man stretched out a stubby arm, but Kate did not need the introduction. She already knew his name.

'Lewis Carter,' he said. 'My sympathies, at this time.'

And later, when the three of them sang 'Some Enchanted Evening' in the corner of the living room, Kate was not surprised. She had expected that too.

Natalie

Natalie put me straight. Who knows what Natalie wants or what she likes, but we know what she doesn't like, that's for sure. At least we do now.

'Well,' I said, after I put the phone down, 'I won't be getting in your way again.'

Natalie should be a star. When she grows up, that is. Natalie should be something really impressive. Because if she isn't, then it'll get pretty lonely, won't it? I mean, how many friends has she got, to lose?

I will be a writer when I grow up and I will put it all down on the page, the tangle between Natalie and me, which is supposed to be about Billy's mother, but I don't think it is, really. Billy is Natalie's boyfriend. I nearly went out with him once, but that is so long ago and it wasn't even a proper thing. Now he's best friends with my boyfriend, who couldn't care less, and neither could Natalie, so that isn't what this is about, either.

I wake up in the middle of the night I am so upset. I mean, when I put down the phone I didn't know what to think – Natalie is so polite, you could hardly call what we had a fight – and then I am lying there with my eyes wide open; looking at what turns out to be the ceiling (duh!), wondering what terrible thought just woke me up.

My sister is asleep across the room – she has a kind of glowing pebble night-light that changes colours, very slowly, and she is lying in this sea of stuff: books and broken Nintendos and inflatable Bratz cushions, and God knows what else is in the pile, except from somewhere deep inside the heap, her breathing. And it makes me think of the milk inside a coconut, and I also think of Natalie's room that I was in once, and it was really tidy. That's all. It was just really tidy.

Natalie is an only child. She says it's OK. She says she doesn't know if her parents really, really love her or really, really couldn't care less. She has nothing to compare it to. They never shout at her anyway, they just have 'little conversations' – which sounds like hell to me but she says it's OK.

Here are the four of us: I am the fat, jokey one with the flaking nail polish, though it is always interesting flaking polish, like mirror silver or navy blue – still, you can tell by the way the stuff jumps off me that I don't really mean it. Natalie is more a *Rouge Noir* sort of girl. She might have her doubts, but that polish stays put.

Natalie has the kind of looks you have to get used to – but once you do, it is as though you have personally discovered her. Her features are sort of see-through, her skin is really pale and she has thin white-blonde hair. Which is why I say she should be a star, because the camera loves all that, close up. She hasn't a single open pore. Though she needs to get her eyelashes dyed professionally. She did it herself once and all around her lids went pink, so she had to stop using anything for a while. Which made her look sort of blinky and peeved.

When I say I am fat – even though, statistically speaking, I'm an eight and a quarter stone *midget* – my boyfriend says that I am not actually fat, I am just sleek. So that's the new word for fat – 'sleek'. But before I go completely self-hating, I do actually like my hair, which is black and really glossy, especially when it is, like, totally saturated with grease.

Who else?

Billy is a lot of trouble and I like him a lot. Hey, I like trouble. Or so I say to my boyfriend when he rolls his eyes up, the way he does. Billy has the kind of looks I used to go for a couple of years ago when I was about fifteen; soulful and soft, with absolutely no hair on his chest.

Though when I say Billy is my boyfriend's best friend, I don't think my boyfriend has a best friend, actually. So maybe that's the real question – Who knows what my boyfriend wants, or who he likes? Does he even like me? It's a mystery.

I am so in love with my boyfriend – at least I know that. He has eyes like George Clooney and beautiful hands. At least, the backs of them are beautiful; inside, they are a bit dry and shattered looking. I tried to get him to use some cream, but that's like trying to put him in a tutu, as far as he is concerned. I literally had to chase him around the room, and he ended up pushing my hand with the cream on it all over my face, even though it is handcream and like lard, basically.

My boyfriend has his own room and his parents gave him a gas heater to help him study in there, and I don't know if it is the smell of the gas or the heat of it that made us feel so fuggy, all last winter. We did a lot of kissing in front of that heater – and yes, we have gone 'all the way'; but that's only when his parents are out, which, these days, is never. But I don't mind. We kiss until we are dizzy, and my boyfriend is just so gorgeous and gentle about it. We tried to go further in the park but it was freezing and dark and I didn't find it sexy at all; in fact, I think it made me a bit upset. (I am not saying I am leaving my boyfriend mad with lust, I am not that sort of person. And, actually, that's all I am going to say about that).

Our debs dance was on Friday evening, and I'm still getting flashbacks; it's like a nightmare – that guy getting sick over my shoulder, and Billy's mother flattened up against the sitting-room wall, and Natalie smiling like some kind of nun. But I am not even thinking about all this, as I lie there in the changing pink light. I am thinking, *It is something else again.*

It all started with Billy's Terrible Time last year, just a little while after he hooked up with Natalie. And we were all delighted he had her, because she is like a flame in the daylight – that's what I think – unwavering, you can hardly see her, but she is always there. And after that mad bitch and, excuse me, cocktease 'Peony' Mulvey, we were really glad he had someone sane. Natalie is above all things sane.

In the middle of the night I think, *Maybe she's not sane at all.*

Anyway.

Billy's mother (who I really like, actually) got cancer last year and she came home from her first chemo session high as a kite from the steroids and she told Billy – told them all, in fact – that she didn't love their father any more, had never loved him in the first place, and once her chemo was over then her marriage was too. It was like, 'I'm alive! I'm alive! I'm not going to waste my life any more!!!' At least, that's how Billy described it. Then all her hair fell out and she was sick as a parrot, and Billy's just looking at his da and his da is looking at him – and you know, there is nothing wrong with Billy's da, he's a genuinely lovely man – and he is bringing her four hundred cups of green tea a day while she lies on the sofa with a face on her that says, As soon as this is done, then I am out that door.

My boyfriend looks it up online and he says ovarian cancer is a complete doozey – and who's going to tell Billy? Like who is going to tell him that her percentages are basically on the floor? We are sitting in the chipper waiting for Billy to get off the phone to his mother – he is outside the plate-glass window trying to get good reception and he is looking at the sky and his face looks so difficult, so old and childish at the same time, that the sight of him is like a pain for each of us. It is like each of us has a pain in our side.

Then Natalie says, 'Fuck the statistics. You just have to be in the right per cent. That's all. You just have to be in the per cent that survives.' And I understand she's a bit defensive, I mean she is literally, actually defending her new boyfriend's peace of mind here, but another part of me thinks that she is also marking her territory, which I quite respect, except I've known Billy's mother for five years now and if she dies, I too will cry.

His mother, incidentally, is what made Billy bonkers – long before she got sick, his mother was what made Billy interesting and unhappy, so she's a bit of a bitch, too, but I don't say that to Natalie, I say, 'You think she is going to survive?'

'I think,' says Natalie after a minute, 'that we don't know. And until we do know, then there's not much point getting in a fizz.'

Which is so like something my boyfriend would say that I think they'd be better off with each other really, they could roll their eyes up to heaven and not get in a fizz together –

while having sex, for example. And afterwards, Natalie could make tea.

So I accuse my boyfriend of fancying her, all the way back to his place, but that is just to get him going – that's just to clear out the memory of Billy coming back in after the phone call, saying, 'No, no. Just the usual,' and pushing his chips away. It is also to distract me from the fact that Natalie's aversion to 'fizz' is not something reasonable, and considered and right; that what she is actually saying is, You don't own Billy's mother.

Dead or alive.

It was only a tiny moment, you know?

As I say, I really did respect Natalie for holding the line, and somehow we seemed to feel, all through that long winter, that if Natalie didn't flicker, if she didn't blink, and if we all stayed nice, and stayed separate, and only had emotions that were appropriate to our actual situation vis-à-vis Billy's mother, then Billy's mother would survive.

I just thought, *What a great sense of decorum Natalie has* – and God knows, there's not much of that around. And I really admired her, that's all. I began to see how beautiful she is close up and I started asking her advice on chip-proof nail polish, even though these things don't interest me as much as I think they do. And that makes it worse, the fact that I don't give a fuck about *Rouge Noir,* really, so a sort of wheedling, messy thing starts to happen, and it is a while before I realise that what I want is for Natalie to *be my friend.*

I say this to my boyfriend and he says, 'She is your friend,' which just shows how much he knows about these things. And after a while she does start to like us, though she doesn't have a lot of choice, really. It can't have been easy: her boyfriend up to ninety, and his mother lying on the sofa, and me gabbling on about some day, maybe, getting my legs waxed – I mean, Natalie just does things, she doesn't talk about them first, and it seems that all those months were about getting nothing done at all.

Then, in the spring, Billy's mother gets her hair back, and it has this amazing red glow that she had as a child, so we are all in and out of Billy's kitchen again, returned from our months as refugees in the chipper, and Billy's mother stays married, and she also stays as mad as she ever was, and also superbly happy, and I just admire her so much for all of this. The next few months are a blur for Billy and my boyfriend, because they both have their last exams, so me and Natalie hang out a little, and the thing about Natalie is, she is a really nice person. It's like I'm making her out to be some kind of bitch or something, but she really isn't. She is actually very cool, and nice.

In the summer, my boyfriend gets a job in the local garage so his clothes smell of petrol, and his hands smell of money, because the guy who owns the place hasn't put soap in the toilets for three months, even though they serve coffees there as well. I say why doesn't he take his own soap in, but my boyfriend just looks at me like I am trying to turn him into a queer.

He is saving for college. And I know that I will lose him, when he goes. So I am on the strictest possible diet, and I am talking non-stop to Natalie about the Dress; the one that I will wear to the debs dance. I mean, I know he loves me, but I will wear this dress and my boyfriend will take one look at me and he will realise that this is what he will lose. All this.

Billy has been accepted into two colleges in England, but I don't think they have the money really, and with his mother still in remission he wants to stay close to home. September is Billy and Natalie's first anniversary, and it is also the anniversary of his mother's diagnosis, and it is the month of our last dance, before the boys go off to war. But I feel so grateful for the turn of the leaves, somehow. I walk through the woods and remember where we nearly did it one time, my boyfriend and me, and I think – a bit like Billy's mother – that when we go, we will go down swinging.

I'm texting Natalie one day and she idly mentions that she has her dress already. 'White! white! white!' And it takes me about two years to spell out, 'very Renee Zellweger!!!'

Eventually I have to bring my little sister into town with me – which feels like a sad-bastard thing to do, but actually she's a demon when it comes to clothes, it's like bringing the entire line-up of a girl band. Between us, we solve everything with a sub-Westwood, sub-goth bustier and my mother's long silk skirt, and a gorgeous second-hand – or should I say vintage – lamé shawl.

Billy's mother says we should go over to their house before the dance so she can frisk us down for naggins of whiskey, and besides, she says, she wants to see me in all my finery. And I say, 'Mrs Casey, I can't even take the smell of whiskey, vodka's the only way to go.'

So when Natalie rings, I ask her to bring her hair straightener and she says, 'Like, it's sort of large.'

'Not to the hotel,' I say. 'Just over to Billy's before we go.'

'Uh . . . OK,' she says, like 'whatever'. So I arrive at Billy's with everything in a huge bag, and Billy's father answers the door.

I don't know where I got it from, this idea that we were going to do it all there: the fake tan and the fake eyelashes and the bow-ties and the zips. When I text Natalie, she just comes back with '???!!?' and Billy's da looks a bit embarrassed, because not even Billy is home. He shows me upstairs into his own bedroom, which is a funny place to be, and I sit at Billy's mother's dressing table, which is a sort of alcove in the fitted wardrobe, and I look at Billy's mother's stuff: lipsticks gone off and pressed powder with one of those pads that look sort of orthopaedic, and industrial-strength night cream. And I know I have to skip the tan for a start, there's no one to do my back. I get a really glossy face on and then I just sit there, looking at myself in Mrs Casey's mirror. After a while there's nothing for it except put on the damn dress. Then I sit on Mr and Mrs Casey's bed, and look at the wallpaper. The bed isn't made. The sheets are a really dark green. I lie down for a moment – just for two seconds, I lie down. Then suddenly everyone's arriving, so I jump up and stuff all the gear into my bag, and I make my grand entrance, sweeping down the stairs and into the hall.

Natalie jigs up and down and screams, and she hugs me from four feet away, not to muss. Then we go into Billy's front room, and his father takes a picture, and then she's there

– Mrs Casey. I was wondering what the silence in the house was, but there she is, flattened against the wall. Actually she swings in round the door frame like a broken gate. She holds the door frame with one hand and slams the other one flat against the wall. Then she goes rigid, and looks to the left, as if there's someone after her, and they're in the hall.

'Hi, Mrs Casey,' I say.

She's really drunk.

'Hiiiii,' she says.

'What do you think?' I do a pathetic little twirl and she lowers her head at me and gives a sort of grunt of approval, then she swings her head around to find Natalie.

She looks at the dress.

'Hnnnn,' she says – which is, actually, the way it comes out of her, quite a friendly and ironic sound. It's a 'White? Interesting choice!' sort of sound, but Natalie just looks at her.

Then she picks up her white skirt with her *Rouge Noir* nails and 'Billy!' she says, like he's a dog or something. She doesn't look to the left or the right. She puts that nun's smile on her face, walks past Mrs Casey and keeps walking until she is out the front door.

'People die,' that's what Natalie said to me on the phone. Because of course, we had a big surge when we got to the hotel and the boys got really trashed. At least, I got really trashed so I assume the boys did too, and I ended up snogging – not Billy, thank Christ – but someone else altogether. There's a little splash of puke on the back of my mother's silk skirt, and I'm pretty sure the guy got sick over my shoulder, and Natalie must hear it in my voice on the phone, the way I blame her for all this. Because when she picked up her white skirt and walked past Mrs Casey, something broke. Something between the four of us broke, for good.

'And anyway she's not dying,' says Natalie, who has no intention of dying, ever. 'She was just drunk.' Which is true.

Like we weren't drunk?

Which I don't think of saying, at the time. I think of saying it later, though – in the middle of the night, when I've just woken up in a sweat of pure shame. Apart from anything else, it's so *gay* – this trailer fantasy I had of me and Natalie swapping mascara, and spraying each other's hair, and fixing the boys' ties. Mrs Casey, downstairs, being tough and smart about my dress; giving me a tough, smart kiss on the cheek before we go. And it's a while before I realise that a) it isn't hairspray that makes you gay, it's sex that makes you gay, and b) I don't even like hairspray.

So that's all right, then.

For a while I just lie there and let all the little moments fly round in my head. Like months ago in the chipper, when Natalie said, 'There's not much point getting in a fizz.'

And I think that Billy's mother will live or die whether or not we get in a fizz. So I say, *fizz away*. You might as well play it as it feels, *Natalie*.

My sister's night light thinks about shifting from blue to lilac, and then seems to change its mind. What do I tell her – precocious brat that she is – what do I tell her, at the age of twelve and a half?

We are not connected.

Because this is what Natalie is saying, isn't it? That we are alone. That there is no connection between me and her, or between Billy and me, or between any of us and Mrs Casey, who might live or who might actually die. Between human beings.

And of course she isn't saying this at all.

I mean, I will still hang out with Natalie. And I know I'll get to like her in some different way – probably her way, actually. And I know the thing I have for my boyfriend isn't love, it's just a stupid kind of bliss. I know all these things – they're not what woke me up. What woke me was a feeling like a horror film – except really boring.

It was the sheets. When I lay down, just for a second, on Mr and Mrs Casey's moss-green sheets. Before the dance, when I was all dolled up in my silk skirt, and I pushed my hands along them and put my cheek against the dark cotton, just for a second. It was the smell of those sheets – cool, unwashed; like something I really wanted, going stale.

That is what woke me up.

HERE'S TO LOVE

I am thirty-nine. My friends tell me that their wives are not happy. My male friends, that is — old boyfriends, some of them. I meet them when I go back home, or they look me up when they come through Paris. It is that time of our lives: they ring, 'Hello, stranger,' and we meet for coffee and we catch up on old gossip and new babies and jobs and, late in the conversation, or the next evening when we meet for a quick drink, they tell me that their wives are not happy.

I don't know what I am supposed to do about it.

I ask how they are and they say that they're fine, and they might say it in a melancholy sort of way, but mostly I believe them — that they are content, or trying to be content. They work, and love their children, and they are interested in something like hiking or a new house — a second house: they like having this house and being in it at weekends.

'And how is Maria?' I say or Annie, or Joyce.

'Oh. She's up and down.'

This from my friend Shay, who I hadn't seen in seven years, and love so much, and not just him, but a little show-off called Peter, whose wife deserves to be miserable, and a guy called Tommy — this odd, impossible boyfriend I had once, who ended up in God knows what sort of nuptial bliss with four 'fantastic' kids: even Tommy at the mention of his wife's name looks vague, as though he can't remember exactly what she is supposed to be doing with her life just now.

I do feel burdened by it, a little; by the great unhappiness of my male friends' wives. Even Shay's wife, Marie, who I never really liked at the time. I do feel burdened by the heigh-ho sadness of his love for her. And I wonder, in a way, why he wants to tell me.

It is easier to say these things to someone you don't see every day, of course. And I never had children, which makes me a kind of throwback – I am still 'fun'. I am still the way we used to be.

Well, yes. Though sometimes I also feel my life closing down. My husband is old, and that makes me feel old too, from time to time. He is not rich. He did not leave his wife – his wife died, some years ago. My husband survived terrible historical events, and then he found me.

'So how are you?' says Shay. 'How the hell are you?' looking me up and down – looking mostly at my breasts, bless him.

'Good, thanks. Really good.'

Actually, they are usually men I have slept with, these guys from home, the ones with the sad wives. If the truth be told. But that isn't the important thing about them. I never did get very fussed about sex. It was all the other stuff that did my head in.

'You're looking well,' he says, by which he means I haven't got fat, or distracted. I am still poised, or I try to be, as I sit at the little table, and engage the waiter in a lot of chat about whether and when we will eat.

Shay looks at me while I do this. He likes it in a way that I find disturbing and nice. He is proud of my expertise. And he heaves a nostalgic sigh when I light a cigarette – the Irish don't smoke any more – I see his fingertips itch towards the pack.

'Sláinte.'

'Cheers.'

It doesn't matter to my husband, this social self; he doesn't care that I am Irish in an old-fashioned way, with a new lick of French. My Agnès B cardigan, and my vaguely hick Hermès scarf: these are certainly not the things that make me beautiful to him. Sometimes I would like to be understood by him, in a venal sort of way, but mostly I am content. I do not know why my husband chose to love me, but I know that, for both of us, it is a great romance.

'Good to see you.'

'So good to see you!'

'So how are you?' says Shay. 'What gives?'

It is lovely to see Shay. We went to the same college in Dublin, but I know him mostly from working together in London. We had this great expat thing going for a while, drinking huge amounts on Friday evenings – probably to stop us ending up in bed together. Not that it worked every time. It all feels like another life now, but there he is, just as big as himself.

'Oh, you know, nothing much.'

What can I say? My husband is sixty-three. He has no job. He is from Saigon. I know exactly what he is thinking when I look into his eyes. He never repeats himself. He told me once what he had witnessed – he told me over the course of one long night, in my old apartment in the Marais, and even now I think of that night as you might think of a dream.

He has a young mouth. I could say that.

My husband's mouth is tight and soft as an opening bud. He is careful in his sexual pleasures. He likes to look at me as I walk around the room. His touch is always specific, and chosen, and light. When he makes love to me, there is very little hesitation. And though we do not make love as much as we used to, it is always 'successful' as these things go.

This is what I would like to tell Shay, because I feel accused – of course I do – of making some deal with desire; some compromise. But my life took an unexpected turn and now I think unexpected thoughts. I think, for example, that many couples are happy in bed – strange, mismatched couples that you see on the metro; ugly ones too. What a great secret! And I wonder if sexual unease – this modern malaise – I wonder if this is not the big lie. I would say that it is the big capitalist lie, but these words make my husband close his eyes, and fail to open them for a long time.

The man with his eyes closed is called Le Quang Hoa.

There are marks on his body. Sometimes he flinches away from things – dogs, of course, and sudden shadows, but also things that I cannot understand: the sound of ice in his glass of water will cause him to flicker, and, for the smallest moment, shut down. I am alert to these signs. I do not look for them, or fear them, but I do recognise them, and I get up and take the glass out of his hand. That is all. He does not need me to do this. He lived alone in Paris for many years, before he met me.

But I take the glass away and I set it down. I wonder what that clinking sound does to his head. And when we make love, I am rarely inventive: I do not exult, or cause pain. I do not take the ice out of the bedside glass, for example, and run it down his spine.

This is what happens when love intersects with history. This is the distance you keep. Or it is the distance the Vietnamese keep. Or old men. Or it is the way my husband and I think about distance and tenderness – it is just the way we are. Who knows? We will have no children. We are very happy. Or, no. We are not happy, exactly. But we love each other very much, and this charges our lives with shape and light.

For the last few years we have lived off the rue Mouffetard. Every morning, when I go to work, my husband walks around to the municipal pool with his towel rolled under his arm. I think of him in the modern, blue water, swimming without a splash. He is like the old ladies you see on the French coast, who paddle out in their sunglasses and hairdos, and paddle back again, gossiping, like so many bodiless heads.

Shay gives in and lunges for the packet of Marlboro Lights. He fusses one to his mouth, and groans, long and deep. Then, when he has fully repented, he lights the match.

'Tastes fucking awful,' he says.

'Well, don't.'

But he doesn't stop. And now that the evening is unleashed, I ask him about his wife.

'How's Maria?'

'Oh. She's up and down,' he says.

'Right.'

Because 'up and down' is Irish for anything at all – from crying into the dishes to full-blown psychosis. Though, now that I think about it, a psychotic is more usually 'not quite herself'.

'I don't know,' he says. 'The moving around doesn't help. We went up to Epsom, to head office, and they talked about – well, they talked about me going to Germany actually, but I didn't think she'd be able for it. It was a tough one to turn down. Of course, the kids were just getting settled too, in their schools.'

I roll the ash off the top of my cigarette and keep nodding. I do love Shay. He has always had a large, and broken, heart. He is the kind of guy who would turn his pockets out in the street, to show he had nothing left to give. And here he is again, flinging his poor soul on to a café table for me; throwing it down – this old rag – because it is all he has.

'I know it's my fault. Or it's the job's fault. But I still love her, you know.'

'Well of course you do.'

'She wants to get back to her singing.'

'Oh? Right.'

'Well, that's what she was doing before.'

Was it? I remember Maria – a tiny, pretty woman – we met once and she hated me, on sight. She was very keen to tell me how she trained as a gymnast, as I recall, but I don't remember any singing. I'm sure Shay is right. I am sure she is a singer. I am sure she is a famous singer disguised as a wife, and that it is all Shay's fault for thwarting her, and shrinking her life. I remember their wedding – her compact little waist under his baggy hand. I think about her doing back flips at the age of nine.

'She's really good,' he says. 'She's brilliant. But it's not something you can just –'

And he lets the sentence drop.

It is five minutes to six. Back in the apartment, my husband has cooked, and decanted, and cooked up again, a beef broth for noodle soup. He won't wait for me to come home. He will pour it, quite soon, and slurp it down. After which, if I am still not back, he will switch on the TV. He likes science fiction: he is especially fond of *Xena: Warrior Princess*. If there is none of this stuff to watch, he will sit and read from a selection of medical books he has, also quack medical books;

pausing occasionally to push at a spot on his abdomen, or to flex and examine his toes.

Five streets away, I touch the back of Shay's big hand and say, 'It's what happens.'

Shay looks at my fingertips, lying there. Then he lifts his large head and looks at me, like, What would I know about it? What would I know about 'what happens'?

'That feeling that you're running out of road. It just hits women quicker. I mean, when they have kids, it hits them. That's all. When they have kids.'

'The thing I like about you,' says Shay, 'is you tell it like it is. "You get old, you get fat, it all turns to shit, you die."'

'Yeah well.'

So now it is my fault – the fact that Shay's wife will never get on the radio, to croon her bedsit jazz. I am the one who is standing in her way.

'It's a very particular thing,' he says. 'Someone else's dreams. It's not something you can control.'

My husband was born in 1943. In the course of his lifetime, he survived invasion by the Japanese, the French and the American armies. At a guess, his family not only survived these occupations, they did quite well out of them. Hoa taught at the French *lycée* in Saigon. He was married during what we call the Vietnam War, and he had two sons. One of his sons lives over the border in Laos, and the other does not want to see his father again. When he was a young man, Hoa thought that Paris was the centre of the universe. After three years in a government re-education camp, he had no thoughts about Paris at all.

'I got married,' I say, suddenly. 'Did I tell you?'

'Christ!' says Shay. 'No, you did not tell me. You certainly did not tell me.'

He looks at me with great excitement. Then something drains from the back of his eyes.

The thing Shay actually likes about me – the thing they all liked about me – is that I didn't want to marry them. I didn't even want to fall in love. As far as I was concerned, you slept with someone or you didn't. It was quite simple. Men really like that; or they think they do. But the only person who understood it – and perfectly – is my husband, who took me by the hand, one ordinary evening, and led me into the next room.

'We only did it for the visa.'

This is a terrible betrayal. It is not even true.

'So tell us,' says Shay. But I have already told him too much. So I make a little story out of it: about my work with refugees, and how we met over a table spread with photographs and chopped-up text and sticks of glue. I could say that the photographs on the table were of this or that victim, but that there was nothing of the victim about Hoa, though I could feel, as I stood beside him, the fact of his pain and the way he transcended his pain. But I don't say this, because Shay will think I am some kind of pervert. And perhaps I am.

He is looking at me now, smiling with a slight and social disgust. He doesn't quite know what to say. Then he comes over all Irish and asks what they think of it 'back home'. Well, I think it is none of their business, actually. My mother died when I was six years old, which means that we are a more than usually fucked-up family; more than usually restrained.

'I haven't told them,' I say.

'No?'

'No.'

'Fair enough,' says my friend Shay, who loves a sad little gymnast and gets her to load his dishwasher for him, every night of the week.

I wonder about my husband's wife; if she too was disappointed by the smallness of her life, before it suddenly got very small indeed. I don't know. I know that I am jealous of her, sometimes; a woman who was born twenty-five years before I was, and who is now long dead. I think that he must have loved her more than he loved me. I say this to him one morning when I wake up and find him sitting by the window in the dawn light. He looks out at the sky for a few moments.

'She was very nice,' he agrees, and thinks about her for a while.

'I don't remember her so well,' he says finally, in his careful sing-song. *Je ne me rappele bien d'elle.*

I realise that I have no idea what it was to love a woman – or just to marry her – in Saigon, in the middle of the war. I have scarcely any idea what it is to love the man that I love now.

'So tell us,' says Shay. 'What brought him over here?'

'What brought him here?'

I start to laugh. Then I stop.

My husband sleeps in the afternoon. When he wakes, he folds the duvet at the bottom of the bed. He is a creature of routine. But he does not shout or cry if the duvet gets messed up again. He does not sit, as Shay's wife might sit – weeping, at the state of the house and the destruction of all her dreams.

'Well,' I say carefully. 'He always liked France. He is a Francophone.'

I talk about him some more and Shay starts to realise how old Hoa is. He does the thing men do when they think I might not be getting the ride; amused but surprisingly vicious, too. *I'd fuck you.*

And I smile.

My husband sleeps every afternoon, quite simply. Sometimes I wander in and out again, without noticing that he is there. I cannot hear his breathing. He might as well be a sheet of paper – a blank sheet of paper – stretched out on the bed. Then he opens his eyes, and sees me.

'So how old is this guy, actually?' says Shay. We are drunk, now. It has come to this.

'Old enough,' I say.

And he lifts his glass to that.

'Here's to love,' he says.

Fifteen minutes later he is making chopping motions on the table with his fat, large hand. He says all our partners can't be refugees or have cancer or what have you but the implication is there – the implication is there – that some day they might be, and that we will still love them, we will still be married to them, no matter what. And I can't disagree with that. I am about to say so, but Shay takes my intake of breath as a stab at recrimination and he fights on.

By now I am almost done with Shay. I watch him and wait for the ruin of our love – the secular, ordinary, drinkers' love we have always had for each other. He is unbearably coarse now; the texture of his skin, the big expressions on his big face. He knows nothing, he says – well, he knows very little – about the history of it all and what went on, but it is important in all of these situations, complex as they are, fucked up as they are, to know who did what. At the end of the day, he says, it is important to know *what your husband did during the war*.

I light another cigarette. Shay sees the look on my face, and subsides.

After which there is truculence, regret, a slow, bitter apology – each of which I have to jolly him through, because this is all my fault, after all. He is depressed now. The whole business of accusing me has worn him out.

'I'm sorry,' I say, because he seems genuinely hurt by it all. Besides, I will never get rid of him unless I confess to something, whatever it is – the nameless thing that I have done wrong – my refusal to live in Epsom and mourn.

Which is all very well, I think, as we hug and separate outside the little café, never to see one another again. Which is all very well, I think, as I walk home to a man who can not pass an Alsatian dog without wetting himself, a man whose left foot and ankle were broken in fifteen different places; an ordinary old man from Vietnam, who snaps at me sometimes like I am a servant girl, and spends ten minutes every morning in a shoulder-stand in order to cure his piles.

Which is all very well.

I turn down rue Rataud and look up, as I always do, at one of the buildings halfway down the street. I saw a man with a gun up there once. It was in one of the corner apartments, and he was leaning over the little balcony. He pointed this large ugly pistol down the cross street. Then he swung around and pointed the gun at me. Or past me.

Those corner apartments are so beautiful; such enviable places to live. I mean, this was the 5th Arrondissement. It was the wrong place for such a thing to be happening – though there was no doubt that it was happening. It was very real. The timing was odd, and there was no soundtrack, and everything about it was too banal. I did not look up again – I did not want to attract his attention, I suppose – and in a few moments I had walked through the intersection in a very ordinary way. Down off the kerb, across the cobbles, up on to the opposite path. I did not look behind me, to check that he was pointing the thing somewhere else, or that he was gone.

I still walk down the street most evenings. And every time I do this, I think about a bullet in the back – about the fact that most of the time, it does not happen to me.

I walk home to Le Quang Hoa, thinking about his body in death; neat and beautiful on our marriage bed. I open the door and wonder if he is real. And if he is still alive.

HONEY

When she tried to think what they looked like, the women who stood in front of him at wine receptions, or at his desk, or at the door of his office, the nearest she could come up with was 'drenched'. They stood with their arms slightly lifted from their sides, as though their fingers were dripping water. Like a childhood picture of the Princess and the Pea, when the princess arrives at the palace door; her dress a sopping sheet, and rain trickling out of her little green shoes.

Of course there would be other things going on – chat, or laughter, or the way they worked their eyes, but none of it so remarkable as this straining stillness; standing at his threshold, or placing some file quickly on his desk, or interrupting his small talk in a crowd to say, quite wordlessly, 'Fuck me again. You must. You must fuck me again,' because this was very clearly what was going on – or what had gone on and would not, at a guess, continue to go on, any more.

It was bad for business, in a mild sort of way. Catherine was a client, after all – but these women ignored her; they just couldn't wrench their heads around to be introduced. And she did feel herself to be elbowed aside: 'You must not speak to her, whoever she is. You must fuck me instead. Now. Any time.'

It happened three, perhaps four times, in the few years she dealt with him. Mostly Catherine was amused by it, though she did find the women really very rude. Each of them so beautiful and distinctive. Of course they didn't last. And she might have felt aggrieved on their behalf – for the way they were pushed out while he continued to make his way up – were it not for their ambition, which was so open, almost livid. Catherine had never slept with anyone for gain, in her life. If you could call it gain.

She wondered if she was missing something. She felt so ordinary beside them, fuddy and intellectual. There was too much pleasure, for her, in the way he just looked at them steadily, and carefully spoke, and then turned back to her to say, 'Sorry, sorry. Go on.'

Phil Brogan. Five foot nine, at a push. Fortyish. Sex machine.

Actually, she liked him. Clever and restless and constantly perceptive – in some ways, he was not like a man at all. And it wasn't as if he was married, as she said to her partner Tom, so why not? There was a story about a stationery cupboard – which she didn't believe – but even so, it said something about the suddenness of him. She assumed this was what got them going. Though she didn't know what it was that brought them back for more.

'Big cock,' said Tom.

'Do you think?' she said.

'Absolutely.'

Which was a brittle enough attempt, as these conversations go. But in the last while, they had other things on their minds.

Catherine's mother was dying, far too young, and far too painfully, of cancer. So as well as all the phone calls and the ferrying, there was the mother thing, which is to say, too much complaining and too much love. She was in chemotherapy: four months in from a late diagnosis, and an unknown number of weeks or months or years from the end of it all. Her mother was so weak she reeled into the car door every time Catherine went around a corner, and when they braked, it was only the seat belt that stopped her from bumping her face on the dash. And she complained all the time. Catherine was going too fast, she was going too slow, she wanted to have a cigarette; what was wrong with high heels, when was Catherine going to lighten up, get something done with her hair.

And then in the hospital, when the pain relief was good, such peace: her mother existing – breath by breath – at her side. Both of them listening to her body, the silent chemicals doing their silent work, and the dent on the side of her breast the largest thing in the room.

Catherine thought about bees in a swarm; the cancer being smoked out of her mother's body to settle in the space under her arm, a drowsy mass. If she could just scoop them up as a beekeeper might, and carry them away, and leave not a single one behind.

In the evening, while Catherine dozed in the chair, a hand might come out to startle her. It would touch her arm or face, her mother's voice behind it, saying, 'Go home, Kitty-kit. Go home to that man of yours.'

Tom was being sadly perfect since these days; there was always food in the fridge and clean T-shirts in the basket, and silence when silence was the necessary thing. But Catherine knew that once the light was out he would break across the space between them, in a rush to comfort her, with hands and mouth and all his large, physical self.

'Don't,' she said. 'Don't make me cry.'

As the months ground on she told him it was as though she was missing something down there – a widget, or a grommet, or a switch you might throw. She did not say that when he stroked her, it felt as though her skin was coming off under his hands.

And so they had some sex – not much – and snapped at each other or did not speak, while Catherine's mother was discharged with no talk of readmission and, around a schedule of home helps and neighbours, work staggered on.

The maddest thing was the way she decided her mother must be better, if the hospital had let her go: the way she thought, very clearly and thoroughly, that even though her mother was not cured – even though she was, in fact, dying – she was also much, much better, in many significant ways. Of course she was better. She was back home.

In the middle of this strange and untrue time, Phil Brogan rang. He needed to bring a client to a conference in Killarney, he said, in May. Would she do it? Would she mind? The hotel was fantastically swish. Call it a freebie. Her Christmas bottle of brandy, arriving early in the year.

'Hang on,' she said, and checked her diary. She could go if

81

her mother was a little better by May. Or she could go if her mother was dead by, say, the end of April. But if her mother was actively dying during those four days in May, then Catherine would not be able to make it. So, because she loved her mother, there was only one answer she could give: 'Yes. No problem. Thanks.' Not even stopping to think whether a conference in Killarney was really her bag.

In the next four weeks her mother's pain became unbearable and, talking to her GP, Catherine realised that she would have to beg for a hospice bed. Once she gave in to the idea of death, she could not stand the wait. People weren't supposed to linger in hospices – who was clogging up all the beds? Keep moving, she shouted in her head. Keep moving.

Nights, she and her sister took turns to sleep in their mother's spare room with a shelf full of medication and a list of times and doses that they checked and re-checked until the writing made no sense. Rolling her mother over to change the soiled sheet, or scolding her while she tried to get a hypodermic into her thigh, Catherine was sustained by a peculiar fantasy – she was riding a horse around the lakes of Killarney, like a bad costume drama, with Phil Brogan in tow. Sometimes, they got down off the horses and went for a swim. Sometimes, they stopped under a spreading oak tree.

And then the hospice. The doctors were generous with their drips and shots – her mother one day wild on morphine, sitting up in bed, applying green eyeshadow and saying, 'These are the things I regret: I never slept with a Frenchman. I never slept with that little fucker whatsisname who went on to make all the money. I didn't enjoy you girls enough when you were still young enough not to thwart me. I deeply resent all that dieting. Deeply. Bitterly. What else? Nothing. I hate the taste of caviar.'

For two weeks, Catherine walked the corridors with sympathetic nurses and murmuring friends and did not give in to the obscene urge she had, which was to say, 'Well, she'll have to die soon. I am going to Killarney in May.'

In the event, her mother made it with more than a week to spare.

Catherine threw twelve white roses into the open grave, and stepped back from the loose earth and the sharp drop. Tom held her by the waist and forearm as though they were skating, and that was what it felt like – an incredible lightness as she walked away from the mess of ground. The air was shocking; pure and sharp, with the smell of early summer rising from the soil. In the distance, someone was mowing the graveyard grass. It was May. The planet was turning. Her feet still touched the ground.

She packed and repacked for Killarney four or five times. She had to bring togs; she had to have business suits, and dresses for the evening, and mid-morning jeans for lounging around in and horse-riding gear. She wondered if she could play golf.

'Have I ever played golf?' she shouted at Tom through the open bedroom door.

'No,' he said.

'I'm sure I played golf with you once. Somewhere high – like Howth, or Bray Head.'

'Not with me,' said Tom.

That evening, he walked into the bathroom as she was waxing her legs, and winced, and went back out again. In the morning, he dragged the oversized suitcase to the car, and kissed her on the forehead and said, 'Relax. Have a good time.'

The hotel was a large old country house. Catherine felt like another person when she walked up the granite steps: she felt like a person who liked hotels. There wasn't a piece of chintz in sight, it was all slate and warm wood and waffle-cloth robes.

She rang Phil's room from the phone beside her bed. She could hear him shift and settle after he picked up, and she knew that he was lying down too.

'So. You made it.' Then he didn't seem to want to hang up, for a while.

They met downstairs and ordered coffee.

'No,' he said. 'What the hell, it's after four, we could have a gin and tonic or a beer, something fizzy, what about champagne? Do you do it by the glass?'

The waitress blushed. Catherine thought he was being really cheesy, until he turned back to her and said, 'Sparkling wine?'

It wasn't the waitress he wanted.

It was true. Phil Brogan wanted to do something very sudden and very urgent with her, Catherine Maguire, recently bereaved. Or, seeing as this was a hotel and not a stationery cupboard, something very urgent and very slow. She felt a rising impulse to giggle, but he held her gaze and did not look away. There was nothing in this guy's pants that liked a joke. This was what all the drenched girls knew. This imperative. This trap.

'A gin and tonic is fine,' she said.

Horrible to be so mirthless, she thought, and wondered if they would end up in his room, or do it in hers.

Phil took out his mobile and went, with a flourish, to switch it off.

'Hang on. Sorry. One last call.'

It was to a florist. The flowers he had ordered for his mother? He had changed his mind.

'Not an orchid – roses. Twelve. Red. Right. "To my darling mother on her birthday."'

What a romantic.

When she thought about it later, this phone call was the weirdest moment of the whole three days – the helpless need he had to mark her cards. He loved his mother. No wonder he was still single. Catherine didn't think they made them like that any more.

But at the time, it was the coincidence that startled her. This wasn't about sex or betrayal, this was about flowers falling into a grave. It was about red roses or white. It was about dying or being alive. It was something she had to do.

Meanwhile, she did not know how these seductions went. Who moved? Who demurred? Did it last for three nights, or half a night? And would she be doomed, ever afterwards, to supplication and hunger; not being able to cross the threshold of his office, but standing in the rain at the door?

She left him to shower and change, then came down to dinner and flirted like crazy over the poached wild salmon.

Her mother would have been proud of her. Actually, though, there was nothing else she could do – she could hardly speak, so she might as well simper. It was unbearable. At half past twelve she fled from the bar with a quick goodnight, and lay awake endlessly in the dark of her room.

She thought about Tom. Sometime before dawn she got out of bed and looked in the mirror: it was a different body in there. Grief had made her thin.

In the morning she called Phil's room from the front desk and he climbed into the car beside her, his hair still damp from the shower. She drove to a larger, cheaper hotel in town, where they walked into the function room and they did their spiel, and were good at it. After which there was the whole afternoon to fill before darkness and sex, or no sex, one more time. Phil seemed amused by all this scheduling – the intimacy of it – and back at their own hotel, he suggested they go their separate ways for a while. What for? Catherine hired a horse and trekked a path behind the hotel that opened into scrubland high above the famous lakes. She looked at them far below; green and grey, as the weather chased across the water. She looked up at the sky, and across at the light, and around her at the lichened, small oaks with their dry, scrubby branches. The horse's mane under her hand was thick and electric. She picked up the reins and turned towards home.

They met for drinks at five, by which time Catherine could not speak at all. Which was fine. Phil told her about himself – his scrambler bike, his trip to Mexico, his teacher with the strap. He was at his interesting best. But every time she opened her mouth, he just looked at her. Why was she always throwing things off kilter? There was something that had to happen before they had sex, a personal thing, and she didn't know what it was.

'Will you have another one?' he said, waggling his empty glass.

'Yes,' said Catherine. 'I think I will. My mother just died.'

He missed a beat.

'I'm sorry to hear it,' he said.

'Well, when I say "just", it was actually quite a while ago, now.'

'I see.'

'Sometimes, it feels closer, that's all. It sort of sneaks up on you.'

'Yes,' he said. 'I think I know what you mean.'

It was, possibly, the rudest thing she had ever said.

Over dinner, she realised that he was trying to impress her. That was why she was supposed to listen and not talk back to him. Her mother used to tell her these things – she was not supposed to impress *him:* it was supposed to work the other way around. So she smiled, in an impressed sort of way, and tried not to think about the look in his eye, or the exact heft of his dick in her hand. She knew that if it didn't happen tonight the whole situation would become unpleasant, so she planned her move, using the moment when they pushed back from the table to suggest a walk in the garden at the back of the hotel. He looked at her and nearly smiled. Good girl, he seemed to say. Well done.

They went out into the moonlight and walked in precoital silence down shallow avenues of clipped box. Some of the roses were out already, white and grey against the black of the bushes, and there were low pools of green where a line of lights showed the way.

It was May. The central path was shaggy with lavender not yet in bloom. Someone had thrown a sweater over the gatepost at the end of the walk that, as they got closer, shifted in the corner of her eye. Catherine looked. Oozing over the concrete ball was a dripping, black, velvet swarm. Clumps of bees fell from the ragged edges, or crawled back up the gatepost to rejoin the mass. It was like watching some slow liquid spill and then unspill itself; honey making its way back into the jar.

'Bees,' she said to Phil, who stood stock-still as she walked forward to stare at them. Then she ducked down to catch a falling cluster and set it back on the pile.

'Jesus,' she heard him say behind her. The bees were bristly and soft, and their tiny legs clung to her fingertips as she shook them back into the mess of black wings. She watched them until she could not tell them apart. Then she started to cry.

But this was not what she was ashamed of, finally, as Phil Brogan lost his moment and walked her back into the hotel. She was ashamed of what she had felt as she stepped away from her mother's grave. That lightness – it was desire. And it was vast. The smell of the air and of the soil and the grass; Tom not supporting her with his arms so much as holding her to the skin of the earth. It was like she could fuck anything: the Killarney lakes and the sky that ran over them, and posh hotels with wafflecloth robes, and the pink scent of a rose that showed grey in the darkness, and the whole lovely month of May. She could swim in it, and swallow it, and cram it into her in each and every possible way.

All of it, that is, except for this unpleasant man, who could not face his own consequences, who stood outside her hotel bedroom and said, 'What about a nightcap? You must have got a fright.'

Catherine looked at him. She did not know where the air stopped and her skin began.

'Not really,' she said.

Switzerland

I.

She did him an injustice, she thought – the American. He was so full of himself. That was the way he arrived in her life, a cup that was brimful; a look on his face that said she didn't know the half of it.

So talk to me, she said. Fill me in.

He was so healthy and new, with his recent blond hair and his fresh white teeth. He might have been made in the airport. He might have materialised in the hum of a security door frame.

Hello, Dublin.

So tell me about your grandfather, she said. About the cups wrapped in old newspaper that you found in a box under the stairs. Tell me about coffin ships and how you came from Connemara, really. Tell me about potatoes.

My great-aunt Louise, he said. When she went mad.

In the old country, she said.

In Connecticut. Rubbed the eyes off potatoes because she thought they were looking at her.

You just made that up.

No, it is true, he said. She went dotty. Quite literally. Ants, flies, mildew, mould – it was the spots that drove her crazy. She thought they were eyes. She thought the world was boiling with eyes. Gravel, for instance. Think about it.

Eyes or eyeballs? she said.

Actually, I made it up.

He wore a little fake history on his back; a white shirt, very thick cotton. It smelt of coppers and laundry blueing and the valet's hands. It looked like something that fell out of a Lancashire loom into a little mill girl's lap. But the cloth probably came from China – she told him – it fell out of a loom into a little China girl's lap. Because everyone has money, these days.

He told her about the Mississippi Delta, the endless flat fields, and the cotton bales that are the precise size of the lorries that come to take them away. And the houses, which are the precise size of the cotton bales, as if the field workers live in lorry containers with a porch slapped on the front. He told her about a parade of African Americans walking down the road in the middle of nowhere, fantastically well dressed, following a slow hearse in the heat. Not another car in sight.

You win, she said. Take off that shirt.

What is this?

It is a competition. It is a poetry competition.

All right, he said. What about you?

Me. I'm the girl in the silk dressing gown with a magnolia tree flowering up the back. I am tired and overused. I like dark lipstick. Who are you?

As you said, I'm the American.

In the street he is handsome and long, but his legs – that look so easy under him – are large and massively hinged when he is in bed. He makes her feel like a child; his big body so indifferent and easy to scale.

I wish there was some other way of doing this, she said. Sex is just a shortcut, that's all.

Well, yes it is, he said. But what the hell?

2.

In Dublin, he thought, the women fuck like we're all in it together, like the place is one big orphanage and they've gone home for the night, and left us to play.

And it is all a joke. That's the other thing about Dublin. The thing you don't understand is that they are always only joking, even in bed. Until you leave – then they stand outside your window in the middle of the night screaming and throwing bottles. Or they take an overdose, maybe, just for a joke.

So he watched her.

Walking around her flat on the North Circular Road, or in his room in Harold's Cross, trying to put a date on her, or a place – naked as she was – trying to fix her, even as he lost her to some small thing; the angle of her eyelashes, or the grain of skin pulled to a slant, when she turned to reach for the bed-side lamp.

She said that sex was an act of the imagination, but he said it was a speech act. He felt that he was blurting something into her. And afterwards, he told her about his father's death.

He remembered his mother's friend, Caitlin, taking him and his brother to the park, to get them out of the house, leaving his mother to the extravagance of her grief. He was so young when it happened, he didn't want to leave his mother be-hind. He thought she was being punished, somehow. He pictured her reeling from window to window, smashing things, stuffing her mouth with the back of her hand, when, what is more likely, she sat quietly in the dark, in a chair. There was no question that she loved his father. No question at all. And two years later she put on her gloves and walked out the door and got herself another one, another husband, just like that.

He liked the new guy well enough, but between the smil-ing lover and the dead father, he sometimes wondered how he grew up straight. For this, of course, they must thank his mother. Thank you, Mom. They must thank the extravagance of her grief. Because this is where he travelled now – into the heart of that disturbance. He was always running back to the house to look for her, and he found – sometimes one thing, sometimes another. In Thailand, he saw a model boat made out of chicken bones. In Berlin he saw a woman breastfeeding in a pavement café, and her eyes were animal; those big wide pavements with plaques every three yards to mark the houses of the slaughtered Jews. And in Dublin, he found . . .

You.

Ah, she said.

You know what I like about Irish women? he said. I like the way they still call themselves 'girls'. And I like the weather in their hair. Which is romantic of me, but I am Irish too, you know. So I like your big family; all those brothers and sisters bubbling up, like the froth on milk. And, I hate to say this, but I love your accent. Also your dark lipstick, and all the history flowering up your back.

3.

They went to Venice for the weekend, and bought an umbrella.

They found it in a poky shop that sold umbrellas and nothing else. She thought it should be a black umbrella with a wooden handle – old-fashioned, because they were in Venice – but he picked up a green telescopic thing and said, What about this?

It has to be black.

What do you want a black one for?

Because we're in Venice.

Already, the man behind the counter despised them. Tim picked up a big striped golf umbrella and tried to open it in the shop. Elaine ran into the street.

Come out. Come out here, she said. But he just kept working at the catch. She had to reach in to the dark shop and drag him out.

What? *What?* he said.

You can't open it inside.

Why not?

The umbrella-seller was, by now, just about sickened by them; he was about to reach for his antacid tablets, or his gun.

It's unlucky, she said.

Tim looked at her. Then he cocked his head and looked, for a long time, at the Venetian sky.

It was still raining.

All right, he said, and they went back in and asked for a black umbrella and they walked back out with it tucked under her arm and hoisted it in the narrow street, and then they lost it before dinner-time.

Everywhere they went in that town, she remembered the last time she was in Venice, with a different man some years before. It was like another town shifting under this one, a *pentimento* of cafés and churches that had all become smaller or bigger since she had last seen them; shops or squares that were always around the next corner, until she realised that the corner itself had disappeared. She chased a black-and-white church all the way into the Grand Canal and nearly walked into the water, so convinced she was that the church should be there. When she found it, somewhere quite different, the cool white-and-black marble had been overlaid with baroque gold. When did that happen? she said.

She had not been happy in Venice. The last time she was here the city had accused her of not being in love; or of being in love in some wrong or wrong-headed way. So here she was with Tim, making amends.

He insisted on using a map. Elaine said that if he didn't bother with the map, then they wouldn't get lost, because it didn't matter where they went, it was all beautiful and all the same. Or all awful, maybe. After dinner, they ended up walking the periphery in the dark. There was a puzzle of streets to the left of them and, to the right, the open waters of the lagoon with real waves, just like the real sea. They walked a hopeful semicircle until the causeway came into view, then they cut back into the ghetto. They came across a fiesta in a small square, with trestle tables and bunting, accordion music and jugs of wine. The real people of Venice sat and laughed under a home-made banner for the Communist Party. They did not see the tourists pushing their way through the square, in the way that they did not see the pigeons at their feet.

Elaine lay in the hotel room, which was cheap for Venice, but which had, even so, a slightly tatty chandelier. It also had damp. She read the guidebook. It said that during the time of the Doges the prostitutes had to wear their underwear on the outside. Another guidebook said that they had to wear their clothes inside out. There was a problem of translation here – the prostitutes had to wear their inside clothes on the outside. They had to wear their hearts on their sleeves, they had to wear their wombs in a prolapse – not that that would be much use. She thought of wearing her bra outside her T-shirt, just here in the room, as a conversation piece, as a precursor to some vaguely syphilitic Venetian sex. But she just lay there until Tim came back, which he did, with a pistachio-flavoured ice cream to cheer her up. And because it was Venice, she had her period, so his penis was stained with the brown blood of it, marinating half the night, until he suddenly woke and went over to the wash-hand basin on the wall.

She thought that it was the cuttlefish in its dark ink that had brought it on. Or perhaps it was the canal, running black outside the restaurant door.

4.

In Mexico, they booked a beach hut from an old man who had lost the fingers of his right hand. He waved the stubs at them and mimed hauling in nets over the side of a boat.

'Fiss,' he said. 'Fiss.'

They swam all day or hung in hammocks and tried to forget their diarrhoea. The coast road was full of crazy pick-ups with kids hanging off the back, but at dusk the people sank back into the forest and there was nothing left, except for a rare murmuring under the trees. The locals did not seem to shout much, or even speak. When they ate, their plates and spoons made no clatter.

Zipolite, the next beach up, was full of tourist trash who slept on the sand with their surfboards tied to their wrists; older types too, hippies and junkies who were madder than his great-aunt Louise.

One of them sat on the sand nearby as they were having dinner. He looked about seventy years old. A beach-bum, afflicted by sores – they were infected mosquito bites, or needle marks, perhaps. He stretched out his legs and looked in horror at the scabs, his face puzzling and straining, as though he expected maggots to crawl out of them. Then he attacked one with his nails, tearing at the skin.

It put them off their food.

Tim said he might have come down to dodge the draft. They looked at him. History, there on the beach. Elaine said he looked more like a prisoner of war – the last GI, the one who couldn't go home.

They paid the bill, and Elaine felt, as he put the money down, the pull in him to Be An American – a man who looked at the movies and saw his own home up there on the screen.

Do you ever want to go back?

You have no idea what my high school was like, he said. Everyone had a car. Everyone crashed their car. It wasn't enough to score a girl, you had to score the girl's coked-up mother. I went to school with guys so stupid, you look at them on the football field and you think, Why don't we just eat them? The whole herd of them. That might be more useful.

The sun was sinking like a stone. The meal and the beer made their skin crawl in the heat. The food pulled at their blood, leaving the surface of them a sheet of sensation; prickles and irritations and the sense of someone at your shoulder, leaning in to whisper – what? – your name, or your other name, your secret. At the end of every day in Mexico they were brushed by shame; a dirty bird's wing someone had dropped on the sand.

For fuck's sake, she said. The whole world is about America, these days. It's not a country, it's a fucking religion. And I don't mind. I am perfectly happy with you as you are. I am perfectly happy with you as an ethnic *product*. But can we, from now, for ever, forget the froth on the milk and the weather in my fucking hair?

The next morning at breakfast, she looked at the fried eggs on her plate and thought she must be pregnant, and she gripped the edge of the table in her fright.

But it was Tim who got sick. They went inland, and he stayed in the hotel room, while she took a day trip out of San Cristóbal de las Casas. There was talk of rebels in the hills. Elaine sat in the back of a pick-up truck, high up in the scrublands, and watched a group of men labouring uphill with sacks of coffee beans on their backs.

After an hour or so, they stopped at a café – just a roof with a table under it, and a broken fridge full of a bright pink cola. In the middle of the table there was a bowl of powdered coffee, turning to gleaming syrup on the communal spoon. A filthy little girl looked at them, with perfect awe as they drank out of plastic cups. Her eyes were the only clean things about her, apart from, when she laughed, the inside of her mouth.

The other people in the pick-up were Swiss. They worked for FIFA, the football organisation, they said: two men and a sharp, hilarious woman, all wearing company baseball caps. She didn't know what they were here for. She didn't see boys playing football in the villages they passed; she saw a lot of wooden, evangelical churches, and dirt.

They passed a coffee plantation and Elaine said it was a pity the people didn't drink the coffee that was growing right there on their own hillsides, that they had to drink horrible dried Nestlé instead. The Swiss looked at her. After a moment, one of the men said, 'Well, that's the way the world goes.' He glanced at the woman and gave a little smirk. She smirked back at him. Then the other man chanced a sneaky little smile. They turned away from each other, airily, and went back to looking at the poor people on the side of the road.

The fucking Swiss. They spoke perfect English to her and perfect Spanish to the guide. They could probably say, 'Well, that's the way the world goes,' in French, Italian and German too. *So geht es. C'est comme ça.*

Is the war over yet? *La guerre, est-elle terminée?*

She tried to figure out which one of the men was sleeping with the woman; a good-time sort of girl, who wasn't a girl any longer. Forty-five at least. She was having a brilliant time on the back of a pick-up truck in Chiapas.

The men were middle-aged. It happened to men all of a sudden, she thought. First the baldness thing, and then Boof! big lunches, cars, overtime, fat already. Well, that's the way the world goes. She wondered if it would happen to Tim, stuck back in the hotel with what might be amoebic dysentry – at least that is what they thought it was, opening the guidebook every few hours to peer at diagrams of what looked like little shrimp, wondering if these were the things that were swimming around in his gut.

When she got back, he was feeling a bit better, and she told him about the Swiss bastards who were so pleased with the way the world went, because it always went their way. Tim started giving out about Nestlé reps going around in white coats with powdered-milk samples, telling women not to breastfeed. But this really annoyed her, somehow. This was not what she was talking about. He did not understand. She said it was almost a sex thing. They smirked because – all three of them – they liked being *bad*.

The way she said 'bad', they might have had sex themselves, if it weren't for his little shrimp. Instead, they got irritated and fought. She found herself defending Switzerland, when she meant to say the opposite. The Swiss didn't actually do anything wrong, she said, they just let other people do it. They made their money out of other people's greed. Because that is the way the world goes. And, Yes, he said. Yes, exactly.

Later, in the dark, she said she was tired of the hurt she caused, just by being alive. She was tired of her own endless needs. And him too. She was tired of him, and of the fact that she would hurt him, too. She could do it now, if he liked, but certainly she would hurt him, over time.

He said it was up to him, really. All of that.

They were in San Cristóbal de las Casas. It was a beautiful town and there were books in the shops and real coffee in the tourist cafés. It was the centre of the rebel movement in Chiapas, Mexico, and Elaine felt that she was in an important place at an important time. She hoped it would work out well for the people here, and also for her and Tim, that they would always be in love, and drink good coffee, and that he would always keep his hair.

5.

Back in Dublin, she unpacked the dressing gown with the flowers on the back and said, I have to get another job, I have to do something, I can't stand this fucking country. It's all right for you.

We could live in France, he said.

She rounded on him and said, What do you do? What are you *for?*

He lifted his empty hands in the air.

This fucking country, she said. You have no idea. Come down to Cork with me. That'll change your mind.

But he loved them all, and they loved him. Her brothers bringing him down to the local for a pint and her father talking about tornadoes in America, and was he ever in one, at all? And it was all the Big Yank in the front parlour, and no one asked them once about Italy, or Mexico, or the North Circular Road for that matter. No one asked anything, except would he like a cup of tea, because in this house, it became clear, questions were out of the question. She had never noticed this before. Questions were impolite. And Tim better at this game than any of them – not looking at the tablecloth or at the cup in his hand, or at any of their sad, accumulated objects, but instead engaging in a vast discussion about all kinds of weather, from the ice on Lake Michigan to the storm in Bucharest that made your hair stand up with the static.

You don't say, said her father, his small stash of books behind him, dead on the shelf.

They gave him the sofa to sleep on, so Elaine crept downstairs in the middle of the night and they had the quietest sex known to mankind. They inched their way along the floor and ended up under the table where, looking up, Elaine saw a crayoned boat she had drawn, one endlessly idle afternoon, when she was nine or ten. A green boat with a blue sail. Her own secret sign.

Where do you want to go? he said. Where do you want to go, now?

WHAT YOU WANT

If I had three wishes; the thing to do is get three more. 'Hello,' says the angel, says the fairy, says the devil even, 'What do you want? One. Two. Three.' And I say, 'Well, first off, I'll have three more of those please,' and then you have five, you see, to play with, which is two extra, because there's always a trick.

Like you might say, 'Well, for my first wish, I'd like to have a beautiful body,' and azzakazzam, 'There's your beautiful body,' says the angel and, when you look down, you're still the same old yoke and the angel says, 'Well, it is beautiful – the way one bone fits into another, and the blood flows, and the brain works and all that,' and maybe, yes – in the scheme of things – but, 'No!' you say, 'No!' and you blurt out something like, 'I want a body like Raquel Welch,' and of course she's ancient, these days, so all you get is a heap of silicone and arthritis. Or even worse, you ask for a body like Marilyn Monroe, who is actually dead, not to mention rotten, or you ask for the body of 'a film star' and the angel gives you Marlon Brando. Or you get the actual body of an actual film star like, say, Nicole Kidman's body, and she sues – quite right too – because there she is wandering around in your old sack and everyone says it's just prosthetic, like that stupid nose she wore. Serve her right.

So the third wish then, has to put it all right. You think about it really hard and you say nothing for ages, and then very carefully you say, 'I'd like a body like the one Raquel Welch had in *One Million Years B.C.,*' and dah dah! – the full thing down to the furry bikini, except it leaves out your face, and you're some sort of monster oul' wan with a dynamite bosom, like those plastic things men wear on stag nights. Or your face does change – because your face is part of your body, of course it is – and your grandchildren don't recognise you and no one will let you back into your own house and you end up in a state of semiprostitution just trying to get the bus fare back to the place where the angel disappeared into the clear blue sky.

It's all just semantics, as my son Jimmy would say.

The thing to do, I say, is to ask for the extra three wishes first, then you have enough to put it right. And the way you put it right is to ask for the body you had in the first place, of course, the same heap of old bones that gets you up on to the bus in the morning, and after that you still have a couple of wishes left. And with the next wish you say, 'I would like to have three more wishes, please.'

You see?

Mad. It's the kind of thing that rolls through your head, in this job, when you're sweeping or wiping – it's very repetitive, cleaning. It's all over and back: over and back again. Your mind starts to run in some terrible groove, and you have to pick the right one or you end up with bombs on the underground and everybody you ever loved lying in the morgue. I can go from a cigarette butt to the Great Fire of London before I have the ashtray cleaned, so I stay in late and listen to the singing. I stand in the dark at the back of the hall, because you have to watch your head, you have to pick something positive to think about, as my son Jimmy tells me, like winning the lottery, though he doesn't approve of that, either. Because I've had my ups and downs.

It never ends. Cleaning. It never ends. Here we go, back to the start, clean what has been cleaned and then clean it again. I start at the top of the house and work down, parterre, boxes, stalls. I hear the other girls hoovering or calling, and we pass each other on the stairs. I don't smoke. A lot of the girls smoke. But it puts miles on you, trekking up and down to get out to the back door. No. I get an early start – something pleasant – the brasses, or the woodwork, way at the back where no one goes. Sometimes they start rehearsing before we are done, just bits and scraps, but I love the singing. And the odd time, there's something special on, and the audience are in on top of you before you know it. Not that they notice me. People don't. They look but they don't see – which is fine by me. I'm the invisible woman, that's what I say. I could shimmy backwards across that stage on my hands and knees and no one would bother, so long as I had a floorcloth going. Everyone so dressed up, they see nothing, except looking for their own reflection in the fancy togs.

I was down there on the circle steps, one time, trying to get some chewing gum out of the carpet, horrible stuff, when a man walks by, in his full rig, and he says to me, 'You're singing!' and I said, 'Am I? I didn't even notice,' and he says, 'Ah! you're Irish. Isn't it marvellous the way the Irish sing while they work?' And I said, 'Yes, isn't it?'

And you know, I have about sixteen things to say to him if he ever stopped by again. Like, 'Oh, that's not me, that's just a tape of Maria Callas I've got stuck up my arse.' Or, 'A cat can look at a king.' I might say that, 'A cat can look at a king.'

I am allowed to like the music. My son Jimmy loves it. He has a voice, he never touched a cigarette. He might come here, even, only he doesn't want to bump into his old mother rooting for the dustpan in the cupboard by the bar.

I might like the opera, you see, but my son Jimmy owns the opera. Jimmy has all the CDs in their box sets. Jimmy was even gay for a while, and then he wasn't gay, and I said to him, I can't keep up. And I think, after all, that he wasn't looking for sex of one kind or another, he was just looking for an education. Which he got. And he has it all now, down to the slice of lime in his gin and tonic, and he never – he very rarely – gives himself away.

Oh, be careful what you want.

I never wanted money – wasn't that lucky? Because if I'd wanted it I might have got it, and wouldn't that be an awful tragedy, an endangerment to my soul? And I never wanted fame. I just wanted stupid things, like knowing the right thing to wear for a christening, or my mother not dying so early, or someone to help out at home.

So, maybe my first wish would be that my mother was still alive – but alive at the age she was before she died, not the age she would be, if she hadn't died in the first place, like a

hundred and two. So, with all her faculties and the body of –
here we go again – the body of a fifty-year-old. A healthy
fifty-year-old. A healthy fifty-year-old woman. As opposed to
man. Or horse.

'Oh, be careful what you want.' It was my mother who
used to say that to me – when I was young, and all I wanted
was Séamas Molloy. When all I wanted was the fella in the
whitest shirt in the crowd outside the dance hall, on a long
summer's evening that was turning into night.

And if I had the devil himself appear to me, on the stairs,
like your man in his tuxedo – 'Aren't the Irish marvellous!' –
he was a good-looking man, I remember that about him. But
if Old Nick came up to me in white tie and tails, and he took
me up on the roof and he said, 'Look out over London town
– all of this can be yours,' I'd tell him that I've heard that guff
before. I heard it from the boy in the whitest shirt, that I spent
the next six years of my life trying to keep white. My Bobby
Dazzler.

Or if he said, 'Fling yourself down there and the angels will
catch you before you hit the ground.' Well, what sort of a
temptation is that? You go to all the trouble of killing yourself and you don't even die? That's what I call a swizz. Besides,
it just sounds like falling in love, to me. Which Jesus never did,
when you think about it. Which I did, like a fool – because
my mother was right, of course: he was an awful messer,
Séamas Molloy.

It's a nice view up there – all the lights of London town. I
go up, sometimes; the last little flight of steps. No one has to
know.

We didn't need the devil, Séamas and me: we thought the
town was ours for the taking. Except of course he couldn't
take it at all. He couldn't take not knowing who anyone was;
he couldn't take the humiliation every time he opened his
mouth and the accent came out: it didn't suit him at all. Because Séamas Molloy was a big man, he was the man in the
whitest shirt, and I had to throw him out, finally, before the
baby came to any harm.

I have a terrible dread of finding him on the street some day, his beautiful eyes all bloodshot, with the memory of me held somewhere behind them, and the kisses we had. Something about me; my hands or my ankles – they're still slim – some giveaway.

But sure drink wipes everything, even your soul.

Come on, Old Nick, offer me London town, and free flying lessons and – what was the third thing? Stones into bread. We'll call that getting your breakfast brought in to you on a tray. He was just trying to get Jesus to show his hand. 'Go on,' he was saying. 'Prove it. Prove it!' And Jesus didn't prove it. He wasn't bothered.

I know what he meant, sometimes. Up there on the roof on a summer's night with the city sparkling and you feel you could just close your eyes and blast it all away. One big hot breath. And when you opened your eyes again the place would be reduced to cinders. Every light gone out. Every miserable room I slept in with baby Jimmy after his father left. Every hall and office and sitting room that I swept and hoovered and polished and shone. Whooosh. Gone.

And then you do open your eyes, and it is still there. Gorgeous. Never mind Old Nick.

I stopped going to Mass for the religion long ago. I just go for the company. I had my lapse, I gave up God, but I said, I'm not going to give up every sinner I know too. They don't know it, of course – that I don't believe a word the priest says, that I am laughing up my sleeve at him, and at his God – they would find it very sort of blasphemous. But I don't care. There were years when these people were all I had.

Except for Jimmy, of course. I always had him.

Talking to that child – that's been my education. His little face. If you ever want to know what you really think, talk to a four-year-old. Is there a heaven? Where do we go when we die? Why do people shoot each other? Why does purple not go with green?

And there you are, lying your head off, and trying to tell the truth at the same time. You offer them the world, worse than any devil. You say, 'When you grow up, my darling, you can be anything you want, you can earn your own money and buy as many toys and records as you like, and you can fly all the way to Timbuctoo.' He comes home crying from school because Shane Fox says he's a nancy boy, or whatever word it was in those days, and I say, 'In twenty years' time you won't care a bit what Shane Fox says,' because you only have to take one look at that child to know where he will end up. And sure enough, time goes by and Jimmy gets his money and his toys and Shane Fox gets ten years for aggravated assault. There's my amazing son, who changes jobs the way men used to change their shirts. He takes a year out to travel, goes to Asia and South America, and he comes back to another job, with even more money. And now he has a wife, who is really quite nice, and they've no plans for babies, he says, even though they can afford it, and she's thirty-nine.

I don't know.

Jimmy tells me I'm wasting my time on the lottery. He says, anyway, rich people don't spend their money, they invest it. And I say, You might as well not have any in the first place – but I see what he means, he means the only way to keep it is pretend it isn't there. He says that rich people live cheap, they're the meanest lot. They have holidays in other people's summer houses, and dinner on expenses, and some company sends them tickets for the ballet or the opera, and all they have is the hire of the suit. Except they don't hire the suit, they use their grandda's suit. And so on. Jimmy wanted me to cut up my credit card, he said it wasn't plastic money it was plastic debt, and I said he sounded like a socialist, which is the last thing he is, the absolute last thing. His father shouting at the radio, throwing it out into the back yard when Kennedy made that speech over Cuba. But sure I never got into debt.

I never wanted much.

I wanted Jimmy, though, and I had him. *Violà!* So I thought he might break the curse of it, somehow. I thought my child could want things, and have them, all at the same time. I thought he could love someone and it would go right for him. And it does go right for him. Though I don't know who he loves, properly speaking. I don't know if Jimmy ever loved anyone at all.

Except, of course, for his dear old ma.

Then he turns around the night before his wedding day, and he says, 'I never had a father,' like it was all my fault. 'I never had a father,' shouting it. 'Better off, too,' I said – which we both know is true. But still.

All right, here it is; it's an angel, it's the devil, it's anything you want. It's three wishes. And what you have to watch for, is the trick.

So, pick something small. You want to get rid of the creaks in your knees and the one that is moving into your right hip. You say, 'I wish that my body was twenty years younger.' Hang on. Careful. Careful does it. 'I wish that my body was twenty years younger – not including my brain, which must remain the same age as it is now, with the same experiences to remember.' Or. Hang on. 'Not including my brain, which must remain the same age as it is now, but with no early Alzheimer's in it, like the Alzheimer's that stops me from remembering my own mother's maiden name.' Now is that one wish or is it three? It sounds like six.

'Oh, be careful what you want,' said my mother. Whose maiden name was Mary Kearney, thank you very much.

She would have loved this: the opera. She would have loved the glam.

All right, I'll tell you what I want. 'I want a small win on the lottery, just a small one, just a few thousand, so I could feel, for once, LUCKY. I want my son to call me on the mobile phone he bought me for a present, that never, ever rings. I also want him to have sex with the right people, meaning female people, in particular the female person who is his wife. I want grandchildren. More than anything, I want grandchildren. Because grandchildren are simple. You wish for them and you have them. And I don't care if they are ashamed of me. I want my son who has everything to have something, for once. Something real. To have a heart that isn't withering in his chest. That little smile when he looks at me.

'Hello, Mum.'

And when the man stops on the circle stairs, I want to look up at him, in his tux. I want to peruse the length of him, and meet him, eye to eye. Old Nick, my friend. I want him to know me, and be very scared of me. And I want to open my mouth, and sing.

The Bad Sex Weekend

He said he had been in New York for a while. He talked about a rat in his sleeping bag in a hostel on Forty-second Street and a guy who got his kidney stolen in the next bed. He said the cockroaches poured out of every hole: the pipes, the flooring, the plasterboard; the room felt like a ship that was sinking in a sea of cockroaches. He was a boy – he did not talk about skating in Central Park, he talked about vermin in a Sligo accent. What did she expect? (What did she ever expect? He had nice eyes.)

She knew Sligo. It was beautiful. She got drunk there once, with some local heads who had a rockabilly band. One of them was in plaster up to the thigh – a car crash, he said. Then he sank nine pints and left to drive home again, pivoting with a hoot, at the door of the pub, on his little prosthetic heel. Sometimes, in her sleep, she tried to figure out how he managed the accelerator and the clutch, jabbing one or the other foot into the duvet and waking up dead. That was Sligo. A place where it rained all day and the rent-boys hung out for the blokes down from Northern Ireland, and they called a housing estate after W. B. Yeats, and you could rot, or you could run, as he did, to somewhere far away.

Now he was back, living in Dublin, talking about the whores in Bangkok, where he had never been, and the way they could blow smoke rings with their pussies, and she liked the way he said 'pussies' in a Sligo accent. He was such a sexy boy. All that self-loving self-loathing – that was very Sligo, and the little business with the razor blade after they did a couple of lines, the way his bad eyes said, 'You can be the edge and you can be the cut.'

It did not turn her on much, truth be told – the promise of damage. It hit her in the heart and not in the groin and, 'Oh, shit,' she thought. Chaos. That was what was on offer. Driving home pissed with only one leg working. Total, sneering hatred, and then crying on her chest with his dick still wet. Oh, shit. The sex, when it happened, an aimless battering around the nub of him, which was sadly distant and, she supposed, numb with drink.

'What do you do?' he said afterwards, like it had turned into a job interview, now that he had (sort of) come.

'Music stuff,' she said. 'I work with bands, coming through town.'

To which he said nothing, not even, 'Which ones?' And in the dull gap of his surprise, she fell asleep.

She dreams about a boy walking along a cliff road in the wet light; the mountains spilling water, the sea pushing against the cliff.

The boy's wellingtons are worn to cloth, but that is the least of it. The socks are wriggling off his feet, putting a clump in his stride, leaving the bare backs of his calves to be sucked and left by the boots at every step. His shirt has a tinge of lilac to it and is riding up. You can see the elastic of his underpants and the pearly lump of his hip, where the hand-me-down trousers gape.

She tries to laugh in her sleep but the boy is not funny, or he is not funny enough. Still, there is a joke around him somewhere – she casts about to find it, but all she can see is an old fridge with the door open, abandoned in the ditch.

The boy's nipples flower under his shirt, and refuse to flower, and the dream moves on, leaving him, nearly hilarious, with no one left to see.

It was afternoon when they woke. He said he had been to Tijuana and the smell of the jacks in the morning was enough to make you puke. He told her that he had crossed the Shenandoah River once in the Shenandoah Mountains and he slept in a town called Shenandoah, and he cased her vinyl collection; hunkered down like a picture of a wild boy, with the thin bones of his backside dabbing at the floor. He asked to borrow her toothbrush and then jumped back in under the duvet for the hangover ride, which was unexpectedly sweet.

He said a woman he was with in America had an abortion once, but he didn't know if it was his. That there was something about foreign women – you didn't believe your stuff would stick. But it did. It did even more than usual. Sex loved those Benetton ads.

'Do you think?' she said.

'Little brown babies,' he said.

'So are you back now?' she said. 'Have you come back for good?'

He thought about it. He said he had driven halfway across America; put the boot down until he ran out of gas, ended up empty in a place called Dewey, Wisconsin. And he got out of the car and looked at people on the sidewalk and he wondered what the hell they were doing here. Maybe it was love. They fell in love, and were amazed by it – by the the fact that All This could happen in Dewey, Wisconsin.

'And?'

'No wonder they shoot each other,' he said, swinging out on to the edge of the bed.

She knew he was leaving. He stood beside the dressing table, poking a finger through the little basket of mascara and lip pencils. He reached up to touch a painted Mexican belt and, in the mirror, his underarm opened to view.

She said, 'I don't believe you were ever in America at all.'

'Oh, I was there all right,' he said.

Then he looked at her and seemed to change his mind.

No, he said. He stayed. He actually lived out there for a while, in the middle of nowhere, in Buttfuck, Wisconsin. He picked up a job working security in the local mine. Two old guys and a big Italian called Alfie and himself; they flicked through porno magazines all night, sitting in front of TV screens that showed the plant in the weird green of infrared. One of the men was always on a round – you could see his torch leave one screen, then, a few minutes later, you would see it wander into the next. It got so it felt they were floating. Two old guys and Alfie and him. And one morning, around six, Alfie turns around and invites him to a pot-luck barbecue that weekend.

Pot-luck! He was so astonished he actually made something – a mix of Jell-O and whipped cream, from a recipe on the back of the packet. He drove around looking for the house, the dessert shivering on the seat beside him – finally finds the party by the number of people on the front lawn. It is a clear, beautiful day in Dewey, Wisconsin. There's a bunch of guys on the front porch talking golf, cracking open too many beers. The wives are there, the kids squealing and running, and there is a smell of ironed cotton off these people, even in the open air.

Alfie is wearing a chef's hat. He belts him between the shoulder-blades and takes the mutant dessert out of his hand.

'Mnn, mnn!'

After a while, he's tranced by the sun and the beer. Just looking at these people, the way they talk and laugh, and the little things with kids. It gets so he can't breathe. He wanders into the garage, where it is dark and cool. A couple of small boys are pushing plastic soldiers through the front grille of the car and a woman's legs are sticking out of a back door. One of her feet is dangling a sandal. When he looks in, he sees Alfie's wife lying in the back seat, flat out, with her arms stretched up, playing with her beautiful blonde hair.

'Good party,' he says.

'Glad you could make it.'

The sandal hits the ground. And he knows he could have sex with her. He knows he could just drive her out of there – one shoe on, the other left behind. He could just gun the motor and go, the kids running for cover, the car door swinging open, across the summer lawn, down over the kerb and away.

He swung out from under the duvet and sat on the edge of her bed. She looked at the bones running down his back.

'So, why didn't you?' she said.

That wasn't the point, he said. The point was him going back out into the garden and looking at these people having their good time. The sun going down. Alfie checking him as he came out the garage door. The point was that he realised that there was nowhere else to go.

He didn't know how to explain it. This garden, this pot-luck bloody barbecue, was all there was. And that's why people stayed in Dewey – because we all lived in Dewey. There was nowhere else to go.

'So welcome home,' she said.

She made scrambled eggs for him and her hands were trembling. She did not know how to keep him in the flat, or what to do, so she broke open a bottle of vodka and mixed it with the cranberry juice, which was all there was in the fridge, and he stuck his nose into his glass and laughed, 'Nyack nyack nyack.'

He said he had a mad brother. He said mad people aren't like they're supposed to be. They're just very dull. They talk about football all day, like anyone else – only more so. Then you see a smear of shit on the side of the bath. Uh-oh.

The other brother was a builder, he said.

He said he grew up in one of those houses that nobody likes; a big bungalow hacienda stuck out in the middle of a field. Though he missed the weather up there, it was better than the telly. And the bog out along the road to Strandhill, he loved it as a kid – playing Aztecs with pyramid stacks of turf, or staging the entire siege of Stalingrad all by himself, running through the trenches. Rat-a-tat-tat. Much slaughter.

And he pointed his finger and shot her.

There was a lot of stuff that wasn't sex, just pawing and tormenting; while the sun appeared and left, in oblongs on the floor. He worked his way through the vodka while she trickled it into her tea and they watched children's television and tried to have sex in the shower. She pulled him back from shouting out the window and late that night he said, or she thought he said, that he had fisted a woman once, and also that he used to meet a guy out on the Strandhill Road when he was a kid and that this guy would fuck him a bit and that he actually quite liked it. *Actually*.

She did not know if she slept or not.

In the morning he came out of the bathroom, beautiful and clean. He said that Elvis never went the whole way. Elvis was better than sex, he said. That was the problem. He knew there would be this shortfall, that in bed, he would never be as good as 'Elvis Presley'.

'What time is it?' she said.

His chest was pale and freckled, all flat – he was arranged in slabs and blocks with a funny, bendy dick curled in the middle of it all. There was no sign or mark of the man he went to meet as a child and she wondered was that something she had dreamt too, because the road was still in her head and the boy walking along it, all night; and her face, in the dream, was pulled after him like toffee. His eyes were clear, amnesiac, and she thought that maybe he told everyone his bog story when he was really pissed; safe from remembering what he had said. Or maybe it was a lie. Maybe something terrible had happened to him – a different thing. Or nothing terrible had happened to him, and she would never find out what it was. Maybe he had never driven all the way to Dewey, Wisconsin.

'Listen,' she said. 'I have to pick up my niece at half one, I promised to bring her into town.'

'Your niece?' he said.

'Yes.'

'How sweet.'

'Fuck off,' she said.

And still he sat in her yellow dressing gown, waiting for the paracetamol to work and flicking through an old copy of *Vogue,* like some parody of her Sunday-morning self.

She made a pot of tea.

He said that he met a transsexual in Reno with breasts you wouldn't believe, but then you get down to the pants and . . . Surprise! And the problem is these breasts are still driving you crazy, you just want to lick them or have them; they just hit your override function, or something.

'Kinky,' she said.

And because she doesn't believe him – or not in the way he would like her to believe him – he is at her again. And she can't tell this person, this liar, two days in, that she doesn't want him touching her any more. Though that is what this is turning into now – two people who don't want to sleep with one another, snogging and clawing, and pushing each other against cupboards. But it doesn't go any further, as she sort of knew it wouldn't. He breaks away, and goes into the bedroom and starts to get dressed. Finally.

He comes back in and she is sitting at the table smoking a cigarette, and he is eight years old. Eight, or maybe nine. That's the look on his little, slapped face.

'So . . . hey!' she says.

'Hey, gorgeous.'

He pushes his boxers into his backpack, which means his little ass is bare under the jeans. And he leaves with big promises, and she shuts the door with big smiles and she showers and picks up her little niece; feeling a bit guilty, now and then, when she remembers the ruin between her legs.

The dream comes back to her all day. She thinks about it in the evening; sitting at the kitchen table and smoking while dusk turns to night. The thump and slap of the boy's wellingtons on the road. The lilac-coloured shirt. The old man's trousers that gape at the waist to show the lump of his hip and the elastic line of his underpants – an unwashed nylon stretch of mermaids, maybe, that his mother didn't even notice when she bought them, or string pants that leave mesh marks on his skin, catching him like a fish.

The boy walks down the road, and he doesn't know his own skin, or his tender little prick at the centre of this landscape and of these clothes. He walks down the road and into his own white breath – even his breath loves him, and the man who is watching from the ridge loves him, and so does the goddamned bog.

And she thinks that maybe she should have loved him too. Maybe she should have tried.

The boy sits down to take off a wellington, and the sight of his bare heel, a flush of red on white, puts him in mind of something.

DELLA

Della thought about the stream again, which was black and broad, and the naked boys who played on its sloping banks, all very white. One of them reached towards the water with a stick, but the stick did not touch the water. You could see him leaning sideways off the steep bank. There was a scrubby tree leaning in from the other bank and its leaves were small and greyish against the black water. Della had no idea of where the river was, or who the boy was, or whether he was about to fall into the water. She did not know if this was something she had seen once, or whether she would see it some time in the future. It was a dream, or something off the telly. She thought it had something to do with the River Blackwater, but it was probably not even Irish. In Ireland, boys didn't swim in the nip.

Della knew there was nothing important in the river – a clump of twigs and leaves, or a different-shaped stick. The boy was reaching out just for the pleasure of it; to see if he could.

She thought it might be in Russia, the river was so black and the trees were birch trees. Or maybe the boys' bodies just reminded her of birch trees, that looked always so fresh and hopeful. But they looked sad too, she thought, like a picture of boys that was taken before a great war.

The man next door was going blind, but he didn't seem to notice it. Della felt she should point it out to him, even though it was none of her business. They had lived side by side for over fifty years but they never got on much. Della had liked his wife once, but the wife was dead a long time, and he had never been chatty. Besides, there was a thing he had about children that stung Della when she was rearing her own. Her five and his two, now gone.

At least hers came back now and again – his didn't darken the door – but they were very scattered and Della, left to herself for long stretches of time, was prone to forgetfulness and thoughts about birch trees and naked boys that she had never known. Sometimes, from next door a scratching or tapping, like, What could he be up to in there? Other times so much silence she wrote it down: '16th April – no noise', trying to keep track of things, in case the man died. Despite the fact that she couldn't remember what year it was, sometimes, if the truth be told.

She pushed the scraps of paper behind the mantelpiece clock. The noises happened behind this wall, in his kitchen, which was the mirror to hers. Domestic scrapings, and the odd bump or clatter. You might think, as she sometimes did, that he was doing something odd in there, but who would have guessed the real oddness of it; that he could not see what he was doing, at all.

It took her months to realise it. She met him outside the local newsagent's – it might have been a day in February – and he neglected to salute her. And this put her in mind of the last time he passed, without a nod or a sign. So either he was fighting with her, or there was something else astray. Still, he had always been such an irritating person that the weather turned to spring before her conscience got to her and she finally said, 'Hello, Tom,' in a voice so loud it might have been sarcastic.

He started and looked around.

'Della?' he said, and she would have thought then that the eyes were going, if it weren't for the daily paper tucked under his arm. Also, she knew by the way he said her name that he was more intimate with her than she liked, on the other side of their brick wall.

Then, one day in April, she saw the newspapers in a clump for the binmen, and a curious sense about them that woke her up in the middle of the night with the fact that they had not been opened, let alone read, and the man next door, whether he knew it or not, was blind.

There was nothing worse than knowing all this. If it was just his mind that was going then at least he would forget, from one minute to the next, how miserable he was. But the noises behind the wall were not the vague scrabblings of old age. He was looking for something. He was getting it wrong, over and over again. She thought of him in there in the gathering filth and she hadn't even a phone number to ring. And even if she had – if she looked one of the children up in the book – what would she say? They would be in their fifties by now, Colm and Maureen, with families of their own. They would be older than her doctor, older than most people. Imagine asking them to remember their own father – the shame of it. Imagine being turned down.

She looked up the book anyway and found the son's name, Colm Delaney. Della had a vision of him at the age of five; such a charmer and bold as brass. Though she felt, even then, that the brass would win out in the end and the charm sour into his father's, who was always so quick to pass remarks. And she did not lift the phone.

He was a most provoking man, Mr Blink, Mr Blunderbuss, the soft white stick that lived next door. One of the first things he said to her – she was out walking her new baby, they couldn't have been three weeks in the place; it was the summer of 1950 and there she was with her beautiful first son, pushing him in front of her for all to admire, and he looked into the pram and said, 'He's small for an Aberdeen Angus.' By which she was to take all sorts of implications. Poor Della, the innocent young wife, with a nine-pound baby coming out of her – the fright of it at the time and the whole world turning inside out. He's small for an Aberdeen Angus. A tone he had that walked into your head and made itself right at home. Laughing at the wreck of her private parts, somehow, or at the size of her husband's – her husband was off working in Scotland at the time. Laughing at her foolish pride in the baby and, worse than all this, obliging her to laugh, too.

And she would have forgotten it, if it weren't so much the nature of the man.

'You're very dressed up,' he might say, meeting her in the kitchen over a cup of tea with his wife. Like she was getting above herself. Or his wife was letting herself go. Whatever he meant, he managed to make everyone unhappy, in a radius.

'Oh, you'd know all about that,' he'd say, over something innocuous, like buying a pork chop.

'About what? What!?' Sometimes she wanted to remind him that he did not actually know her. That anyone could have bought the house next door. Anyone at all could be playing with their baby in the little front garden as he walked by and said, 'How's the brat?' over the wall.

It was midsummer by now and Della was awake at four and asleep again at three in the afternoon, and it was very aggravating to be so out of step with the world, snoring through the Lotto results and waking with the worst kind of film spilling unheeded into the room. She would switch the telly off and in the after-image came the picture of the boys playing on the riverbank. She would try to hold that, and fix the place in her mind. The white forks of their legs; the ease and grace of them as they stood and watched the boy with a stick leaning out over the water. The flatness of the river below.

Della was expecting to die any moment. But it didn't seem to be happening, somehow – river or no river. Still, this was another reason she put off doing something about the man next door, feeling in a childish sort of way that no one would expect her to help him if she was dead: no one would blame her if she was slumped in a chair while the telly panicked and begged for someone to turn it off, night after night. But she didn't die. She didn't even feel dizzy when she stood up out of her chair. All that came to her were the alien tang and the drifting nights of old age, while darkness gathered next door and the scratching and tapping went on. Getting under the skin of his own house: the world's most irritating man.

'Where are you off to?' he'd said to her once. 'In your good shoes.'

Maybe, she thought all these decades later, he had been talking about sex. And this was what got to her. The nerve of him – thinking she might be interested; horrible person that he was, the kind of man who'd be sarcastic to a dog. But she had left herself open to it: by being pregnant, maybe, by pushing prams, by whatever passed between herself and her husband in the dark. So it was just as much as she deserved (her whimpering, maybe, coming through the wall), he could say what he liked about her shoes, or her pork chops, or the vegetables she bought from the vegetable man. It was enough to drive you demented. She began to feel thought about, and watched. She did not like passing their windows, any more.

She wouldn't have kept up the connection except that they were neighbours and she felt sorry for his wife, Noreen, who was a terrific person, especially when Della was off in the Coombe. She fed the abandoned children and doted on the new babies, each of them as they came in the door, this woman who was sneered at day and night by a husband who only gave her two.

Though he was mad about her, in his way; couldn't move without her. And there was a whole year he sat in their front room and nothing was said – about his job, or what was happening, or why he was sitting there in the dark. After which time, his comments never seemed to hit home. They were getting a bit old for all that anyway, Della bagged out by five pregnancies looking in the mirror and seeing her mother looking back: still, she felt, in those years, uncommonly strong, with all her children growing around her. Until the day her little daughter, Margaret, came in crying because Mr Delaney said her chest was getting fat. Such a peculiar and wrong thing for a man to say, and the whole street going, 'Isn't he a ticket, ha ha ha.' She thought it was wrong at the time and she thought so now and, though her own husband said she was silly, hysterical, call it what you like, Della, burning with shame and sorrow for her daughter's poor breasts, did not address a word to Tom Delaney, or laugh at his jokes, or stop in the street, from that day out. She did not fight him, she just failed to respond, and his wife she spoke to less and less and then not at all. And this was a great loss to her – his wife Noreen, who was always such a terrific person – it cut a small notch out of her. By the time she died, Noreen had no friends left, of course, and that too may have been part of his plan – the spoiler. Della went to the woman's funeral and wondered if things could have been otherwise, and realised that they could not.

He must be covered in bruises, she thought, with the sound one day of a dish hitting the kitchen floor: the crash followed by three more, so regular they may have been deliberate – and how was he going to clear that up? Coming down in the morning with his feet bare. She picked her own feet up in sympathy, quickly. One. Two.

It was unbearable. Della went upstairs and cleaned the mirror of the bathroom cabinet, and looked at the picture of herself in there: an old woman she didn't know. Nothing to do with the young woman pushing a pram, or the middle-aged woman watching, as he walked behind his wife's coffin, the face of Tom Delaney made frank and obscene by grief. It was indecent, she thought at the time, to go to a funeral with no forgiveness in your heart. There was no luck to it.

Was that what had gone wrong? Della tried to see herself in the bathroom mirror but she saw, instead, Any Old Woman: someone whose kindness did not matter.

She took the soap dish and banged on the pipe that led down from the cistern to the back of the toilet; a thin, unsatisfying sound, of plastic against plastic. She cast about, found the Olbas Oil in its little thick bottle, and reached for the ceramic of the cistern itself. Then she tapped three times.

It came that evening – mortifying: One. Two. Three. He was knocking on the spot directly behind the mantelpiece clock. Della picked up the poker and, with a dangerous surge in her thin old heart, tapped back, twice. The silence that followed reminded her of leaning in for a kiss, or deciding to lean in, and when the returning knock came she was off at the sink making a cup of tea. Enough was enough. She would have to buy a packet of biscuits tomorrow, and pretend that nothing had ever happened, and ring the bell next door.

The boys playing by the river did not have private parts, she realised, when she woke at dawn and found herself still in the old chair downstairs. They were blurred at the crotch, as angels might be blurred. It was not that their penises did not exist, it was just that she could not picture them – the one that belonged to the boy with a stick, for example, hanging down as he leaned out over the water, straight as a plumb line. She could think of it, but she could not see it, even though she knew it was there.

The lump of twigs and leaves, on the other hand, became more clear, cut the water more sharply; it pulled through the flow like an opening zip. Della could not imagine it as anything else: a dead dog, for example, or a living water rat, or the periscope of some unlikely submarine. The twigs and leaves remained just what they were. For which she would always be grateful.

Because there was something about the scene that she had not noticed before; a different quality. If she thought very hard about the black of the river and the whiteness of the boys (were there four boys, or five?), if she let them be – let the boy with the stick reach for the water, let the watching boys shift from one foot to another, and the water flow on – if she did not try too hard, she could sense it, there in the picture. Music. Very beautiful. It was hard to say what kind.

'Hello, Tom,' she said at the door.

'Della?' he said. And she was reminded of his tone outside the newsagent's, saying her name with a voice that, if you shut your eyes, was the voice of true love.

'I have some biscuits,' she said, obliging him to let her in. And when he did – the devastation of the place.

'Ah, Tom,' she said. 'Would you not think of the Meals on Wheels?'

'I did, sure,' he said. 'Until they took my radio.'

'They did not.'

'They were cute enough. They left me this one, instead. Except it's full of holes.'

And he made his way unerringly to the radio on the table, which was an ordinary radio with ordinary holes in it, for the sound to come through. Della's own sight wasn't the best –

she had to admit it – but at least she knew what she could or could not see. It was typical of Tom Delaney that he wouldn't go blind just because his eyesight deserted him. It was typical of him not to let on. Della was so annoyed with him she forgot herself, and spoke as if they had been close, all these years.

'I'm too old to be cleaning up after you,' she said.

Though there was a solace to it, too, getting a brush and shoving the whole stinking lot out the back door. Much easier, she thought, than cleaning up your own place. Lord Lucan sitting behind her at the table patting the holes in his radio or reaching his soft fingertips to the plate of biscuits. You couldn't even begin to tackle the sink. She would have to get Margaret on to it – at least get her to ring the social services. Poor Margaret, with three teenage children and no husband in Glasnevin, and the breasts that Tom Delaney had mocked in 1964 just a nuisance now, when she ran for the bus. And it seemed so absurd to Della – the thirty years that these things mattered, out of the eighty years that made up a life, eighty or more – that she found herself laughing out loud.

'What's the joke?' said Tom Delaney.

'Nothing,' she said.

'Don't let me stop you,' he said.

'I won't, so,' she said.

And he turned his face to her; gleeful, like he could see her quite clearly – a woman in his own kitchen who was far from being a virgin, a woman who would, no doubt, find him quite attractive, in the end.

GREEN

I like Gertie, but she just doesn't get it. Her and that pair of vultures she works with, always sniping – a sort of dizzy silence when I walk into the restaurant and then all business as usual; wipe the fingerprints off a glass, smooth a tablecloth down just so. Of course they're jealous – the vultures I mean: young women you can see closing up over the years, getting bitter. But I expected more from Gertie.

Sometimes I feel like packing it all in. I said as much to my mother, I said I wanted to start over somewhere else. France – why not?

'Oh, this town is very small,' she said, and she looked out of the window at the passing street.

'No, Mam,' I said. 'That's not good enough.' But she is right, of course. It's the little things that get to you. It's the little things that make you turn to the window and wonder how long you have left, before you can decently die.

Mam was a beauty: she had that to contend with. There are still women who will not talk to her after Mass because of what their dead husbands said once, or did not say, when she walked by.

And of course I went to the 'better' school – St Matilda's. Years of chilblains and semolina; the French teacher whacking you over the head with Maupassant, in hard-back – Miss Nugent that was, or should I say *Mamselle Noojong* – six years of misery so you could catch a man with a better-cut suit and maybe a four-wheel drive.

'You are the future,' said Sister Albert, sending us back to be hated in hotel bars from Birr to Crossmolina for our T-strap stilettos and our taste in Campari and lime. I'd rather be dead, I said. But, 'Why not?' said Mam. 'Why not marry a nice, well-to-do man?' I said there's better ways to earn your new

Sanderson curtains than on your back – I'd get the money myself. Or no money, if that's the way I wanted to play it. And I packed my bag for uni and shook the dust of that damn town off my feet.

Now here I am. Back again.

Gertie was a Matilda's girl too, of course. She was three years ahead of me, and I thought she was really beautiful, and really dull. Or something worse than dull – the way Sister Albert smiled so sadly at her, and Gertie smiled so sadly back. Gertie was a saint. She tried to use a tampon once and fainted against the toilet cubicle door: ker-klunk. She never did leave the town. She married the man she was supposed to marry, and she got the curtains she was supposed to get: he drinks every day now from half past twelve, and Gertie says he's infallible when it comes to a good Bordeaux.

Go for it, Gertie. St Matilda's is proud of you yet.

She rang me up yesterday. She actually rang me up. She was terribly nice. I was terribly nice. I was smiling and nodding at the phone receiver like something demented.

'Aha!' I said. 'Unhum!' Then I put down the phone and went out and hacked down the sycamore that had suckered by the back wall. And of course it was too big for me, so the place is a mess of branches now, with an ignorant-looking stump left, all mutilated and half alive.

Because, strange to relate, I did marry a local man. And he does have a four-wheel drive. Which we need for the farm. But whatever way you cut it, eleven years after I left, I was back again in a white dress, walking down the aisle of the town church, that Gothic barn, the ghost of my childhood shifting her sticky knees on the green leatherette, *Behave yourself now*. The place was so cold my arms were mottled red and orange, poking out of the white dress like chicken legs. I was shaking – and not just with the cold. But sure they loved that too. Walking like something plucked in front of the sentimental, small eyes of that town. *Isn't she lovely?* Saying later I had terrible circulation problems because of the drugs I did in New

York, was it? Or Paris? Believe me, this is an outrageous place. But all places are outrageous, and I was in love.

Still am.

I don't think Gertie understands 'organic'. She rings me up yesterday out of the blue, and says she wants enough radicchio for forty.

'Also,' she says, and then a list as long as your arm. *Well,* I thought, the pure gall of it. But, 'Aha!' I said. 'Unhum!' I said I'd see what I had, because 'with organic you don't always have it on demand'.

'Oh,' she said.

I went out to polytunnels and I couldn't find J.P. so I went to the toolshed and got out the handsaw and hacked at the poor sycamore until it was just a bleeding mess of green. It is very satisfying, cutting down a tree. You work small and the result is catastrophic: stand out of the way and, whoosh, the sky falls.

J.P. came up after a while.

'What gives?' he says.

'Gertie wants radicchio for forty,' I said.

'Well, that's good.'

'Jesus, J.P.,' I said. 'Never buy a chainsaw.'

That evening I was all depressed. I walked under the plastic and listened to the sprinklers. I am not sentimental about vegetables, but I think I was crying. All the beautiful rows of green. I felt like ringing Gertie and saying that rabbits had got into the crop, or sawfly. Paraquat in the irrigation system. Anything. No more radicchio. The radicchio is all dead, Gertie.

Mam said, 'Maybe it's the start of something new. A change of heart. She'll be ringing you up now, all the time.' I don't think Mam understands about the way my business is these days. I gritted my teeth and said, 'Mam . . . I have two refrigerated vans a day going up to Dublin. One of them goes all the way to the airport because they eat my cima di rapa, which are just fancy turnip leaves, let's face it, in effing London town. And now Gertie rings up *ten years too late* and says she wants my product. Ten years of her saying my carrots were delicious, of course, but a bit funny looking, and there was no demand for cima de rapa around here, and some of her customers actually picked the basil leaves out of their pasta and so what could you do?'

'So what?' says Mam. 'You've won now.'

But it doesn't feel like I've won. It didn't *sound* like I'd won when I was talking to Gertie on the phone. It was a wedding, she said. The bride wanted organic – was very firm about it. And why wouldn't she be, when her father ran half the cattle in the county? 'If anyone knows what's in the beef,' said Gertie, 'she does.' And we had a bit of a laugh about that, before I hung up and went looking for some implement of destruction – any implement of destruction – and a tree to cut down.

I'm throwing my radicchio before swine.

When I married J.P. and turned him organic, Gertie ran the only restaurant for fifty miles. For the first five years we put off having kids, worked all the hours God sent – all that – and Gertie did take some stuff, now and then, to help us out. But she had one cook who was a demon for 'posh' food, everything drowned in 'French' sauce, and lots of spuds of course, and *Has your daddy had enough?* I think Gertie was afraid of her, actually. The other one had done a course at Ballymaloe and was very uppity for the first while. Of course, my problem was that I was uppity all the time (thank you, St Matilda's) and so neither of them would touch one of my crooked, delicious carrots if her life depended on it. All that *cleaning,* they said. I know this because, for five years, every Saturday night, in the dim hopes of rustling up a bit of business, myself and J.P. took off our wellingtons, put on something half decent and went to eat in Gertie's restaurant in town. We ate until it choked us. We ate, more precisely, until the children came along. And when we stopped, I actually missed it – there was nowhere else to go.

We have sandy soil, red and light. I went all the way to Westmeath for the organic manure, and brought the first lot back by trailer. We couldn't afford a lorry. I made five trips.

'Muck into gold,' said J.P., shovelling it on. 'Muck into gold.' Now the tilth is so fine, it crumbles under your hand.

In year three I swung a deal with a small supplier in Smithfield. In year four I got our organic stamp. Prices went up. Over at Gertie's, Has-Your-Daddy-Had-Enough said that there were 'maggots' in the potatoes, and the uppity one said that she 'quite liked' organic, but 'you could get better organic elsewhere'. I bought my first van. I bought my second van. Every day they roared past Gertie's door.

'You know what kills me?' I used to say to J.P. 'If they started taking the stuff now, they'd say it was because it had improved. Or they'd decide the cos was OK, but the rest was as bad as ever. They'd tell me I should stick to cos. And there I'd be, selling cos to them and smiling. That's what kills me.'

J.P. is out of sorts with all this. He is a reluctant sort of man. He likes working the land. I pretend this drives me mad, but of course it's the thing that keeps me sane. Tonight he takes off his clothes as though they are a trial to him, as though that shirt of his has been at him all day. He puts them into the laundry basket and slaps the lid shut. Then, naked, he gets into bed: my organic man. He closes his eyes, rolls over to kiss my shoulder, rolls back, and sleeps.

At four in the morning I look out the bathroom window and see the poor sycamore oozing sap under a scudding sky. Such greedy trees, sycamores, nothing grows in their shade. I look into the mirror and think about Gertie. The sight of her praying in the school chapel at fifteen, with those lumpy-looking white gloves that girls used to wear when they were all overcome by the Virgin Mary. I think about the little bully she married; her mother, who always had some vague symptom. Her mother's funeral, then, later. And my own father's funeral, later again. Shaking Gertie's hand.

'I'm sorry for your trouble.'

God, I hate that woman. I put my hands on the side of the sink and lean forward and close my eyes. And I think of the food I must gather for Gertie: the beautiful plump lettuces, the purple sprouting broccoli, the early beans. I think about pulling them from the earth when they are still cool with the morning; settling them into their boxes, with the sweet air trapped among their leaves. I think about how I will gather them up, and pick them over, and pack them with a little knotted sprig of rosemary and thyme. I think how Gertie will take this little bouquet, and look at it, and like it. And I sigh.

Ronan, our youngest, comes in, holding the front of his pyjamas, his face muddled with sleep. I help him go to the toilet and he says something about camels which makes me smile, about how camels hold their water for such a long time.

'Hydroponics,' I say to J.P. as I get back into bed. 'Ebb and flood.'

'You always say that,' he says. It is nearly dawn. He might get up now, and let me sleep on. The light outside our window is undecided and we lie there, intimately awake. J.P. has heard it all before – a dream I have of water, an infinity of lettuce, row upon row of the stuff, coming out of a lake smooth as glass, so all you see is the lettuce and the reflection of the lettuce. And maybe, as I fall asleep, me also, floating in there, utterly still amidst the green.

SHAFT

As soon as I walked in, I knew he wanted to touch it. It was a small lift, just a box on a rope really. You could hear the churning of the wheel high above, and the whole thing creaked as it wound you up through the building.

I stood over to give him room – not easy when you are so big. Then, of course, I realised I hadn't pressed the button yet, so I had to swing by him again, almost pivot, my belly like a ball between us. I was sweating already as I reached for the seventh floor.

You know those old bakelite buttons – loose, comfortable things, there's a nice catch to them when they engage. If someone's pushed it before you, of course, they just collapse in an empty sort of way and your finger feels a bit silly. So I always pause a little, before I hit number seven. And in that pause, I suppose, I get the feeling that this bloody box could go anywhere.

'Oh, I'm sorry,' he said, even though there was no need for it. American. In a suit. Quite tall.

'Oh. Sorry.' I said it too. Well, you do, don't you?

The button went in with a soft crunch – wherever he was going, it wasn't to my floor. He eased back into the far corner and we waited for the doors to close.

This blasted lift. Six times a day I go up and down in this box, maybe more, waiting for the machine to make up its mind; waiting for it to finish thinking; checking the building, floor by floor. It's so ancient – it should have those screechy trellis gates, like a murder mystery. (I should have an ash-blonde permanent wave, the American should be packing a snub little gun.) But it doesn't. There are just these two endlessly reluctant doors of metal, that click and surge, as though to close, and then change their mind.

I gave a little social sigh – *Well, here we all are* – and flicked a glance his way. He was looking at my stomach, but staring at it. Well, people do. So I blinked a bit and smiled my most pregnant smile, all drifty and overwhelmed, *Isn't nature wonderful?* These days, my skin smells of vegetable soup. I mean quite nice soup, but *soup* – you know? I tell you – reproduction, it's a different world.

He looked up at my face then, and smiled. The doors heaved a little in their furrows and then decided against it. Very serious eyelashes. Very bedroom.

'So. When's the happy day then?' he said.

As if it was any of his business. As if we had even been introduced. When you're pregnant, you're public property, you're fair game. 'Well, hello,' they say in shops. 'How are *you* today?' It's as though the whole world has turned American, in a way, and here was the genuine article, corn fed, free range; standing there in his nice suit and inquiring after my schedule.

'What do you mean?' I wanted to say. 'I am just suffering from bloat.' Or, 'Who says it's going to be happy? It might be the most miserable day of my life. I might be, for example, screaming in agony, or haemorrhaging, I might be dead.'

'Oh.' I looked down at my belly like I'd just realised it was there – *What, this old thing?*

'Six weeks,' I said.

'Hey!' he said back. Like a cheerleader. I thought he might reach out and give me a playful little punch on the arm – *Go for it!*

I turned and jabbed the 'doors close' button. At least I thought it was the 'doors close' button, it was actually the 'doors open' button – there is something so confusing about those little triangles – so the doors which were, at that exact moment, closing, caught themselves – *Ooops!* – and slid open again.

We looked out into the small lobby. Still empty.

'Well, good luck!' he said.

And he gave a little 'haha' laugh; rocking back on his heels a bit, while I jabbed at the other button, the correct one this time, the one where the triangles actually point towards each other, and, *OK,* said the doors – *Now we close.*

Someone got a pot of gloss paint and dickied them up, years ago. Thick paint, you can see the swirl of the brush still in it, a sort of 1970s brown. The doors meet, and sigh a little, and you look at the place where the paint has flaked. You look at the place where the painter left a hair, in a big blond S. You stand three inches away from another human being, and you think about nothing while the lift thinks about going up, or down.

Decisions decisions.

Good luck with what? The labour? The next forty years? The lift started to rise.

'I'll need it,' I said.

This building used to be a hotel. I can't think of any other excuse, because there is dark green carpet, actual carpet, on the walls of the lift, up to what might be called the dado line. Above that, there's mirror made of smoked glass, so that everyone in it looks yellow, or at least tanned. Actually, the light is so dim, people can look quite well, and basically you look at them checking themselves in the glass. Or you look at yourself in the glass, and they look at you, as you check yourself in the glass. Or your eyes meet in the glass. But there is very little real looking. I mean, the mirror is so hard to resist – there is very little looking that goes straight from one person across space to the other person, in the flesh as it were, as opposed to in the glass.

Or glasses. One reflection begs another, of course, because it is a mirror box – all three walls of it, apart from the doors. So your eyes can meet in any number of reflections, that fan out like wings on either side of you. The American in the corner was surrounded by all my scattered stomachs, but he was staring straight at the real one. And, *No, you can't,* I thought. *Don't even think about it.*

I look so strange anyhow these days. I misjudge distances and my reflection comes at me too fast. I felt like I was tripping over something, just standing there. The American's hands were by his sides. The left one held his document case and the right one was unclenching, softly.

And then, as a mercy, we stopped. The third floor. Ping.

'You'll be fine,' he said, like it was goodbye. But when the doors opened, he didn't leave, and there was no one there. They stayed open for a long time while we looked at an empty corridor; then they shut, and it was just me and him, listening to the building outside, listening to our own breathing, while the lift did absolutely nothing for a while.

I always look people in the eye, you know? That is just the way I am. Even if they have a disability, or a strangeness about them, I look them straight in the eye. And if one of their eyes is damaged, then I look at the good eye, because this is where they *are,* somehow. I think it's only polite. But I am not always right. Some people want you to look at their 'thing' and not at them. Some people need you to.

There was that young transvestite I met in the street, once; I used to know his mother, and there were his lovely eyes, still hazel under all that mascara and the kohl. Well, I didn't know where else to look at him, except in the eye, but also, I think, I wanted to say hello to him. *Himself.* The boy I used to know. And of course this is not what he wanted at all. He wanted me to admire his dress.

Or Jim, this friend of mine who got MS. I met him one day and I started chatting to him of course. And then I found I was talking faster, like really jabbering, because it was him I wanted to talk to – him and not his disease – and he was sliding down the wall in front of me, jabber jabber jabber jabber, until a complete stranger was saying to him, 'Would you like me to get you a chair?'

I would prefer it if he looked at me, that's all – the American. Even if I was sliding down the mirrored wall in front of him, even if I was giving birth on the floor. I would prefer it if he looked at the person that I am, the person you see in my eyes. That's all. I put my hand on my stomach to steady the baby, who was quiet now, enjoying the ride – and silent, as they always are. But sometimes they leave a bubble of air in there, with their needles and so on. They leave air in there by accident and, because of the air, you can hear the baby cry – really hear it. I read that somewhere. It must the loneliest sound.

We are all just stuck together. I felt like telling him that too.

Anyway, what the hell. There was this guy looking at my stomach in the lift on the way up to the seventh floor one Tuesday morning when I had very little on my mind. Or everything. I had everything on my mind. I had a whole new person on my mind, for a start, and the fact that we didn't have the money really, for this. I had all this to worry about, a new human being, a whole universe, but of course this is 'nothing'. *You are worrying about nothing,* my husband says. Everything I think about is too big, for him, or too small.

Of course, he is right. I pick the things off the floor because if I don't *our life will end up in the gutter.* I put the tokens from the supermarket away because if they get lost *our child will not be able to afford to go to college.* My husband, on the other hand, lives in a place where you don't pick things up off the floor and everything will be just fine. Which must be lovely.

'It's perfectly natural,' he says, when I tell him the trouble I am having with the veins in my legs, or the veins – God help us – in my backside. But sometimes I think he means, *We're just animals, you know.* And sometimes I think he means, *You in particular. You are just an animal.*

By the time we passed the fifth floor I had the sandwich in my mouth. Roast beef, rare, with horseradish sauce. That's why I was in the lift in the first place, I had just waddled out for a little something, and God, it tasted amazing. I lifted my chin up to make the journey down my throat that bit longer and sweeter, and maybe it was this made him breathe short, like laughing, almost, made me look at him finally, sideways, with my mouth full.

'Well, that sure looks good,' he said.

This American laughing at me, because I am helpless with food. And because I look so stupid, and huge, this man I have never met before being able to say to me, 'Would you mind? May I touch?'

I could feel the lift pushing up under my feet. My mouth was still full of roast beef. But he stretched his hand out towards me, anyway. It looked like a hand you might see in an ad – like that old ad for Rothmans cigarettes – slightly too perfect, as though he was wearing fake tan. I turned around to him, or I turned the baby round to him, massively. I did not look him in the face. I looked sideways a little, and down at the floor.

I wanted to say to him, *Who is going to pay for it?* Or love it. I wanted to say, *Who is going to love it?* Or, *Do you think it is lonely, in there?* I really wanted to say that. I swallowed and opened my mouth to speak and the lift stopped, and he set his hand down. He touched all my hopes.

'It's asleep,' I said.

The doors opened. So we were standing like that, him touching my belly, me looking at the ground, like some sort of slave woman. Thinking about his eyelashes. Thinking that, no matter what I did these days, no matter what I wore or how I did my hair, I always looked poor. Lumbered.

He said, 'Thank you. You know, this is the most beautiful thing. It's the most beautiful thing in the whole world.'

Well, he would say that, wouldn't he.

In the Bed Department

Kitty was suspicious of the escalator, or more properly the escalators, as there were two of them, one falling and one rising, anchored side by side in the middle of the main shopping floor. She disliked the push of the motor, and under that, the loose, light clacking sound of something she could not analyse. A chain perhaps, that ran freely deep in the machine.

They were new. The space where they appeared had been boxed in for months, floor to ceiling, with cheap wooden panelling, painted blue. First they knocked a hole in the floor, and then another in the ceiling above, she supposed. They worked at night, but even during the day, men came out from behind the panelling, filthy and smiling, and went back in again. Ordinary Dublin men who worked whenever, and installed escalators in the middle of the night. She wondered how much they were paid.

Kitty tried to take to them, but she couldn't. She was disturbed by the sight of them out among the merchandise. She disliked the way they talked to each other loudly and laughed as if they owned the shop. They interrupted the conversation, somehow. You'd be selling a bed, talking about springs, you'd be with a young couple, pushing into the mattress in a cosy sort of way, and who would stroll past but the lean blond one, maybe, with the dirty-looking tan, adjusting his zip on the way back from the loo.

Not that she minded men. She had two grown sons at home, so she was used to it: the cheerfulness, the indifference and the mess. Though sometimes she turned around in the kitchen and was shocked by the sheer size of them – all that protein and carbohydrate, the muscle and milk of them, as though she had fed a couple of potted plants, and grown triffids.

Then one morning, she walked in and the men were gone. The place was perfect; the carpets fresh and new, the hoarding dissolved into thin air and, in the middle of the floor, a pair of escalators, one going up and the other coming down. The steps tugged lightly at each other as they passed, snagging and loosening all day long. It ticked in the corner of her eye, making her feel balanced, or dizzy, depending on the light. They were so clean. The up escalator always mounting itself, step over step, the down escalator falling like syrup; burying itself slowly in the flatness of the floor.

They were beautiful and they never stopped and finally they got on her nerves. Nothing happened in the bed department. People bought a bed, or they did not buy a bed. Kitty used to like the open space, the hummocky slabs of mattress, the headboards like tombstones in a giant graveyard. 'Who's been sleeping in *my* bed?' But all her satisfaction was gone, now. The way people lay down and curled up, in the middle of the crowd. The old couples sitting on either side of the mattress and looking over their shoulders at each other in a way that was almost coy; the giggles and the silences. Most people buying a bed were in love, she used to think, or hopeful at least of finding love. Now, they just bounced up and down, or put their dirty feet up, or looked as though they could kill for a decent night's sleep.

Kitty was at home one evening, washing the dishes, when the phone rang. It was a young man who said he was looking for a Kevin Daly. She was listed as K. Daly in the phone book, and Kitty didn't want to give too much away. She said there was no Kevin Daly at that number and the young man asked was she sure. He said that he was looking for a Kevin Daly he used to know, a man who had gone to school in Malahide. 'I'm sorry,' Kitty said, but they were talking to each other now. He told her that Kevin Daly was his brother, long out of touch. Then he said that, actually, Kevin Daly was his father, but that he did not know he was his father, at least he did not know that *he* was his son. He said he was looking for his father because his mother was sick and that was why she had given him his father's name, finally – Kevin Daly – and the fact that he'd gone to school in Malahide. It was a schooltime romance, he said. Kitty just said, 'Sorry,' a lot, the way you might say, 'I see.'

'Sorry,' she said.

'So that's why – you know?'

'I'm sorry.'

He asked did she have a brother called Kevin Daly, or a cousin, and she just said, 'No, sorry.' But he was quite insistent, as though she might be harbouring the man. 'No, really, I'm sorry,' she said, and put down the phone.

The next day, Kitty expected someone to float down the escalator into the bed department and call her by name. She did not know who it might be, or how they might be dressed. A girl, maybe, with green eyes, or a slender young boy. She imagined a man in a perfect black suit – something extra about him, anyway, like Cary Grant. A young man with curly red hair gazed at her – or through her – all the way from the floor above and she wondered, bizarrely, if he might be the person she was waiting for. Also, what he might say to her, if he was.

Then a figure did appear that made her heart turn, and it took a while before Kitty realised it was her own mother, sailing down from fabrics and soft furnishings like a queen.

'I didn't recognise you,' Kitty said.

Her mother was in town looking for a shower curtain and thought she would pop in to say hello. But after that, there was little enough to talk about. Kitty was used to seeing her at home: out in the open, she seemed surprisingly well dressed and mute.

'Well, you always know where to find me,' Kitty said to her, with a stranger's smile.

Kitty ended up seducing a man from the local drama society, a little to his surprise. He had been courting her for months, but in an old-fashioned sort of way. He was sixty-plus and Kitty was forty-plus, but that was the kind of age gap you could expect, with two nearly grown sons. They were both in a production of *Johnny Belinda,* a play about a deaf mute who gets pregnant, though it comes out right in the end. Kitty did the interval coffees and had a walk-on in the final scene. Tom, for that was the man's name, did the set. He was good with his hands, he said, as he bent over a saw-horse in the scene dock, and Kitty flicked a glance at him to see what he meant – but all he meant was that he was good at making things. Nice. In a way. He drove her home after rehearsal most nights, and one evening they stopped out to eat. After which, Kitty asked him in for a drink.

Tom. He said all he needed was a couple of hours to fit two dimmers where the old light switch was, but she'd need to redecorate, after. He looked at the photos on her mantelpiece. He was recently bereaved. His daughter had told him to join the drama society, so there he was. In a moment, Kitty thought, he would tell her about his teeth, that they were all his own. Faded brown eyes, silver hair, a handsome where-did-it-all-go-wrong face. They were safe enough. Kitty's eldest lumbered in from the pub, and stayed to be introduced. Her youngest was upstairs with his own TV. They were nice boys. They did not expect their mother to seduce old geezers in the front room, and neither did the geezer. It was awkward all the way through, and quite satisfying. Kitty did not tell him about her ex-husband, as he did not talk about his dead wife. She did not tell him that her husband had strayed, that she had done every-thing to keep him – up to, and including, porn videos in the bedroom – and that when she stormed out, the judge had held that desertion against her and awarded him the house. She did not tell him how her husband moved a woman in two weeks after they walked out of court, how the boys had followed her finally to her bedsit and looked after her, as only young boys can, how together they had made their way here, to the outer suburbs and a decent life. Nor did she tell him that she was pregnant, when she realised that she was pregnant. She just let him, and the drama society, lapse, soon after the curtain had rung down on *Johnny Belinda,* and before anyone could be surprised.

At first she thought it was the change of life. She stood in the bed department and waited for hot flashes. She did not mind growing old as long as it meant growing easy, but it did not seem to be working out that way. There was an agitation, a turbulence in her blood. She rode all the way up to accounts to query her payslip, and she landed back down in the bed department with a thump. She walked the floor and sat on the beds. She had a terrible need to lie down on one of them. One Monday evening during stocktaking, she actually did lie down. She simply reclined. She let her back sink into a double-sprung Slumberland, and felt she might never rise again.

It was not until she bought three pots of apricot jam that the penny dropped. She did not even bother to take a test. She felt that swooping blankness she had felt with each of the boys, so delicious, like diving into a pool and finding you could breathe. The child was no bigger than a pip in the flesh of her stomach. She took it for walks and little outings. She gave it a go on the escalators and on a park swing, scuffing the coarse sand under her feet and feeling a little mad. What would she tell the boys? As for the people in the bed department – Jackie, who shared the floor with her, and the customers who came in to look or buy – they all looked empty to her, like husks. As though she were the only real thing left. It was like that film with the pods, and she wanted to run away somewhere, to a deserted lighthouse, or a shack by the beach, and sit in a shaft of light while her baby grew.

Tom rang. His voice was a shock.

'I just thought I'd check up on you.' He sounded close, he sounded right inside her ear. Kitty had to remind herself that there were miles of cable between them, a maze of electricity and static.

'I'm fine,' she said. 'How are things?'

'Good. Good.'

In the pause, she felt sorry for him. He wasn't used to this kind of thing.

'And yourself?' he said.

'Oh, flying,' she said. 'Flying form.' And he took the hint and let it go.

Then one morning the down elevator sighed and stopped. People clumped down the steps carefully, almost aslant, squinting at the lines that were strangely solid, though they still seemed to shift beneath their feet. Kitty was glad she wasn't on the thing when it ground to a halt. It would make you look so foolish. As it happened, the escalators had been empty apart from a young woman on the other side, who seemed to surge suddenly up. Whoosh.

Kitty knew it didn't mean anything, but she feared for her baby, that was now just eleven weeks old. She could not bear the lopsided sight of the stalled steps, like someone endlessly limping at the other end of the shop floor. She took a very long lunch and when she came back a man had taken the panel off the bottom of the broken side. She was right about the chain – there it was, looping around the steps that were wedges, actually, when you looked at them side-on. They packed around the central pivot like big slices of metal pie, then separated out on the way up, dangling their triangular bases into space.

The escalator man glanced at her as she stared into the works, and then went back to his phase tester, tipping the metal gently here and there. He had hair on the backs of his hands, fine and light: one of those big, furry men with cushioned muscles and uncertain eyes. Kitty stood for a long time, making him uneasy. He glanced over his shoulder again, but he did not really see her – which was fine.

Kitty lost the baby at thirteen weeks, or lost something, at any rate. She looked at the blood on the wad of toilet paper and wondered if it was the change of life, after all. Perhaps she had imagined the baby, perhaps it had never been there in the first place. She called in sick and went to bed and could not cry.

At the weekend she drove her youngest to his soccer game in the Phoenix Park. She had to park a distance away, because he was embarrassed by the car. Also, he did not like having his mother on the sidelines any more, so Kitty, amused, went for a walk instead. She thought she might look for the deer. And almost as she thought it, there they were, a herd of does and their fawns, standing or lying, and all of them chewing; watching, as she now watched, a pair of children and their toy plane buzzing at the other end of the glen.

She felt sure it was a baby, now – that she had not been fooled. Her stomach was still warm and aching from it. The deer chewed on and did not mind her, while the toy plane buzzed and sputtered and fell to ground.

The change of life.

Her life was changing, that was for sure, though she seemed to be standing still. But, 'Up or down?' she wondered. 'Up or down?' The children threw the plane back in the air and it circled again on the end of its wire. Kitty walked on. It had been a baby, she knew it. She had been visited. How could it be down, when she felt such joy.

LITTLE SISTER

The year I'm talking about, the year my sister left (or whatever you choose to call it), I was twenty-one and she was seventeen. We had been keeping our proper distance, that is to say, for seventeen years. Four years apart – which is sometimes a long way apart, and sometimes closer than you think. Some years we liked each other and some years we didn't. But near or far, she was my sister. And I suppose I am trying to say what that meant.

Serena always thought she would pass me out some day, hence the underage drinking and the statutory sex. But even though she was getting into pubs and into trouble before I was in high heels, I knew, deep down and weary, that I was the older one – I always would be the older one, and the only way she would get to be older than me, is if I got dead.

And of course, I liked it too. It was fun having someone smaller than you. She always said I bossed her around, but I know we had fun. Because with Serena you are always asking yourself what went wrong, or even, Where did I go wrong? But, believe me, I am just about done with all that – with shuffling through her life in my mind.

There was the time when she was six and I was ten. I used to take her to the bus at lunchtime, because she still only had a half-day at school. So I spent my break waiting at the bus stop with my little sister instead of playing German jumps in the playground, which is not me complaining, it is me saying that she was cared for endlessly, by all of us. But there are just some things you can not do for a child. There are some things you can not help.

This particular day, we were walking out of the school lane and on to the main road when a girl sailed through the air and landed on the roof of a braking car. Serena said, 'Look!' and

I pulled her along. It was far too serious. And as if she knew it was far too serious she came along with me without a fuss. A girl landed on the roof of a braking car. She turned in the air, as though she was doing a cartwheel. But it was a very slow cartwheel. There was a bicycle, if you thought hard about it, skidding away from the car, the pedal scraping the tarmac and spraying sparks. But you had to think hard to remember the bike. What you really remembered was this girl's white socks and the pleated fan of her gymslip following her through the air.

The next day there were rumours of an accident, and my mind tells me now that the girl died but they didn't want to tell us in case we got upset. I don't know the truth of it. At the time there was just the two of us on an empty road, and a girl turning her slow cartwheel, and my hand finding Serena's little hand and pulling her silently by.

That was one incident. There was another incident when she was maybe eight and I was twelve when a man in plaid trousers said, 'Hello girls,' and took his thing out of his fly. Maybe I should say he let his thing *escape* out of his fly, because it sort of jumped out and curled up, in a way that I now might recognise. At the time it looked like giblets, the same colour of subdued blood, dark and cooked, like that piece of the turkey our parents liked and called 'the pope's nose'. So we ran home all excited and told my mother about the man in plaid trousers and the pope's nose, and she laughed, which I think was the right thing to do. By the lights of the time. And we had the same three brothers, who went through their phases of this or that. Nothing abnormal – though the year Jim wouldn't wash was a bit of a trial. Look at me, I'm scraping the barrel here. We had a great childhood. And I'm fine, that's the bottom line of it. I'm fine and Serena is no longer alive.

But the year I am talking about, it was 1981 and I was finished uni and starting a job. I had money and was buying clothes and I was completely delighted with myself. I even thought about leaving home, but my mother was lonely with us all growing up. She said she felt the creak of the world turning and she talked about getting old. She cried more; a general sort of weep, now and then – not about *her* life, but just about the way life goes.

I came home one day and Serena was in the doghouse, which was nothing new, because my mother smelt cigarettes off her, and also Something Else. I couldn't think what this something else might be; there was no whiff of drink – perhaps it was sperm, I wouldn't be surprised. It was three weeks before her final school exams and Serena was trashing our bedroom while my mother stood in the kitchen – wearing her coat, strangely enough – and chopping carrots. I went in and sat with Mam for a while, and when the silence upstairs finally settled, I went to check the damage. Clothes everywhere. One curtain ripped down. My alarm clock smashed. A bottle of perfume snapped at the neck – there was a pool of Chanel No. 5 soaking into the chest of drawers. I had a boyfriend at the time. The room stank. I didn't blow my top. I said, 'Clean yourself up, you stupid moron, Da's nearly home.'

None of us liked our father, except Serena, who was a little flirt from an early age. I don't think even my mother liked him – of course she said she 'loved' him, but that was only because you're supposed to when you marry someone and sleep with them. He had a fused knee from some childhood accident and always sat with his leg sticking out in front of him. He wasn't a bad man. But he sat and looked at us shouting and laughing and fighting, as though we were all an awful bore.

Or maybe I liked him then, but I don't like him since – because after Serena he got a job managing a pub and he started sleeping over the shop. So that's another one, now, who never comes home.

For three weeks the bedroom was thick with the smell of Chanel, we did not speak, and Serena did not eat. She fainted during her maths exam and had to be carried out, with a big crowd of people fanning her on the corridor floor. All of June she spent in the bathroom squeezing her spots, or she sat downstairs and did nothing and wouldn't say what she wanted to do next. And then, on the fourteenth of July, she went out and did not come home.

We waited for ninety-one days. On Saturday the thirteenth of September there was the sound of a key in the door and a child walked in – a sort of death-child. She was six and a half stone. Behind her was a guy carrying a suitcase. He said his name was Brian. He looked like he didn't know what to do.

We gave him a cup of tea, while Serena sat in a corner of the kitchen, glaring. As far as we could gather, she just turned up on his doorstep, and stayed. He was a nice guy. I don't know what he was doing with a girl just out of school, but then again, Serena always looked old for her age.

It is hard to remember what it was like in those days, but anorexia was just starting then, it was just getting trendy. We looked at her and thought she had cancer, we couldn't believe this was some sort of diet. Then trying to make her eat, the cooing and cajoling, the desperate silences as Serena looked at her plate and picked up one green bean. They say anorexics are bright girls who try too hard and get tipped over the brink, but Serena sauntered up to the brink. She looked over her shoulder at the rest of us, as we stood and called to her, and then she turned and jumped. It is not too much to say that she enjoyed her death. I don't think it is too much to say that.

But I'm stuck with Brian in the kitchen, and Serena's eye sockets huge, and her eyes burning in the middle of them. Of course there were tears – my mother's tears, my tears. Dad hit the door jamb and then leant his forehead against his clenched fist. Serena's own tears, when they came, looked hot, as though she had very little liquid left. My mother put her to bed, so tenderly, like she was still a child, and we called the doctor while she slept. She woke to find his fingers on her pulse and she looked as though she was going to start yelling again, but it was too late for all that. He went out to the phone in the hall and booked her into hospital on the spot.

Ninety-one days. And believe me, we lived them one by one. We lived those days one at a time. We went through each hour of them, and we didn't skip a single minute.

I met Brian from time to time in the hospital and we exchanged a few grim jokes about the ward; a row of little sticks in the beds, knitting, jigging, anything to burn the calories off. I opened the bathroom door one day and saw one of them in there, checking herself in the mirror. She was standing on a toilet seat with the cubicle door open and her nightdress pulled up to her face. You could see all her bones. There was a mile of space between her legs, and her pubis stuck out, a bulging hammock of flesh, terribly split. She pulled the nightdress down when she heard the door open, so by the time I looked from her reflection to the cubicle, she was decent again. It was just a flash, like flicking the remote to find a sitcom and getting a shot of famine in the middle, or of porn.

Serena lay in a bed near the end of the row, a still shape in the fidgeting ward. She read books, and turned the pages slowly. I brought her wine gums and LLC gums, because when she was little she used to steal them from my stash. Serena was the kind of girl whose pocket money was gone by Tuesday, and who spent the rest of the week in a whine. Now, it was a shower of things she might want – wine gums, Jaffa Cakes, an ice-cream birthday cake, highlights in her hair – all of them utterly stupid and small. We were indulging a five-year-old child, and nothing was enough, and everything was too late.

Then there was the therapy. We all had to go; walking out the front door in our good coats, as though we were off to Mass. We sat around on plastic chairs: my father with his leg stuck silently out; my mother in a welter of worry, scarcely listening or jumping at some silly thing and hanging on to it for dear life. Serena sat there, looking bored. I couldn't help it, I lost my temper. I actually shouted at her. I said she should be ashamed of herself, the things she was putting Mam through. 'Look at her,' I said. 'Look!' I said I hoped she was pleased with herself now. She just sat there listening, and then she leaned forward to say, very deliberate, 'If I got knocked down by a bus, you'd say I was just looking for attention.' Which made me think about that car crash when she was small. Perhaps I should have mentioned it, but I didn't. Brian, as official boyfriend, sat in the middle of this family row with his legs set wide and his big hands dangling into the gap. At the end of the session he guided her out of the room with his palm on the small of her back, as though he was her protector and not part of this at all.

It takes years for anorexics to die, that's the other thing. During the first course of therapy they decided it would be better if she moved out of home. Was there another family, they said, where she could stay for a while? As if. As if my parents had a bunch of cheerful friends with spare rooms, who wanted to clean up after Serena, and hand over their bathroom while she locked herself in there for three hours at a time. We got her a bedsit in Rathmines, and I paid. It was either that or my mother going out to work part-time.

So Serena was living my life now. She had my flat and my freedom and my money. It sounds like an odd thing to say, but I didn't begrudge it at the time. I just wanted it to be over. I mean, I just wanted my mother to smile.

Five months later she was six stone and one ounce, and back in the ward after collapsing in the street. I expected to see Brian, but she had got rid of him, she said. I went to pick up some things from the flat for her, and found that it was full of empty packets of paracetamol and used tissues that she didn't even bother to throw away. They were stuck together in little lumps. I don't know what was in them – cleanser? Maybe she spat into them, maybe her own spit was a nuisance to her. I had to buy a pair of rubber gloves to tackle them, and I never told anyone, not the therapist, not the doctor, not my mother. But I recognised something in her face now, as though we had a secret we were forced to share.

I went through her life in my head. Every Tuesday night before the goddamn therapy, I sifted the moments: a cat that died, my grandmother's death, Santa Claus. I went through the caravan holidays and the time she cried halfway up Carantoohill and sat down and had to be carried to the top. I went through her first period and the time I bawled her out for stealing my mohair jumper. The time she used up a can of flyspray in an afternoon slaughter and the way she played horsey on my father's bocketty leg. It was all just bits. I really wanted it to add up to something, but it didn't.

They beefed her up a bit and let her go. A couple of months later we got a card from Amsterdam. I don't know where she got the money. The flat was all paid up till Christmas and I might have taken it myself, but one look at my mother was enough. I could not do a thing to hurt her more.

Then one day I saw a woman in the street who looked like my gran, just before she died. I thought it was my gran for a minute: out of the hospice somehow ten years later and walking towards St Stephen's Green. Actually, I thought she was dead and I was terrified – literally petrified – of what she had come back to say to me. Our eyes met, and hers were wicked with some joke or other. It was Serena, of course. And her teeth by now were yellow as butter.

I stopped her and tried to talk, but she came over all adult and suggested we go for coffee. She said Brian had followed her somehow to Amsterdam. She looked over her shoulder. I think she was hallucinating by now. But there was something so fake about all this grown-up stuff, I was glad when we said, 'Goodbye, so.' When I looked after her in the street, there she was, my sister, the little toy walk of her, the way she held her neck – Serena running away from some harmless game at the age of seven, too proud to cry.

The phone call from the hospital came six weeks later. There was something wrong with her liver. After that it was kidneys. And after that she died. Her yellow teeth were falling out by the end, and she was covered in baby-like down. All her beauty was gone – because, even though she was my sister, I have to say that Serena was truly, radiantly beautiful in her day.

So, she died. There is no getting away from something like that. You can't recover. I didn't even try. The first year was a mess and after that our lives were just punctured, not even sad – just less, just never the same again.

But it is those ninety-one days I think about – the first time she left, when it was all ahead of us, and no one knew. The summer I was twenty-one and Serena was seventeen, I woke up in the morning and I had the room to myself. She was mysteriously gone from the bed across the room, she was absolutely gone from the downstairs sofa, and the bathroom was free for hours at a time. Gone. Not there. Vamoosed. My mother, especially, was infatuated by her absence. It is not enough to say she fought Serena's death, even then – she was intimate with it. To my mother, my sister's death was an enemy's embrace. They were locked together in the sitting room, in the kitchen, in the hall. They met and talked, and bargained and wept. She might have been saying, 'Take me. Take me, instead.' But I think – you get that close to it, you bring it into your home, everybody's going to lose.

So, it was no surprise to us when, after ninety-one days, Serena walked back into the house looking the way she did. The only surprise was Brian, this mooching, ordinary, slightly bitter man, who watched her so helplessly and answered our questions one by one.

I met him some time after the funeral in a nightclub and we ended up crying at a little round table in the corner, and shouting over the music. We both were a bit drunk, so I can't remember who made the first move. It was a tearful, astonishing kiss. All the sadness welled up into my face and into my lips. We went out for a while, as though we hoped something good could come of it all – a little love. But it was a faded sort of romance, a sort of second thought. Two ordinary people, making do. Don't get me wrong, I didn't mind that he had loved Serena, because of course I loved her too. And her ghost did not bother us: try as we might, it did not even appear. But I tell you, I have a child now and who does she look like? Serena. The same hungry, petulant look, and beautiful, too. So that is my penance I suppose, that is the thing I have to live with now.

I am trying to stop this story, but it just won't end. Because years later I saw a report in the newspaper about a man who murdered his wife. The police said he was worried she would find out about his financial problems, and so he torched the house when she was asleep. He made extraordinary preparations for the crime. He called out the gas board twice to complain about a non-existent leak and he started redecorating so there would be plenty of paint and white spirit in the hall. He wrote a series of threatening letters to himself, on a typewriter that he later dumped in the canal. I read the article carefully, not just for the horror of it, but because his name was Brian Dempsey. The name of the broody, handsome man who had slept with my sister – and also with me. Which sounds a bit frank, but that was the way it was. Brian. I could not get those threatening letters out of my head. He started writing them two whole months before he set the fire. I thought about those eight weeks he had spent with her, complaining about the dinner or his lack of clean shirts, annoyed with her because she did not, *would* not, realise that she was going to die. I even wanted to visit him in prison before the trial, just to look at him, just to say, 'Brian.' When the case finally came to court, there was a picture in the paper, and I thought he looked old, and terribly fat. I looked and looked at the eyes, until they turned into newspaper dots. Then, when I read the court case, I realised it was another Brian Dempsey altogether, a man originally from Athlone.

That was last month, but even now, I find myself holding my breath in empty rooms. Yesterday, I set a bottle of Chanel No. 5 on the dressing table and took the lid off for a while. I keep thinking, not about Brian, but about those ninety-one days, my mother half crazed, my father feigning boredom, and me, with my own bedroom for the first time in years. I think of Serena's absence, how astonishing it was, and all of us sitting looking at each other, until the door opened and she walked in, half-dead, with an ordinary, living man in tow. And I think that we made her up somehow, that we imagined her. And him too, maybe – that he made her up, too. And I think that if we made her up now, if she walked into the room, we would kill her, somehow, all over again.

Pillow

'Alison,' she said.

'Yes?'

'What is a homosexual?'

I did not know what to say.

'It's a man who loves another man.'

'Yes,' she said. 'But what *is* it?'

'They are in love,' I said.

'But how?' she said. 'How are they in love?' And I thought I knew what she meant then. I said they put their things up each others' bottoms, though I used the word 'anuses', to make it sound more biological.

'Ah,' she said and I tried to see what she was thinking.

'Thank you,' she said.

But I didn't feel right about it, so when the next day Karen says to me, 'What are you telling Li about gay sex for?' I felt awful already.

'She doesn't even know the other thing,' she said. 'She doesn't even know what *people* do.' Then she gave me a very hard time. She did not try to make me feel better, at all. I think that is one of the things about Americans: when they decide to blame you for something, they really want you to know that you are to blame.

Karen had requested me from the college accommodations office. She told me this when I arrived; that they liked 'an ethnic mix', so she had asked for someone Irish. I was a bit jet-lagged. I said I'd be Irish for her of a Tuesday, but could I have the rest of the week off? Actually, I couldn't believe this place, the size of it. When they said 'dorm' I expected rows of beds. I put my suitcase down and asked when there was hot water for a shower. Karen didn't understand. She said that there never *wasn't* hot water, unless something was broken – the tap had an 'H' on it because the water that came out of it was 'hot'.

There were four bedrooms off the central living room and she told me to take my pick. They each had a bunk-bed with a desk built in underneath and there were fancy pin lights on the underside of the bed to light the desk. I took the one nearest the hall, climbed the little ladder in all my clothes and lay down in the underglow. I was in college. I was in America. Fly me to the moon.

I stayed in the room for weeks. I couldn't sit in the living room and the kitchen belonged to Li and Wambui. They put things on to marinate before they went to class: bowls of liver covered in honey and chilli, or fish turning grey in some strange sauce. Amazing food. They giggled in there like children and cooked like grown-ups. I didn't even know how to boil an egg. Karen, wouldn't you know, got in takeaway.

I did want to go into the bathroom but she showered three times a day in there. Vast amounts of water, then the sound of her humming, and the low squirt – the slap or squelch of her 'products'. Little grunts, as well. I had to wait until everyone was asleep before I could take a crap. One night I stumbled out in a T-shirt and Karen was sitting at the living-room table. All the time we were talking she looked at my legs like she wanted to retch. I think it was the hair. I think she found it *morally* offensive. Karen would rather have an abortion than a bikini line. Or so I said to Li who looked at me and blinked a few times. Then, chomp!

'Alison.'

'Yes?'

'What is a bikini line?' Of course she knew what an abortion was, being mainland Chinese.

Karen had a boyfriend, who was built like a brick shit house, and made no noise at all. They closed her bedroom door and disappeared. Complete silence. Afterwards, he would sit in the living room and look us over. Wambui stayed out in the hall talking on the phone all evening, which was one way of dealing with it. I just said the first thing that came into my head.

'God,' I said, coming out of the bathroom. 'Why does hair conditioner always look like sperm?'

The next morning the hair conditioner was gone. Bingo. I was good at that sort of thing, though I hadn't really had a lot of sex myself. I mean, I had done it – or I did it that first term – and I liked it, but it also freaked me out. I shaved my head, for example. Though I had wanted to do that for a long time. But the next day I woke up and decided that today was the day to shave my head. So when the guy saw me across the dining hall, he nearly ducked. Physically. He flinched and checked the floor for a piece of cutlery he might have dropped. Anyway. I made him do it one more time, with my bald head, and then I didn't want to see him any more. But I liked the stubble. For a while, I looked pretty jaunty with my bristles and the little Muslim prayer cap I had bought in a thrift shop, embroidered black and gold.

I used Karen's razor to shave my head. I'm pretty sure she noticed, because the next day she had a new electric gizmo and all the old plastic razors were in the bin. Neither of us said anything, but that kind of thing makes you feel dizzy, you could shoot yourself, actually shoot yourself through the head. Or you could just not give a damn. Like the fact that I know Li stole a pair of my knickers; plain cotton knickers, that I saw distinctly one evening being stuffed into her drawer.

'Shit,' said Karen when I told her. 'No shit!'

Neither of us had ever seen her underclothes. We said maybe she didn't have any, but Karen discovered a pair of nylon socks tucked into a pair of plasticky shoes under her desk. They were see-through nylon, like pop socks but even shorter. Like ankle-high tights.

'Oh, God, don't touch them,' said Karen. 'Oh, what are we going to do about her?' she said. 'What are we going to do about the smell?'

It was pretty clear that Li didn't wash her clothes, because the week before she had asked me how the laundry machines worked; so we were looking at three months here. But the smell wasn't that bad – sort of dry and old and sexless.

'Oh, my God,' said Karen. 'Oh, my God.'

We had gone in during Li's early-morning class. Karen wanted to get out of there, but Li never cut a class. She used words like 'catalepsy', and 'dramaturgy', which amazed me. She was from China and knew more English than I did. She was nineteen.

I opened one of the drawers in her desk and found it was full of tablets. Rows and rows of little plastic jars with Chinese labels. I tried an orange one, and a purple one. They were huge. They tasted of talcum.

'Come *on,*' said Karen, who was holding the door handle and bobbing up and down, like she wanted to pee. Karen was at law school. If it didn't work out she would become a realtor. I had to ask her what a realtor was, and when she told me it was selling houses I felt pretty stupid, but not as stupid as she was for wanting to sell them.

The more I got to like her, the more she drove me mad. She said Wambui was a lesbian because she had a friend who slept over all the time. I just looked at her. Every time I got annoyed with Karen, the word 'douche' came into my head. She just had clean and dirty all mixed up. Douche douche douche! Instead, I said, 'You know, girls sleep with each other all over the world and no one says anything. All over the world, except here.'

Wambui's friend was called Brigid and I really liked her. She said she was taught by Irish nuns in Nigeria, then held out her hand for proof. 'Look at the scars.' She was funny, really dead-pan. She told Karen she should consider getting corn-rows in her hair. Karen was really interested and asked a load of questions. After she left, Brigid and Wambui laughed until they were hanging on to the furniture. Li got the joke, about half an hour too late – or some joke – and that set us off again. Li made a funny noise. I think she was uncomfortable laughing out loud.

But as my hair started to grow out I realised how really unhappy I was. I went to the college doctor and said I thought I had a lump in my breast, and he felt both of them and asked me about contraception and gave me some sleeping pills. He told me to go to the counselling service and I did, but the woman there just thought everything I said was really funny. She said she loved my accent. She said the very fact that I was here meant that I was among the brightest, and that I should nurture my self-esteem.

But I didn't think I was among the brightest. I thought some of them were pretty thick actually. Apart from this guy from New York, who was massively clever in a dull sort of way. At mid-term I got my assessment essay back with a B despite the fact that 'you do not know what a paragraph is'. After that I stayed in more, and grew my hair.

At night I walked down to the lake. I stood with my back to the water and checked the lights of all the rooms I knew, to see who was in and where everyone was. It took me weeks to realise that they were all working. Actually working. They weren't having a good time somewhere that I didn't know about. There was no secret good time.

One night I woke up and saw Li standing in my bedroom with a pillow in her hands, or maybe she was clasping the pillow to her chest. It was Li and a pillow, anyway, in the dark, and I had to check that I wasn't dreaming.

'Oh, Li,' I said. And in my half-sleep the words came out all worn and fuzzy. Almost loving. Then she turned and walked out again.

Maybe she just wanted some company. It was the first night of the Christmas break; Karen had gone home and Wambui had friends in Chicago. I didn't have the money to go anywhere and Li, I suppose, had even less. So it was just the two of us, feeling a little left behind.

The next day, I said nothing. There was nothing I could possibly say. I felt a bit sorry for her, that's all. I wondered did she just want to sleep with me, like I told Karen women do everywhere except here. Or did she want to *sleep* with me the way women actually do (especially here)? The thought of her skinny little bones gave me a sort of rush, but it wasn't really a pleasant one.

Meanwhile, she worked in her room as usual, and blew her nose, as usual, under the running tap in the bathroom, making me gag a little at the sound. Other times, she was so quiet I wanted to check if she had died.

We collided from time to time in the living room and she might throw a question at me – What did I think of advertising? or, Was it true they give medicine to children, here, to calm them down? or, Was I short-sighted? Had I read Voltaire? After one particular silence she decided to show me a series of eye exercises they did in China, which meant that many people there 'did not need glasses' (Oh, yeah?). You had to rub your thumbs between your eyebrows and rotate your forefinger on particular points of the eyeball and around the socket, and when you were finished, stare into the distance for a while. So we sat there, in an empty block, in the middle of this deserted campus, while the rest of the Western world hung up fairy lights or wrapped their gifts, and we rubbed our eyeballs. Then we looked out the window.

Actually, I think it sort of worked.

She never knocked at my door, but I still found myself staying up all night and sleeping into the afternoon: I felt safer that way. When I staggered out on Christmas Day, she was working at the living-room table. She got up really quickly and handed me a tiny package saying, 'Happy Christmas, Alison,' with a shy little duck and twist of her head. Inside was a little calendar printed on a plastic card. There were two cutie-pie babies holding a ribbon with the year written on it. I said, 'Oh, thank you, Li. Thank you,' and she seemed horribly pleased.

Later in the afternoon, I stole some late winter roses from a college flower bed and put them on the table along with a burnt chicken and a heated-up tin of sweet-corn. My life was too short to do potatoes. My life would *always* be too short to do potatoes. I said this to Li who stared at her plate with a snake-like fascination. Does everyone do this? What does turkey taste like? Is it a sacrificial animal? I was worn out just listening to her. I tried to make her drink some wine and she finally took a glass, which made her giggle immediately. I drank and ranted on about advertising, which seemed to interest her, and nuclear power, ditto. She asked about Irish 'Catholicism' (with a funny imprecision, I realised she'd never spoken the word out loud before) and I put my head on the table, and said, 'Oh, Li, oh, Li, oh, Li,' which we both seemed to find quite funny.

I'm not very good at drinking, I suppose. I'd only done it three or four times and I felt quite dizzy. Before I knew it, I was tackling her about the whole homosexuality thing. She *did* know about it – she must know – so why did she ask me? She said no, no, they have no such thing in China, they do not even have a *word* for homosexual in China. There must be a word for it, I said, it's nothing to do with culture, it's just a natural thing, but she laughed, as though she was quite sophisticated and I was the simple one. No, she said. Really. Perhaps there was a word once, but not any more.

The phone in the hallway started to ring – my family wishing me a Happy Christmas. So, I did all that 'Yes, you too. Yes, you too,' through brothers and sisters and aunts, shuffled at high speed on the long-distance line. When I came back, Li had washed the dishes. She came into the living room and stood in front of me.

'Thank you for a lovely "Christmas", Alison,' she said, with a little squirm. Then she walked past me, into her room.

They were sweet, nothing days. I managed to sleep through all the hours of daylight; the nights I spent reading or looking at the weather as it fell past the street lamp outside: a slight snow, or drizzle, or just the night itself in a long yellow cone. This little slice of weather made me think that the air is really busy and there is an awful lot of it, and it was good to be inside and small and barely, just *barely*, existing. I felt almost flayed – peeled bare and true. It was so peaceful I jumped at the smallest sound: a plastic bag subsiding in the kitchen; my own breath.

It was a kind of spell, those endless night-days of sitting and pacing and breathing. At four in the morning, I might look at the street lamp and want to cry for the melancholy beauty of the light, or the air fizzing about beneath it, or for the millions of street lamps and the millions of windows and all the drops of rain. Li was in there somewhere too, sleeping her Chinese sleep in those nylon pyjamas: not quite a Buddha but, still, my little plastic charm.

We met over her breakfast, which was my supper, and we murmured at each other like people who live together but have other business in hand. Everything was quite easy. When Karen put her key in the door, I thought we were being burgled. I realised that I had missed New Year's Eve, somehow. And I was sad. Whatever had happened, it was all over now.

Karen was in a complete rage after the holidays. Something about her father's girlfriend and a dog, I think, or a car. Whatever. Her father's girlfriend was Superbitch, and so Karen snapped at us all day and cried herself to sleep at night. We could hear her through the wall. Then, suddenly, I was in love with the massively-clever-but-a-bit-dull guy from New York – completely obsessed. I talked and talked, and paced down to the lake and back again. I finally got him to call for some notes he wanted to borrow and, when he left, I shut the door behind him and slid down it on to the floor. 'Oh, Li,' I said, laughing. 'Oh, Li.'

For some reason it became the roomies' joke. 'Oh, Li!' we said. 'Oh, Li.' When anything funny or desperate happened, like a burnt saucepan, or peculiar-looking hair. It was better when she was there, but we said it sometimes when she wasn't. As for Li, she seemed flattered by the attention: she always made that silly, laughing sound. But it confused her, too.

One evening she announced, quite carefully, that Li was what we call a surname. Her given name, which came second in Chinese, was Chiao-Ping. But mostly Ping. Then she was silent. It seemed that she didn't want to do anything with this information, she just wanted to say it.

'Oh, Ping,' I said, after a moment's silence. 'Oh, Ping.' And we couldn't help it, we just dissolved, we just laughed and laughed until we were on the floor.

The next night, I found myself struggling through a horrible dream. It was one of those dreams that soak right through you, a sickener. I think the guy from New York was in it, and he was absolutely evil. I fought to wake up and the dream lurched. My mother was there, warning me, I swear it. My mother was there saying, 'Wake up, wake up, darling,' though 'darling' was never her sort of word. So I did wake up, and my body was flailing on the bed. My head was stuck and there was something wrong with the darkness. I tried to breathe but it didn't work, somehow. I couldn't catch my breath. My hand connected with something, a face, and I pushed into it with all my strength. I pushed my fingers into the eyes.

Ping was trying to smother me. Finally. I suppose if it hadn't been a bunk-bed I might have died but, when I pushed, she overbalanced on the ladder and fell. I looked down and she was on the floor, scrabbling for the pillow. She grabbed it and looked up at me, then she said something in Chinese. It sounded really strange and vicious. I had never heard her speak Chinese before.

I might have left it. Isn't that funny? Like the razors and the knickers and Karen crying all the time. I might have said nothing and just gone on, or dealt with it in some other, sidelong way. But the noise of her falling woke everyone and, the next thing, Karen was knocking on the door, 'You OK in there?' and when she opened it, Ping was still on the floor, and I was still looking down at her.

After that, everyone tried to make me feel guilty again. Ping was sent back to China (to where? to a camp?) and I had about three college counsellors, just in case I might want to sue. They all talked about racism. They sidled up to it. But I said it wasn't the fact that she was Chinese that mattered, it was the fact that she was insane. Besides, I couldn't tell them that I didn't care. I couldn't tell them what really happened to me, the weird thing, the real thing. Because, sometime after my mother called me 'darling' and before I pushed Ping off the ladder, I felt the strangest feeling. It was a thing, it was me, it was my very self, fluttering in my chest and trying to get out of there, exultant, like it had been living in the wrong person and was finally going home.

Pale Hands I Loved, Beside The Shalimar

I had sex with this guy one Saturday night before Christmas and gave him my number and, something about him, I should have known he would be the type to call. For once, I was almost grateful that Fintan answered the phone. I could hear him through the sliding door.

'Yes, she's here. She's in the kitchen, eating dead things.'
Then, 'No, I'm not a vegetarian.'
Then, 'I mean dead as in dead. I mean people like you.'
I said, 'Just give me the phone, Fintan.'

After the call was finished, I threw out the rest of my dinner, came into the living room and sat down. Fintan was watching a documentary about airports, which turned out to be quite funny. When it was over, I got up to go to bed and he looked up at me and said, 'Do not go gentle.'

And I said, 'Goodnight, Fintan. Goodnight, darling. Goodnight.'

I nearly went out with Fintan, before he was diagnosed. Now, we live together and people say to me, Isn't that a bit dangerous? But he is the gentlest man I know. The ashtrays were the biggest problem; the filth of them. I finally said it to him one day over the washing-up, and he disappeared for a week. Then one evening he was back, sitting on the sofa with a brass box in his hand. It had the most vicious spring lid. I said, 'Where did you get that from, India?' and he looked at me. You can hear him clacking and snapping all over the house now. It's like someone smoking into a mousetrap, but it still makes me smile.

Otherwise I have no complaints. I would get him to wash his clothes more, but I think he is happier with the smell, and so am I. It reminds me of the time when I nearly loved him, back in college when it rained all the time, and no one had any heating, and the first thing you did with a man was stick your schnozz into his jumper and inhale.

These days, he is thinner and his hands tremble. He leaves his coat on around the house, and spends a lot of time looking at the air in the middle of the room – not at the ceiling or the walls, but at the air itself.

You can't trust that sort of thing. I would be the last to trust it. Personally, I don't think he would hurt a fly, but I still check his medication when he is not around. And yet, it was true what he said – when the phone rang that night, I was eating dead things. I was sitting in the kitchen with the condensation running down the black windowpane, forking through the carbonara as though it was all the men I had missed or messed up. All the men I had missed or messed up. If it was a song you could sing it. If it was a song you could Play it, Sam.

I went out and took the receiver and said, 'Hello?' and glared at Fintan until he left the hall. 'Sorry about that.'

'Is that you?' said the guy at the other end. 'Is that you?'

So, he introduced himself – which is odd if you have slept with someone already. Then, he asked me out for 'a date'. I didn't know what to say. There was none of that when I started out. You just bumped into people. You just stayed for one more drink and then by accident until closing time, and then by a miracle, by a fumble, by something slippery and inadvertent, for the night. (But it was a serious business, this accident, I'm telling you. It was as serious as an accident with a car.) This was partly what I had been thinking in the kitchen, as the pasta slithered through the egg and the cream – How do I do this now? How do I crash the goddamn car?

'So, what about Friday night?' he said.

'Sorry?'

'Or Wednesday?'

I checked an imaginary diary in the darkness of the hall, and listened for a while to the dialling tone, after he had put down the phone.

I wasn't sure that I liked him. That was all.

The dinner was hilarious. I should stop whining about my life, but I sat in a restaurant with red velvet curtains and white linen tablecloths and expensive, smirking waiters, and wondered, as I played with the fish knife, what all this was *for*. We went back to his place and I could feel the migraine coming through the sex. It should have been nice – I have no objection to sex – but with the migraine starting I felt as though he was a long way away from me, and every thrust set my brain flaring until I was very small and curled up, somehow, at the bottom of my own personal well.

Of course he was very solicitous and insisted on driving me home. Men say they want casual sex but, when you say thanks-very-much-goodnight they get quite insulted, I find. So he touched the side of my face and asked could he see me again, and when I said yes he undid the central locking system with a hiss and a clunk, and let me go.

In the kitchen I drank four cups of kick-ass black coffee, and went to bed. And waited.

Some time the next day, Fintan came in and closed the curtains where there was a little burn of light coming through. I was so happy the light was gone, I started to cry. There is something unbelievable about a migraine. You lie there and can't believe it. You lie there, rigid with unbelief, like an atheist in hell.

Fintan settled himself on a chair beside the bed and started to read to me. I didn't mind. I could hear everything and understand everything, but the words slid by. He was holding my childhood copy of *Alice in Wonderland* and I wondered were the colours that intense when I was young; Alice's hair a shouting yellow, the flamingo scalded pink in her arms.

He got to the bit about the three sisters who lived in the treacle well – Elsie, Lacie and Tillie. And what did they live on? Treacle.

'They couldn't have done that, you know,' Alice said, 'they'd have been ill.'

'So they were,' said the Dormouse. 'VERY ill.'

I smiled, swamped by self-pity. And suddenly I got it – clear as clear – the smell of treacle, like a joke. The room was full of it. Sweet and burnt. It was a dilation of the air: it was a pebble dropped into the pool of my mind, so that, by the time the last ripple had faded, the pain was gone or thinking of going. The pain was possible once again.

'Oh,' I said.

'What?' said Fintan.

He looked at me in the half-dark. Downstairs, the phone began to ring. I went to get out of bed but Fintan stopped me, just by the way he sat there, in a chair by my side.

A couple of weeks later I was arguing with him, banging his dirty dishes in the kitchen. It is possible Fintan has a problem with water. It is possible all men have a problem with water. Some day they will find the gene for it, but in the meantime, I want a better life.

But of course Fintan never answers back, so the argument is always about something else – something you can't quite put your finger on. The argument is about everything.

Yes, I wanted to say, he is married. But he is separated – well and legally separated – from a wife who is always sick; a daughter who is bright but will not eat; another daughter who is his pride and joy. I liked him; he made the effort. Every time we met, there was some present; usually not to my taste, but 'tasteful' all the same; small and expensive, like some moment from a fifties film. And there was an astonishing darkness in bed. That had to be said. I felt, as he reared away from me, that he was thinking about nothing, that there were no words in his head. He rolled his eyes back into it, and the widening dark was bliss to him. It was like watching a man die. It was like having sex with an animal.

None of which I said as I banged the saucepan from Fintan's scrambled eggs on to the draining board. I didn't mention the too-bright daughters either, or the crumbling ex-wife. What I did say was that Fintan had to find somewhere for the Christmas holidays, because I didn't want to be worried about him in the house by himself.

'Christmas doesn't matter,' he said.

'Right.'

Of course not. Christmas, I went down home. What mattered was the New Year, because when midnight struck I would be in a hotel, drinking good champagne beside bad swagged curtains. I would be in bed with my new squeeze, my big old, hairy old, Mister Daddy-O.

And. And. And.

'And I don't mind your dishes, Fintan, but I really can't take scrambled egg.'

There was a silence.

'Fried?'

'Fried is fine.'

He was right. Fintan didn't care about the champagne, or even about the curtains. I suspect he wasn't even bothered by the sex. He cared about something else. A small flame that he put his hands around, but could not touch.

He is the gentlest man I know.

But it was a gentle feeling I had, too. I wanted to say that, somehow – that this man had too much money and no taste, but he wanted me very hard. I wanted to say how helpless this made him; how violent and grateful I felt him to be. I wanted to say that he had flat, self-important eyes but the back of his neck smelt like a baby's hair.

That evening, as I opened the front gate, I heard the sound of the piano starting up in the house behind me. It was dusk. Across the road, the alcoholic teacher had put up his Christmas lights; a different shape in each of the windows. There was a square and a circle downstairs, upstairs a triangle and what we used to call a rhomboid, all in running, flashing, gold and white. Over by the postbox, an object flew out from among a cluster of boys and landed in the roadway. It was a skateboard. I stood there with my hand on the cold, low handle of the gate and listened to the first bars of *Pathétique*.

You only play when I'm not looking, I thought. Every time I look, you stop.

I stood at the bus stop, but as soon as the bus appeared I pulled my coat around me and walked back to the house. Because, if he was playing again, then the shake was gone from his hands. And if the shake was gone then he was off his pills and all hell was about to be let loose – airport police, Fintan running naked through Dublin or, if he was lucky, Paris; Fintan balanced on the parapets of buildings or bridges, with his pockets full of rocks.

I had never seen him in full flower. I was away when it started, the summer after our finals – in which, of course, he had done indecently well. His notes, they discovered later, were written all in different colours, and some were in code. There was a dried-out pool of blue ink draining out of the bath, staining the enamel. It was still there when I got back to the house – hugely sad. The blue of his thoughts, the blood of his mind, I thought, as I tried to scrub it away and failed, or sat in the bathwater and looked at it.

So when he came out of hospital six months later his room was still there – of course it was. No one was going to let Fintan down. Our other housemate (and my ex), Pat, was setting something up in Germany and was always there and gone again. I had a job. Over the years, the area started to come up. And then it was just Fintan and me.

Now it was just me, crying on the way back from the bus stop, pulled by the sound of his playing along a terrace of pebbledash, painted blue and grey and dark green. The woman we called Bubbles was listening at her front door in a peach-coloured housecoat-negligee. She saw me blowing my nose and I gave her a laugh and waved her away. I didn't know what I was crying for. For the music. For the guy I used to know at college, maybe, with his boy's body and his jumper of royal blue. And the fact, I think, that his were the first hands I ever loved, the whiteness of them.

The playing stopped as I put my key in the door. When I got into the living room he was sitting on the sofa, as though he had never left it. I pulled him into an awkward, easy embrace and we sat like that; Fintan twisted into me, his face pressed against my chest until my T-shirt was wet from the looseness of his mouth. We sat for a long time. We made that picture of ourselves. That pietà. When I closed my eyes, I could see us sitting there – though I could not, for some reason, feel him in my arms.

In the kitchen, drinking tea – the phone started to ring and I went out to answer it. Then I came back and sat down.

'I used to be clever, Fintan,' I said. 'But it is no use to me any more.'

'I know,' he said.

I should have given him his pills then. I should have forced one into his hand, into his mouth, or down his throat – but we were always too delicate with each other, even for words, so we just said goodnight and went to bed.

On Christmas Day, my mother announced that plum pudding was too much trouble any more, and produced one of those shop-bought ice-cream desserts. My brother had brought a few good bottles of wine, and I supplied the paper hats. After the pudding declaration, we had a huge fight about brandy butter and I burst into tears. My mother just looked at me.

On New Year's Eve, I rang the house, but there was no answer. And when I got home on the third of January, Fintan was gone.

On the fourteenth of February I got my Valentine's card and twelve fat, dark roses delivered to my desk at work. I also got a phone call from Fintan's occasional brother in Castleknock to say that they had found him, finally, that they knew where he was.

I took the afternoon off and bought a Discman and some CDs, then took a taxi out to Grangegorman. I had never been there before: it was a joke of an asylum, looming and Victorian, people muttering and whining in the bare wards, and a smell everywhere of bleach and sperm that was like your own madness, not theirs. When I found him, Fintan was lying so still in the bed that you could see every bump and crevice, from the knuckles of his fingers to the high, tender line of his penis, under the thin white counterpane. He opened his eyes and closed them again. Then he opened them and looked at me for a while and turned his head away. Drugged up to the eyeballs.

I clipped the headphones into his ears and put some music into the Discman. He twitched, and I turned the volume down. Then he turned to look at me, as the music played. He took my hand and placed it against his face, over his mouth and nose, and he kissed my palm. He looked at me with great love. I don't know what his eyes said as they gazed at me, over my lightly gagging hand. I don't know what they saw. They saw something lovely, something truly lovely. But I am not sure that they saw me.

The wedding was in November, by which time Fintan was back in the world again, slightly depleted. Every time this happened, I thought, he would become more vague; harder to see. I felt many things – guilt mostly – but the health worker wanted to put him in a halfway hostel, and besides, I was leaving. Whatever way you looked at it, the house was finished for us now. There would be no more snapping ashtrays and trips to the launderette; there would be no more evenings on the bust-up sofa, or chats with Bubbles on the Captains Road.

But I never once thought of saying goodbye to him. I was only getting married. I even brought him along on the hen night – as a sort of mascot, I suppose.

The evening started off slow. My grown-up girlfriends were talking contact numbers and exchanging business cards – I had to start the tequila slammers myself. Two hours later we were off on the Final Bash, the last night ever. I have some recollection of a couple of horse-drawn cabs. I also remember climbing in over the back wall of my new – that is to say, my future – husband's house. It did not occur to us – to any of us – to use my key, or even knock at the front door. There was a light on in the kitchen: I remember that. We stripped a red-brick wall of ivy and wore it in our hair. I lost my knickers to some ritual in the flower beds. My oldest friend Cara took pictures, so this is how I know all this – two of the girls trying to get my shirt off, Breda ripping up the dahlias (saying, apparently, 'Boring flowers. Boring flowers.') and someone, it looks like Jackie, snogging Fintan up against a tree. In the photo, he is all throat. His head is bent back for the kiss, so the flash catches his Adam's apple and the blue-white underskin of his neck.

I kissed him myself once. It was in my second year at college, before he went mad, or whatever. We sat on the windowsill at a party and pulled the curtains around us and talked for a while, with our heads tipped against the cold windowpane. I remember the silence outside, the curtains resting against us, and beyond them the fug and blather of the room. At some stage, I kissed him. And that was all. The skin of his mouth was terribly thin. Even then, Fintan dealt in moments. As though he moved through liquid while the rest of us made do with air.

So, I am married, whatever that means. I think it means that now I know.

Now I am living in that house with its boring flowers and ivy-covered walls, I know that I didn't 'nearly' love Fintan – I loved him, full stop. And there is nothing I can do about it – about the fact that I loved him for years and did not know it. Nothing at all.

I sleep easy enough beside my husband, my greedy old man. Because he was right in a way – Fintan is always right, in a way. So many of the men that you meet are dead. Some of them are dead in a nice sort of way, some of them are just dead. It makes them easy to seduce. It makes them dangerous to seduce. They give you their white blindness.

So it is easy, under the sheets, to lie beside him and think about nothing much. My hairy old baby. Who would do anything for me. He spends money on me, it seems to give him pleasure – more pleasure than what he is buying at the day's end, because dead men don't know the difference between things that are alive (me, for example, or even My Cunt) and things that are dead, namely His Money, which is just so many dried-out turds and not worth living in the house of the dead for. And so I keep talking and he keeps dying, and giving me things that have already decayed (a 'lovely' silk scarf, a car that I might want to drive some place, two books that are quite like real books I might want to read). There is the conspiracy of the dead all around us and the head waiters still smirk, as head waiters do, while the food fucks on the tabletop in an encouraging sort of way.

I am sick now. This life does not suit me. His old wife has cyst problems, something horrible with her back, some disintegration. I hear her silence on the other end of the phone. I see the cheque-book with her name in it, printed under his. I am thinner now. My clothes are more expensive. Weekends he sees his daughters – always a little bit better at their maths, their smiles always sweeter, their ribbons that little bit straighter; their cheekbones beginning to break through the skin of their faces now, too early, beautiful and aghast.

I meet Fintan in the afternoons and we have sex sweet as rainwater. I need the sun more than anything and we undress in the light. I open the curtains and look towards the sea. He is madder now than he ever was. I think he is quite mad. He is barely there. Behind my back I hear the sound of threads snapping. I turn to him, curled up on the sheet in the afternoon light, the line of bones knuckling down his back, the sinews curving up behind his knees and – trembling on the pillow, casually strewn – the most beautiful pair of hands in the world.

I say to him, 'I wish I had a name like yours. When I'm talking to you, you're always "Fintan". It's always "Fintan this", "Fintan that". But you never say my name. Sometimes I think you don't actually know it – that no one does. Except maybe him. I listen out for it, you know?'

Taking Pictures

Words spoil it. They make it sound silly.

When he showed me the ring I just laughed. I don't know what it is to be in love, even less to be married. I thought, 'What can I say?' I wanted to bury his head in my coat. I wanted to wrap my coat around him and tuck him under my arm. Except that he is so big.

'So what brought this on?' said Sarah at work – the bitch.

'Just,' I said.

'Just,' she said. 'You're *just* getting married.'

'Yes.'

'But that's wonderful.'

Later – drunk, of course – she leans back in her chair and says, 'So he's into pain then, is he?'

'Well, obviously.' But in my head later, for days later, I'm saying, 'He is not even interested in pain, Sarah. He will not have it in the room.'

Some nights I stay at his place and some nights I stay back at mine. All this moving around makes us impatient, with the multiplying toothbrushes and a permanent pair of knickers, clean or worn, at the bottom of my bag. But I still don't know what it is to be in love. I know it is different from being married. But just for now, married seems to me more. And less, of course. But mostly more.

Sarah at work, I can't stop believing in Sarah at work, just because I am getting married, just because she is jealous. Here is a description of Sarah. She is a washed-out sort of strawberry blonde with fine bones and small features. She is fading to white. She is constantly insulted by men.

Back at his place, I bite my fiancé on the ear. Sometimes I come up behind him and chew at the muscles of his back. Or when he is sitting down I worry my teeth inside his thigh, along the seam of his jeans. If I hurt him, he reads the paper. If he laughs, we go to bed. Or more often do not go to bed, but rumble a while and then talk. He likes to spoon. He likes to go to bed after it is all over. Which is lovely. Which is always a little bit more.

So Sarah at work has a personality problem. Which is to say, her problem is that she does not like other people's personalities.

My mother had a friend who was always too much, and very clever. I know these things can last a lifetime, so I am careful of Sarah, and careful of my man – too careful to use his name with her. Despite which I end up saying it all the time. 'Oh, Frank,' I say. 'Frank says this,' 'Frank doesn't like that.'

'Really?' says Sarah.

She is seeing a guy herself – sort of. He isn't married, he isn't with someone else, but there is a problem, I can tell – a sick mother, maybe, or even a child. The only thing Sarah will say is, 'The fucker won't do Saturdays'. Maybe he's a bisexual. Sarah has no breasts, truth be told. And you can't win with a bisexual, I say, because bisexuals can't lose.

Of course, I don't say it out loud. Sarah is the witty one. At the time, I just look at her skinny little chest, and think.

We are going over the wedding list for the fourteenth time. I pause over Sarah's name, and Frank says, 'Don't invite her then, if you don't like her. Just leave her out.'

And I say, 'I can't leave her out.'

'Why not?'

'Because it's Sarah,' I say. 'Because it just doesn't work that way.'

The wedding is only four months away. I have a feeling that something massive is going to hit me. I feel like I have been fighting in the surf all my life. Now, out beyond the last, the biggest wave, there is open sea.

I tell Sarah about the dress I tried on over the weekend.

'White, is it?'

'Cream, actually.'

'Sounds lovely.'

'Sarah!!!' I say. We have nipped out for a coffee. Something has to break.

'Sarah what?'

'Just stop it. All right?'

And then, because she is Sarah, she changes the subject, makes me laugh about Gary in security's hairy neck. I talk about my sister's children, while she sprinkles the table with sugar and draws her finger through it, and then she asks about the dress. Seriously this time.

Apparently, I can't do a dropped waist. I'll have to get on a sunbed *now,* and go for white.

Once when she was drunk she said, 'You know your problem? You'll be all right. That's your fucking tragedy, you know that? You'll always be all right.'

But I don't feel all right, Sarah. Just because I don't make a song and dance about it. Doesn't mean I'm always, or even sometimes, *all right.* You know?

'I just wanted to get married,' says Frank.

'Profiteroles,' I say, 'or chocolate mousse. It's just a decision. A stupid decision, that's all.'

But there is an extraordinary thing happening in bed. As if he wants to wreck us both, sink to the bottom, while all the invitations and the profiteroles and the satin shoes wash up on shore.

And because I am more miserable about Sarah all the time, because I think she will spoil everything like the bad fairy at the christening, he says, 'Bring her over. All the two of you do is get hammered and miserable. I'll cook. Bring her over.'

We don't just get hammered, we have a laugh. And we talk too. We talk about lots of things. But when I ask her to dinner, it feels odd. And somehow, because I am getting married, the bisexual boyfriend has to come too.

Frank's flat is better than mine for these things. He has a big living room, split by a kitchen counter, and a table of a decent size. I put candles on the table and on top of the TV. By the time I'm finished cleaning, Frank has all the vegetables on different plates, chopped up and ready to go.

Sarah turns up before it gets dark. She moves sort of sideways and looks at things in the room, picking up an old birthday card, a list of messages, and then Frank's tax cert. which she puts back down again. She is wearing black, and jewellery. I feel I should change, to put her at ease, but it's too late now.

Frank has a dish of olives on the table, but she will not eat them. Like it's all a bit hilarious. When she walked in the door she said, 'Kisses!' as if she'd known him for years. But she still hasn't looked at him. She picks at scraps of paper and touches things. She checks her watch.

'So married bliss, Frank,' she says.

'Yeah,' says Frank.

'What do you mean, "Yeah"?'

'Well, it's . . . I don't know,' says Frank. 'It's such a production.'

And she gives me an arch look, while his back is turned. He comes over to the table with the dips and cut bread. She looks at him then. She gives him a good look, and her eyes falter.

He puts the food on the table.

'Isn't he a treasure?' she says, and I don't want Frank to cook any more. It makes him look silly. I follow him to the kitchen counter and, 'Ack ack ack!' he says, and swipes my hand away from all the vegetables, in their neat rows.

'So, honeybunch,' I say. 'When's this guy of yours going to show?'

At dinner we talk about sex. Everyone is drunk quite quickly, except maybe Frank who is worried about the food. But when it is all served up, he goes too. Wham. There are two red blotches flaring over his cheeks from the side of his nose.

Sarah's man sits all hunched over and bundled up in a T-shirt and a knitted thing and a jacket that he won't take off, so I can't tell what his body is like, but his hands are very small and unpleasant. He reaches on to his plate and lifts little pieces up with glistening fingertips.

So, his name is Fiach. He works part-time for his father and he takes photographs and he wants to get into advertising but more like short films, blah blah, you know the type. When he turns his head you can see the tail end of a tattoo coming out from under his hair.

But it seems that Sarah is mad about him. She looks at him with her entire face, then she gets embarrassed and looks down at her plate. I wonder what he does to her in bed, or makes her do.

And then we are all talking at once. I say that the real porn on the Internet is the property pages from France. A house in the Auvergne for fourteen grand, that's the real porn, and Sarah is trying to tell her hitch-hiking story from Italy and Fiach is talking about the first porn shop he went into in London where the women in the magazines were like house-wives, all trussed up with clothes pegs and Marigold gloves.

Amazing. We are people who have sex. Frank fills the glasses and I see it all stretching out ahead of me. Couples. I look at the rest of my life and despair.

Now everyone is excited, jumping in with their particular tic: politicians who put things up their bottoms, and the one about the lesbian journalists, and then some film star who took a shit, literally, on a beautiful black woman, this last from Sarah.

'Oh, come on,' says Frank.

'Come on, what?'

'It's just because she's black.'

'Well, exactly.'

'I mean, the *story* is just because she's black.'

'Oh, Frank,' says Sarah. 'Oh, you poor boy,' and she squeezes his forearm.

Frank gets up then and goes to the counter and there is a pause around the table. He swings back with the coffee cups and says to Fiach, 'I was looking for a camera in the duty free last month, but it's all gizmos and auto-focus. Like for eejits.'

Sarah snorts into her glass of wine. Then she just keeps laughing. Fiach looks at her and says, 'Don't bother. I started with a second-hand Olympus. Bog basic. Lovely thing.'

'Olympus,' says Frank, but before Fiach can turn away from her, Sarah says,'Fiach likes taking pictures. Don't you, Fiach?'

Then it is her turn to get up. She leaves the room and the two boys talk on about cameras and she doesn't come back. I think she's left the flat; I think she's in the other room doing something dreadful, something I can't even imagine. I try to think of what it might be, but whatever comes to mind isn't really dreadful, after all.

Still, the air of it is in the room, the feel of something appalling, until Sarah comes back with her hair brushed and the eyeliner wiped away from under her left eye. She sees us looking, sweeps up her drink and decides to dance. Glass in one hand, she waves the other in the air. The skin of her underarm is dark and stained, and not particularly strawberry blonde. I say, 'Sarah.'

'What?'

But, as if she guesses, she lowers her arm, shimmies over and hooks her finger into the neck of Fiach's T-shirt. She smiles close into his face. Then she gives up and slumps back into her seat.

'Oh, for fuck's sake,' she says. 'Let's go somewhere. Let's go for a bop.'

Which is when Frank brings out the brandy, still talking to Fiach about lenses, and I ask Sarah about her mother. Sarah hates her mother, though it is her father who is the manic depressive, probably. But it is the father she loves and the mother she despises, so we talk about this for a while. Then I tell her about Mammy taking the bottle out of the hot press and saying, 'Well, at least I'm not drinking any more,' as she pours herself another vodka. But it is an old conversation. It doesn't work any more. It is time to go – or would be if Sarah weren't so drunk. She leans back and looks at the boys and tests the edge of her front teeth with her tongue.

'Fiach,' she says.

'What?'

On the other side of the table, Fiach is talking about some kind of goose. He says he goes to Bull Island every Saturday to take pictures of this goose. He is throwing it out like it's a sort of trendy thing to do, but he's also actually started listing the names of gulls and terns and Frank is looking at him with a face like setting concrete. I think he's too astonished or too bored to speak, but then I see that he is completely interested, that he is nine years old.

'Maybe Fiach could do the wedding pictures,' I say, but no one is listening. Fiach is on to curlews now, he seems to be talking about their feet.

'I said, maybe Fiach can do the wedding, Frank.'

Beside me, Sarah is trying to set her drink on fire. She has the lighter pushed down into the glass, and she's flicking the wheel. When the spark catches, she pulls back in fright and the glass falls over. The flaming brandy licks out across the table.

For a moment, all four of us watch the flames spill across the wood. Frank lifts his napkin but does not bring it down. It is such a beautiful blue. The fire gathers the air and loses it; drinking it, slurping it down. Fiach pulls his chair back as a rivulet of flame drips over the edge of the table and lands on the floor. Then I pick up a bottle of water and put it all out.

Sarah is silent in the bedroom, putting on her coat. Then she turns to say that she is delighted. Of course, she said it when I first showed her the ring – with a big fake scream like the rest of them – but now she says it properly, she takes both my arms and says she is just delighted, just so pleased. She says that Frank is just so brilliant.

'Thanks,' I say. 'Oh, Jesus, Sarah, I'm scared.'

We hug then, and I show her back into the big room.

After they are gone I go over to the stereo, turn it up and start to dance. I swing my backside. I sit down on the air and then push up into it. I say, 'Fuck *you*, Sarah. Hey, fuck *you*,' pushing up with my joke penis, made of air.

Frank sits on the sofa and looks at me. Then he closes his eyes and seems to sleep.

THE HOUSE OF THE ARCHITECT'S
LOVE STORY

I used to drink to bring the house down, just because I saw a few cracks in the wall. But Truth is not an earthquake, it is only a crack in the wall and the house might stand for another hundred years.

'Let it come down,' I would say, perhaps a little too loudly. 'Let it come down.' The others knew what I meant alright, but the house stayed still.

I gave all that up. We each have our methods. I am good at interior decoration. I have a gin and tonic before dinner and look at the wallpaper. I am only drunk where it is appropriate. I am only in love where it stays still. This does not mean that I am polite.

Three years ago I hit a nurse in the labour ward, because I had the excuse. I make housewife noises in the dark, to make your skin crawl. I am glad he has given me a child, so I can drown it, to show the fullness of my intent.

I boast, of course.

Of all the different love stories, I chose an architect's love story, with strong columns and calculated lines of stress, a witty doorway and curious steps. In the house of an architect's love story the light is always moving, the air is thick with light. From outside, the house of the architect's love story is a neo-Palladian villa, but inside, there are corners, cellars, attics, toilets, a room full of books with an empty socket in the lamp. There are cubbyholes that smell of wet afternoons. There are vaults, a sacristy, an office with windows set in the floor. There is a sky-blue nursery where the rockinghorse is shaped like a bat and swings from a rail. And in the centre of it all is a bay window where the sun pours in.

It is familiar to us all. At least, it was familiar to me, the first time I walked in, because all my dreams were there, and there were plenty of cracks in the wall.

The first time I didn't sleep with the architect was purely social. We were at a party to celebrate a friend's new extension. There had been connections, before that, of course, we were both part of the same set. If I ever wanted an extension, I would have come to him myself.

I asked him about terracotta tiling and we discussed the word 'grout'. I was annoyed by the faint amusement in his face when I said that white was the only colour for a bathroom sink. 'I am the perfect Architect,' he said, 'I have no personal taste. I only look amused to please my clients, who expect to be in the wrong.' There was a mild regret in his voice for all the cathedrals he should have built and we talked about that for a while.

The second time I didn't sleep with the architect was in my own house. I shouldn't have invited him, but the guilt was very strong. I wanted him to meet my husband and go away quietly, but he spent the time pacing the room, testing the slope of the floor. He knocked on the walls too, to see which were partitions; he sniffed slightly in front of my favourite picture and told me the bedroom was a mistake. 'I know what you mean,' I said, and then backed away. I said that I could live in a hole at the side of the road, so long as it was warm. 'Do you ever think of anything,' I asked, 'except dry rot?' We were perfectly at home with one another. Even so, there were many occasions in that first year when we did not make love.

The reasons for this neglect were profound, and not to be confused with an absence of desire. The architect and I had both built our lives with much deliberation. The need to abandon everything, to 'let it come down' had been mislaid long ago. We understood risk too well. We needed it too much. There was also the small matter of my husband and a child.

It is a quiet child with red hair. It is past the boring stage and runs around from room to room, taking up my time. It would be a mistake to say that I loved her. I *am* that child. When she looks at me I feel vicious, the need between us is so complete, and I feel vicious for the world, because it threatens the head that I love. On the other hand, wives that are faithful to their husbands because they are infatuated by their offspring don't make sense to me. One doesn't have sex with one's children.

I am unfaithful with my husband's money – a much more pleasing betrayal. My life is awash with plumbers and electricians, and I change all the ashtrays twice a year. I watch women in fitting rooms, the way they stick their lips out and make them ugly when they look into the mirror. I wonder who they are dressing for and I wonder who pays.

My husband earns forty thousand pounds a year and has a company car. This is one of the first things he ever told me. But I fell in love with him anyway.

After I hadn't slept with the architect a few times, I took to riding buses as though they were the subways of New York. I sighed when the air-brakes loosened their sad load, and sat at the front, up-top, where I could drive with no hands. I became addicted to escalators, like a woman in a nervous breakdown. Stairs were for sitting on, with my child in my lap. I joined the local library for that purpose.

These were all things I dreamed about long before I met the architect, which makes this story dishonest in its way. Under excuses for sitting on library steps I could also list: simple fatigue, not winning the lottery, not liking the colour blue. Under excuses for getting rid of a baby I could list: not liking babies, not liking myself, or not liking the architect. Take your pick.

I don't mean to sound cold. These are things I have to say slowly, things I have to pace the room for, testing the slope in the floor. So. The architect is called Paul, if you must know. His parents called him Paul because they were the kind of people who couldn't decide on the right wallpaper. Paul has a mind as big as a house, a heart the size of a door and a dick you could hang your hat on. He never married; being too choosy, too hesitant, too mindful of the importance of things.

I wanted to function in and around his breakfast. I wanted to feel panic and weight. There was the usual thing about his smell, and where I wanted that. (I felt his body hard against me. His eyes opened so slowly, I thought he was in pain. 'Oh Sylvia,' his breath was a whisper, a promise against my skin. The green flame of his eye licked my mouth, my neck, my breast.) But I'm sounding cold again. The architect's smell would have spiralled out from me to fill uncountable cubic feet. I loved him.

Not sleeping with the architect helped my marriage quite a bit. I discovered all kinds of corners in my husband, and little gardens in his head. I was immensely aware of how valuable he was as a human being, the presence he held in a room, the goodness with which he had given me his life, his salary and his company car. I was grateful for the fact that he still kissed for hours, as though the cycle of our sex lives was not complete. (Sex with my architect would have been horribly frank, nothing to say and nothing to hide.)

My husband came in to breakfast one morning, and his hands were shaking. He said 'Look what I have done.' He was holding a letter that he had picked up in the hall. 'I tore it up,' he said. 'It was for you, I'm sorry.' He was very bewildered.

If it was wartime, we could have clung to each other and burnt the furniture, we could have deceived the enemy with underground tunnels and built bombs out of sugar. As it was, I rode the buses and he worked and we loved each other well enough.

The idea of the house grew into our marriage. I don't know who suggested it in the end, but I rang Paul and said 'Aidan wants you to think about some plans. We want to build. Yes at last. Isn't it exciting?' and my voice echoed down the phone.

I needed this house to contain, to live in his love. It would be difficult of course. There would be a lot of meetings with the door ajar, talking about damp-courses. The arguments over where the walls should be would mean too much. I would listen to the architect's big mind and his big heart and look at his shoes. His voice would ache and retract. The green flame of his eye would lick me quite a bit. All the same, I would not fling my life into his life and say that he owed me something (which he did; which he knew), calls for responsibility being impolite these days, even with parents who gave birth and bled and all the rest. Besides, all he owed me was a fuck and whatever that implied. I had not slept with the architect seventeen times, incidentally.

I chose the site, a green field as near to a cliff as I could find – something for the house to jump off. We would take risks. From the front it would look like a cottage, but the back would fall downhill, with returns and surprises inside.

Of course he was good at his job. The place rose like an exhalation. The foundations were dug, the bones set, and a skin of brick grew around the rest. It was wired and plastered and plumbed. Much like myself, the first time I slept with the architect.

It was in the finished house. We were walking the empty shell, making plans to fill it in. I was joking most of the time. There would be no banisters on the stairs. The downstairs toilet, I said, should be in Weimar Brown and Gun Metal Grey, with a huge lever set in the floor for the flush. The bathroom proper would have an inside membrane of glass filled with water and fish. The master bedroom would be a deep electric blue, with 'LOVE' like a neon sign hung over the door. *Trompe-l'œil* for the dining room, even though it was no longer the rage, forests and animals, built out of food. I would coat the study walls with dark brown leather and put a cow grazing on the ceiling.

'It's just a house, Sylvia,' he said. 'Quite a nice house, but a house all the same,' as he led me through the flexible, pro-portioned spaces that he made for me. It was all as familiar to me as my dreams: the kitchen, where we did not make love, with wires and tubes waiting in the walls; the dining room, where he did not eat me; the reception room where he did not receive me, the bedrooms where he did not bed me.

I should tell you who made the first move and what was said. I should say how I sat down on the stairs and how his big, hesitant heart cracked under the strain.

So we did it on the first landing and it was frank, compre-hensive, *remarkably* exciting and sad. I thought the house might fall down around our ears, but it stayed where it was.

★ ★ ★

The payment of debts is never happy. All he owed me was a fuck and whatever that implied, which in this case is a child. I loved the architect and the architect loved me. You think that makes a difference.

In my childhood book of saints there were pictures of people standing with ploughshares at their feet, cathedrals in their hands. This is the church that St Catherine built. If I painted myself now there would be a round hazy space where my stomach is, and a cathedral inside. This baby is a gothic masterpiece. I can feel the arches rising up under my ribs, the glorious and complicated space.

I can feel it reaching into the chambers of my heart, and my blood runs to it like children into school. We have the same thoughts.

Women used to kill their children all the time: it was one of the reasons for setting up the welfare state—this 'unnatural act'. As if money were nature and could set it all to rights. Money is not nature. I have plenty of money.

I don't want anything so bland as an abortion. Killing something inside you is not the same, we do that all the time. Don't be shocked. These are just words I am speaking. Perhaps I will love it instead. Perhaps I will never find out what is inside and what is outside and what is mine.

We had Paul over for the celebration dinner in our new house, with its avocado bathroom, the bedroom of bluebell white, the buttercup kitchen, the apple-green dining room, and the blue, blue, blue-for-a-boy nursery, with clouds on the wall. I was a beautiful hostess, dewy with pregnancy, surrounded and filled by the men I love. Aidan is a new man. The house, the child, would have saved our marriage, if it needed saving. 'Let it come down,' I say, but the house is inside my head, as well as around it, and so are the cracks in the wall.

MEN AND ANGELS

The watchmaker and his wife live in a small town in Holland and his eyesight is failing.

He is the inventor of the device which is called after him, namely 'Huygens' Endless Chain', a system that allows the clock to keep ticking while it is being wound. It is not perfect, it does not work if the clock is striking. Even so Huygens is proud of his invention because in clocks all over Europe there is one small part that bears his name.

Two pulleys are looped by a continuous chain, on which are hung a large and a small weight. The clock is wound by pulling on the small weight, which causes the large weight to rise. Over the hours, the slow pull of its descent makes the clock tick.

The small weight is sometimes replaced by a ring, after the fact that when Huygens was building the original model, his impatience caused him to borrow his wife's wedding ring to hang on the chain. The ring provided a perfect balance, and Huygens left it where it was. He placed the whole mechanism under a glass bell and put it on the mantelpiece, where his wife could see the ring slowly rise with the passing of the hours, and fall again when the clock was wound.

Despite the poetry of the ring's motion, and despite the patent which kept them all in food and clothes, Huygens' wife could not rid herself of the shame she felt for her bare hands. She sent the maid on errands that were more suited to the woman of the house, and became autocratic in the face of the girl's growing pride. Her dress became more sombre and matronly, and she carried a bunch of keys at her belt.

Every night Huygens lifted the glass bell, tugged his wife's ring down as far as it would go, and left the clock ticking over the hearth.

Like Eve, Huygens' wife had been warned. The ring must not be pulled when the clock was striking the hour. At best, this would destroy the clock's chimes, at worst, she would break the endless chain and the weights would fall.

Her mistake came five years on, one night when Huygens was away. At least she said that he was away, even though he was at that moment taking off his boots in the hall. He was welcomed at the door by the clock striking midnight, a sound that always filled him with both love and pride. It struck five times and stopped.

There are many reasons why Huygens' wife pulled the ring at that moment. He put the action down to womanly foolishness. She was pregnant at the time and her mind was not entirely her own. It was because of her state and the tears that she shed that he left the ruined clock as it was and the remaining months of her lying-in were marked by the silence of the hours.

The boy was born and Huygens' wife lay with childbed fever. In her delirium (it was still a time when women became delirious) she said only one thing, over and over again: 'I will die. He will die. I will die. He will die. I will die FIRST,' like a child picking the petals off a daisy. There were always five petals, and Huygens, whose head was full of tickings, likened her chant to the striking of a clock.

(But before you get carried away, I repeat, there were many reasons why Huygens' wife slipped her finger into the ring and pulled the chain.)

★　★　★

When his first wife died, Sir David Brewster was to be found at the desk in his study, looking out at the snow. In front of him was a piece of paper, very white, which was addressed to her father. On it was written 'Her brief life was one of light and grace. She shone a kindly radiance on all those who knew her, or sought her help. Our angel is dead. We are left in darkness once more.'

In Sir David's hand was a dull crystal which he held between his eye and the flaring light of the snow. As evening fell, the fire behind him and his own shape were reflected on the window, a fact which Sir David could not see, until he let the lens fall and put his head into his hands.

There was more than glass between the fire, Sir David and the snow outside.

There was a crystalline, easily cleavable and nonlustrous mineral called Iceland spar between the fire, Sir David and the snow, which made light simple. It was Sir David's life's work to bend and polarise light and he was very good at it. Hence the lack of reflection in his windows and the flat, non-effulgent white of the ground outside.

Of his dead wife, we know very little. She was the daughter of James MacPherson, a poet who pretended to translate the verse of Ossian, an ancient Scottish bard, into English. Unfortunately, Ossian, son of Fingal, existed only because the age found it necessary to invent him: he moped up and down the highlands, sporran swinging poetically and kilt ahoy, while MacPherson campaigned for a seat in the House of Commons – which, in time, he won.

All the same, his family must have found sentiment a strain, in the face of the lies he propagated in the world. I have no reason to doubt that his daughters sat at his knee or playfully tweaked his moustaches, read Shakespeare at breakfast with the dirty bits taken out, and did excellent needlepoint, which they sold on the sly. The problem is not MacPherson and his lies, nor Brewster and his optics. The problem is that they touched a life without a name, on the very fringes of human endeavour. The problem is sentimental. Ms MacPherson was married to the man who invented the kaleidoscope.

Kal eid oscope: Something beautiful I see. This is the simplest and the most magical toy; made from a tube and two mirrors, some glass and coloured beads.

The *British Cyclopaedia* describes the invention in 1833. 'If any object, however ugly or irregular in itself, be placed (in it) . . . every image of the object will coalesce into a form mathematically symmetrical and highly pleasing to the eye. If the object be put in motion, the combination of images will likewise be put in motion, and new forms, perfectly different, but equally symmetrical, will successively present themselves, sometimes vanishing in the centre, sometimes emerging from it, and sometimes playing around in double and opposite oscillations.'

The two mirrors in a kaleidoscope do not reflect each other to infinity. They are set at an angle, so that their reflections open out like a flower, meet at the bottom and overlap.

When she plays with it, her hand does not understand what her eye can see. It can not hold the secret size that the mirrors unfold.

She came down to London for the season and met a young man who told her the secrets of glass. The ballroom was glittering with the light of a chandelier that hung like a bunch of tears, dripping radiance over the dancers. She was, of course, beautiful, in this shattered light and her simple white dress.

He told her that glass was sand, melted in a white hot crucible: white sand, silver sand, pearl ash, powdered quartz. He mentioned glasswort, the plant from which potash is made; the red oxide of lead, the black oxide of manganese. He told her how arsenic is added to plate glass to restore its transparency, how a white poison made it clear.

Scientific conversation was of course fashionable at the time, and boredom polite, but David Brewster caught a spark in the young girl's eye that changed all these dull facts into the red-hot liquid of his heart.

He told her how glass must be cooled or it will explode at the slightest touch.

After their first meeting he sent her in a box set with velvet, Lacrymae Vitreae, or Prince Rupert's Drops: glass tears that have been dripped into water. In his note, he explained that the marvellous quality of these tears is that they withstand all kinds of force applied to the thick end, but burst into the finest dust if a fragment is broken from the thin end. He urged her to keep them safe.

Mr MacPherson's daughter and Dr (soon to be Sir) David Brewster were in love.

★ ★ ★

There is a difference between reflection and refraction, between bouncing light and bending it, between letting it loose and various, or twisting it and making it simple. As I mentioned before, Sir David's life's work was to make light simple, something he did for the glory of man and God. Despite the way her eyes sparkled when she smiled, and the molten state of his heart, Sir David's work was strenuous, simple and hard. He spent long hours computing angles, taking the rainbow apart.

Imagine the man of science and his young bride on their wedding night, as she sits in front of the mirror and combs her hair, with the light of candles playing in the shadows of her face. Perhaps there are two mirrors on the dressing table, and she is reflected twice. Perhaps it was not necessary for there to be two, in order for Sir David to sense, in or around that moment, the idea of the kaleidoscope; because in their marriage bed, new forms, perfectly different, but equally symmetrical, successively presented themselves, sometimes vanishing in the centre, sometimes emerging from it, and sometimes playing around in double and opposite oscillations.

(One of the most beautiful things about the kaleidoscope is, of course, that it is bigger on the inside. A simple trick which is done with mirrors.)

In those days, these people had a peculiar and terrible fear of being buried alive. This resulted in a fashionable device which was rented out to the bereaved. A glass ball sat on the corpse's chest, and was connected, by a series of counterweights, pulleys and levers, to the air above. If the body started to breathe, the movement would set off the mechanism, and cause a white flag to be raised above the grave. White, being the colour of surrender, made it look as if death had laid siege, and failed.

Death laid early siege to the bed of Sir David Brewster and his wife. She was to die suitably; pale and wasted against the pillows, her translucent hand holding a handkerchief, spotted with blood. It was a time when people took a long time to die, especially the young.

It is difficult to say what broke her, a chance remark about the rainbow perhaps, when they were out for their daily walk, and he explained the importance of the angle of forty-two degrees. Or drinking a cup of warm milk with her father's book on her lap, and finding the skin in her mouth. Or looking in the mirror one day and licking it.

It was while she was dying that Sir David stumbled upon the kaleidoscope. He thought of her in the ballroom, when he first set eyes on her. He thought of her in front of the mirror. He built her a toy to make her smile in her last days.

When she plays with it, the iris of her eye twists and widens with delight.

Because of her horror of being buried alive, Sir David may have had his wife secretly cremated. From her bone-ash he caused to be blown a glass bowl with an opalescent white skin. In it he put the Lacrymae Vitreae, the glass tears that were his first gift. Because the simple fact was, that Sir David Brewster's wife was not happy. She had no reason to be.

Sir David was sitting in his study, with the fire dying in the grate, his lens of Iceland spar abandoned by his side. He was surprised to find that he had been crying, and he lifted his head slowly from his hands, to wipe away the tears. It was at that moment that he was visited by his wife's ghost, who was also weeping.

She stood between him, the window and the snow outside. She held her hands out to him and the image shifted as she tried to speak. He saw, in his panic, that she could not be seen in the glass, though he saw himself there. Nor was she visible in the mirror, much as the stories told. He noted vague shimmerings of colour at the edge of the shape that were truly 'spectral' in their nature, being arranged in bands. He also perceived, after she had gone, a vague smell of ginger in the room.

Sir David took this visitation as a promise and a sign. In the quiet of reflection, he regretted that he had not been able to view this spectral light through his polarising lens. This oversight did not, however, stop him claiming the test, in a paper which he wrote on the subject. Sir David was not a dishonest man, nor was he cold. He considered it one of the most important lies of his life. It was an age full of ghosts as well as science, and the now forgotten paper was eagerly passed from hand to hand.

★ ★ ★

Ruth's mother was deaf. Her mouth hung slightly ajar. When Ruth was small her mother would press her lips against her cheek and make a small, rude sound. She used all of her body when she spoke and her voice came from the wrong place. She taught Ruth sign language and how to read lips. As a child, Ruth dreamt about sound in shapes.

Sometimes her mother would listen to her through the table, with her face flat against the wood. She bought her a piano and listened to her play it through her hand. She could hear with any part of her body.

Of course Ruth was a wonder child, clever and shy. When her ears were tested the doctor said 'That child could hear the grass grow Mrs Rooney.' Her mother didn't care. For all she knew, the grass was loud as trumpets.

Her mother told Ruth not to worry. She said that in her dreams she could hear everything. But Ruth's own dreams were silent. Perhaps that was the real difference between them.

When Ruth grew up she started to make shapes that were all about sound. She wove the notes of the scale in coloured strings. She turned duration into thickness and tone into shade. She overlapped the violins and the oboe and turned the roll of the drum into a wave.

It seemed to Ruth that the more beautiful a piece of music was, the more beautiful the shape it made. She was a successful sculptor, who brought all of her work home to her mother and said 'Dream about this, Ma. Beethoven's Ninth.'

Of course it worked both ways. She could work shapes back into the world of sound. She rotated objects on a computer grid and turned them into a score. This is the complicated sound of my mother sitting. This is the sound of her with her arm in the air. It played the Albert Hall. Her mother heard it all through the wood of her chair.

As far as people were concerned, friends and lovers and all the rest, she listened to them speak in different colours. She made them wonder whether their voices and their mouths were saying the same thing as their words, or something else. The whole message was suddenly complicated, involuntary and wise.

On the other hand, men never stayed with her for long. She caused the sound of their bodies to be played over the radio, which was, in its way, flattering. What they could not take was the fact that she never listened to a word they said. Words like: 'Did you break the clock?' 'Why did you put the mirror in the hot press?' 'Where is my shoe?'

'The rest is silence.'

When Ruth's mother was dying she said 'I will be able to hear in Heaven.' Unfortunately, Ruth knew that there was no Heaven. She closed her mother's eyes and her mouth and was overwhelmed by the fear that one day her world would be mute. She was not worried about going deaf. If she were deaf then she would be able to hear in her dreams. She was terrified that her shapes would lose their meaning, her grids their sense, her colours their public noise. When the body beside her was no longer singing, she thought, she might as well marry it, or die.

She really was a selfish bastard (as they say of men and angels).

(She Owns) Every Thing

Cathy was often wrong, she found it more interesting. She was wrong about the taste of bananas. She was wrong about the future of the bob. She was wrong about where her life ended up. She loved corners, surprises, changes of light.

Of all the fates that could have been hers (spinster, murderer, savant, saint), she chose to work behind a handbag counter in Dublin and take her holidays in the sun.

For ten years she lived with the gloves and beside the umbrellas, their colours shy and neatly furled. The handbag counter travelled through navy and brown to a classic black. Yellows, reds, and white were to one side and all varieties of plastic were left out on stands, for the customer to steal.

Cathy couldn't tell you what the handbag counter was like. It was hers. It smelt like a leather dream. It was never quite right. Despite the close and intimate spaces of the gloves and the empty generosity of the bags themselves, the discreet mess that was the handbag counter was just beyond her control.

She sold clutch bags for people to hang on to; folded slivers of animal skin that wouldn't hold a box of cigarettes, or money unless it was paper, or a bunch of keys. 'Just a credit card and a condom,' said one young woman to another and Cathy felt the ache of times changing.

She sold the handbag proper, sleek and stiff and surprisingly roomy – the favourite bag, the thoroughbred, with a hard clasp, or a fold-over flap and the smell of her best perfume. She sold sacks to young women, in canvas or in suede, baggy enough to hold a life, a change of underwear, a novel, a deodorant spray.

The women's faces as they made their choice were full of lines going nowhere, tense with the problems of leather, price, vulgarity, colour. Cathy matched blue eyes with a blue trim, a modest mouth with smooth, plum suede. She sold patent to the click of high heels, urged women who had forgotten into neat, swish reticules. Quietly, one customer after another was guided to the inevitable and surprising choice of a bag that was not 'them' but one step beyond who they thought they might be.

Cathy knew what handbags were for. She herself carried everything (which wasn't much) in one pocket, or the other.

She divided her women into two categories: those who could and those who could not.

She had little affection for those who could, they had no need of her, and they were often mistaken. Their secret was not one of class, although that seemed to help, but one of belief, and like all questions of belief, it involved certain mysteries. How, for example, does one *believe* in navy?

But there were also the women who could not. A woman for example, who could NOT wear blue. A woman who could wear a print, but NOT beside her face. A woman who could wear beads but NOT earrings. A woman who had a secret life of shoes too exotic for her, or one who could neither pass a perfume counter nor buy a perfume, unless it was for someone else. A woman who comes home with royal jelly every time she tries to buy a blouse.

A woman who cries in the lingerie department.

A woman who laughs while trying on hats.

A woman who buys two coats of a different colour.

The problem became vicious when they brought their daughters shopping with them. Cathy could smell these couples coming, all the way from Kitchenware.

Cathy married late and it was hard work. She had to find a man. Once she had found one, she discovered that the city was full of them. She had to talk and laugh and be fond. She had to choose. Did she like big burly men with soft brown eyes? Did she like that blond man with the eyes of pathological blue? What did she think of her own face, its notches and dents?

In the end, she went the easy road with a kind teacher from Fairview and a registry office do. She stole him from a coltish young woman with awkward eyes. Cathy would have sold her a tapestry Gladstone bag, one that was 'wrong' but 'worked' all the same.

Sex was a pleasant surprise. It was such a singular activity, it seemed to scatter and gather her at the same time.

Cathy fell in love one day with a loose, rangy woman, who came to her counter and to her smile and seemed to pick her up with the same ease as she did an Argentinian calf-skin shoulder bag in tobacco brown, with woven leather inset panels, pig-skin lining and snap clasp. It was quite a surprise.

The woman, whose eyes were a tired shade of blue, asked Cathy's opinion, and Cathy heard herself say 'DIVE RIGHT IN HONEY, THE WATER'S JUST FINE!' – a phrase she must have picked up from the television set. The woman did not flinch. She said 'Have you got it in black?'

Brown was the colour of the bag. Cathy was disappointed by this betrayal. The weave would just disappear in black, the staining was everything. Cathy said, 'It's worth it in brown, even if it means new shoes. It really is a beautiful bag.' The woman, however, neither bought the brown nor argued for black. She rubbed the leather with the base of her thumb as she laid the bag down. She looked at Cathy. She despaired. She turned her wide, sporting shoulders, her dry, bleached hair, and her nose with the bump in it, gave a small sigh, and walked out of the shop.

Cathy spent the rest of the day thinking, not of her hands, with their large knuckles, but of her breasts, that were widely spaced and looked two ways, one towards the umbrellas, the other at the scarves. She also wondered whether the woman had a necklace of lines hanging from her hips, whether she had ever been touched by a woman, what she might say, what Cathy might say back. Whether her foldings and infoldings were the same as her own or as different as daffodil from narcissus. It was a very exciting afternoon.

Cathy began to slip. She made mistakes. She sold the wrong bags to the wrong women and her patter died. She waited for another woman to pick up the tobacco-brown bag to see what might happen. She sold indiscriminately. She looked at every woman who came her way and she just didn't know anymore.

She could, of course, change her job. She could drive a bus. She could work as a hospital maid in, for example, the cardiac ward, which was full of certainties.

Because women did not get heart attacks. They would come at visiting time and talk too much or not at all. She could work out who loved simply or in silence. She could spot those who might as well hate. She would look at their bags without judgement, as they placed them on the coverlets, or opened them for tissues. They might even let a tear drip inside.

Cathy emptied out her building-society account and walked up to the hat department with a plastic bag filled with cash. She said, 'Ramona, I want to buy every hat you have.' She did the same at Shoes, although she stipulated size five-and-a-half. She didn't make a fuss when refused. She stuffed the till of her own counter full of notes, called a taxi and hung herself with bags, around her neck and down her arms. All kinds of people looked at her. Then she went to bed for a week, feeling slightly ashamed.

She kept the one fatal bag, the brown calf-skin with a snap clasp. She abused it. She even used it to carry things. She started to sleep around.

The Portable Virgin

Dare to be dowdy! that's my motto, because it comes to us all – the dirty acrylic jumpers and the genteel trickle of piss down our support tights. It will come to her too.

She was one of those women who hold their skin like a smile, as if she was afraid her face might fall off if the tension went out of her eyes.

I knew that when Ben made love to her, the thought that she might break pushed him harder. I, by comparison, am like an old sofa, welcoming, familiar, well-designed.

This is the usual betrayal story, as you have already guessed – the word 'sofa' gave it away. The word 'sofa' opened up rooms full of sleeping children and old wedding photographs, ironic glances at crystal wineglasses, BBC mini-series where Judi Dench plays the deserted furniture and has a little sad fun.

It is not a story about hand-jobs in toilets, at parties where everyone is in the van-rental business. It is not a story where Satan turns around like a lawyer in a swivel chair. There are no doves, no prostitutes, no railway stations, no marks on the skin.

So there I was knitting a bolero jacket when I dropped a stitch. Bother. And there was Ben with a gin and tonic crossing his legs tenderly by the phone.

'Thoroughly fucked?' I asked and he spilt his drink.

Ben has been infected by me over the years. He has my habit of irony, or perhaps I have his. Our inflections coincide in bed, and sometimes he startles me in the shops, by hopping out of my mouth.

'Thoroughly,' he said, brushing the wet on his trousers and flicking drops of gin from his fingertips.

There was an inappropriate desire in the room, a strange dance of description; as I uncovered her brittle blonde hair, her wide strained mouth. A woman of modified adjectives, damaged by men, her body whittled into thinness so unnatural you could nearly see the marks of the knife. Intelligent? No. Funny? No. Rich, with a big laugh and sharp heels? No. Happy? Definitely not. Except when he was there. Ben makes me too sad for words. I finished the row, put away my needles and went to bed.

Judi Dench came out of the wardrobe and decided that it was time that she had an affaire herself. She would start a small business in the gardening shed and leave her twin-sets behind. And just when she realised that *she* was a human being *too* – attractive generous and witty (albeit in a sofa kind of way) – some nice man would come along and agree with her.

Mrs Rochester punched a hole in the ceiling and looked at Ben where he sat at the end of the bed, maimed and blind. She whispered a long and very sensible monologue with an urgency that made the mattress smoulder, and we both had a good laugh about that.

Karen . . . Sharon . . . Teresa . . . all good names for women who dye their hair. Suzy . . . Jacintha . . . Patti . . .

'What's her name?' I asked.

'Mary,' he said.

My poor maimed husband is having sex in the back of our car with a poor maimed woman who has a law degree and a tendency to overdress. She works for a van-rental firm. You would think at least she could get them something with a bigger back seat.

My poor maimed husband is seriously in danger of damaging his health with the fillip this fact has given to our love life. And while he bounces on top of his well-loved sofa, Satan turns around in the corner, like a lawyer in a swivel chair, saying 'Go on, go on, you'll wake the children.' (Or is that me?)

She is the silence at the other end of the phone. She is the smile he starts but does not finish. She is the woman standing at the top of the road, with cheap nail-polish and punctured ears. She is the girl at the front of the class, with ringlets and white knees and red eyes.

The phonecalls are more frequent. It is either getting serious or going sour. He used to head straight for the bathroom when he came home, in order to put his dick in the sink. Then they stopped doing it by accident and started going to her flat instead, with its (naturally) highly scented soap. Should I tell her the next time she rings? Should we get chatty about Pears, fall in love over Palmolive? We could ring up an agency and do an advert, complete with split screen. 'Mary's soap is all whiffy, but *Mary* uses X – so mild her husband will never leave.' Of course we have the same name, it is part of Ben's sense of irony, and we all know where he got that from.

So Ben is tired of love. Ben wants sad sex in the back of cars. Ben wants to desire the broken cunt of a woman who will never make it to being real.

'But I thought it *meant* something!' screams the wife, throwing their crystal honeymoon wineglasses from Seville against the Magnolia Matt wall.

I am not that old after all. Revenge is not out of the question. There is money in my purse and an abandoned adolescence that never got under way.

I sit in a chair in the most expensive hairdresser in Grafton Sreet. A young man I can't see pulls my head back into the sink and anoints (I'm sorry) my head with shampoo. It is interesting to be touched like this; hairdressers, like doctors, are getting younger by the day. My 'stylist' is called Alison and she checks my shoes beneath the blue nylon cape, looking for a clue.

'I want a really neat bob,' I say, 'but I don't know what to do with this bit.'

'I know,' she says, 'it's driving you mad. That's why it's so thin, you just keep brushing it out of your eyes.'

I am a woman whose hair is falling out, my stuffing is coming loose.

'But look, we're nearly there,' and she starts to wave the scissors (like a blessing) over my head.

'How long is it since you had it cut last?'

'About ten weeks.'

'Exactly,' she says, 'because we're not going to get any length with all these split ends, are we?'

'I want to go blonde,' says the wet and naked figure in the mirror and the scissors pause mid-swoop.

'It's very thin . . .'

'I know, I want it to break. I want it blonde.'

'Well . . .' My stylist is shocked. I have finally managed to say something really obscene.

The filthy metamorphosis is effected by another young man whose hair is the same length as the stubble on his chin. He has remarkable, sexual blue eyes, which come with the price. 'We' start with a rubber cap which he punctures with a vicious crochet hook, then he drags my poor thin hair through the holes. I look 'a fright'. All the women around me look 'a fright'. Mary is sitting to my left and to my right. She is blue from the neck down, she is reading a magazine, her hair stinks, her skin is pulled into a smile by the rubber tonsure on her head. There is a handbag at her feet, the inside of which is coated with blusher that came loose. Inside the bags are bills, pens, sweet-papers, diaphragms, address books full of people she doesn't know anymore. I know this because I stole one as I left the shop.

I am sitting on Dollymount Strand going through Mary's handbag, using her little mirror, applying her 'Wine Rose and Gentlelight Colourize Powder Shadow Trio', her Plumsilk lipstick, her Venetian Brocade blusher and her Tearproof (thank God) mascara.

I will be bored soon. I will drown her slowly in a pool and let the police peg out the tatters to dry when they pick up the bag on the beach. It affords me some satisfaction to think of her washed up in the hairdressers, out of her nylon shift and newly shriven, without the means to pay.

My revenge looks back at me, out of the mirror. The new fake me looks twice as real as the old. Underneath my clothes my breasts have become blind, my iliac crests mottle and bruise. Strung out between my legs is a triangle of air that pulls away from sex, while my hands clutch. It used to be the other way around.

I root through the bag, looking for a past. At the bottom, discoloured by Wine Rose and Gentlelight, I find a small, portable Virgin. She is made of transparent plastic, except for her cloak, which is coloured blue. 'A present from Lourdes' is written on the globe at her feet, underneath her heel and the serpent. Mary is full of surprises. Her little blue crown is a screw-off top, and her body is filled with holy water, which I drink.

Down by the water's edge I set her sailing on her back, off to Ben, who is sentimental that way. Then I follow her into his story, with its doves and prostitutes, its railway stations and marks on the skin. I have nowhere else to go. I love that man.

INDIFFERENCE

The young man in the corner was covered in flour. His coat was white, his shoes were white and there was a white paper hat askew on his head. Around his mouth and nose was the red weal of sweating skin where he had worn a mask to keep out the dust. The rest of him was perfectly edible and would turn to dough if he stepped outside in the rain.

He was with a pal. They were assessing her as she sat across the room from them with a glass of Guinness and an old newspaper that someone had left behind.

'What do you think?' asked the white man.

'I wouldn't go near her with a bag of dicks,' said his companion, who was left-handed – or at least that was the hand that was holding his pint. He had the thin Saturday-matinée face of a villain; of the man who might kidnap the young girl and end up in a duel with Errol Flynn. She saw him swinging out of velvet drapes, up-ending tables and jumping from the chandelier, brandishing, not a sword, but a hessian bag from which come soft gurgles and thin protesting squeaks.

Errol Flynn wounds him badly and is leaning over his throat ready for the final, ungentlemanly slash when the bag of dicks escapes, rolls down a flight of steps, shuffles over to the beautiful young girl and starts to whine. She unties the knot and sets them free.

'What a peculiar language you speak,' she said mentally, with a half-smile and a nod, as if her own were normal. 'Normal' usually implied American. I am Canadian, she used to say, it may be a very boring country, but who needs history when we have so much weather?

Irish people had no weather at all apart from vague shifts from damp to wet, and they talked history like it was happening down the road. They also sang quite a bit and were depressingly ethnic. They thought her bland.

Of course I am bland, she thought. You too would be bland if you grew up with one gas pump in front of the house and nothing else except a view that stretched over half the world. Landscape made me bland, bears poking in the garbage can stunted my individuality, as did plagues of horseflies, permafrost, wild-fire, and the sun setting like a bomb. So much sky makes ones bewildered – which is the only proper way to be.

She rented a flat in Rathmines where the only black people in the country seemed to reside and the shops stayed open all night. The house was suitably 'old' but the partition walls bothered her, as did the fact that the door from her bedroom into the hall had been taken off its hinges. The open block of the doorframe frightened her as she fell asleep, not because of what might come through it, but because she might drift off the bed and slide through the gap to Godknowswhere. (In the shower she sang 'How are things in Glockamorra?' and 'Come back, Paddy Reilly, to Ballyjamesduff'.)

The white man was beside her asking to look at her paper and he sat down to read.

'Go on, ask her does she want to come,' said the matinée man across the deserted bar.

'Ask her yourself.'

'Where are you from?' said the matinée man picking up their two pints and making the move to her table.

'God that's a great pair of shoes you got on,' he said looking at her quilted moon-boots. 'You didn't get them here.'

'Canada,' she said.

'She can talk!' said the villain. 'I told you she could talk.'

'You can't bring him anywhere,' said the white man, and she decided that she would sleep with him. Why not? It had been a long time since Toronto.

'Would you like a drink?' she asked, and was surprised at the silence that fell.

'I'm skiving off,' said the white man. 'I'm on the hop. Mitching. I'll get the sack.' She still didn't seem to understand. 'Look at me,' he opened up his palms like a saint to show her the thin rolls of paste in the creases. 'I work over there. In the bakery.'

'I guessed that,' she said. 'I could smell the fresh bread.'

She wrote this story in a letter to her flatmate in Toronto. It is a story about A Bit of Rough. It includes furious sex in red-brick alleyways. It has poignant moments to do with cultural distinctions and different breeds of selfishness. Unfortunately the man in question is not wearing leather, nor is he smelling like Marlon Brando. He is too thin. His accent is all wrong. He is covered, not with oil and sweat, but with sweat and flour.

The furious sex took him by surprise. She looked at a man sliding down the wall on to his hunkers with his hands over his face. He had lost his paper hat. There was flour down her front congealing in the rain. 'I've never done that before,' he said.

'Well, neither have I.'

'I've never done any of that before.'

'Oh boy.'

'And I've got the sack.' So she brought him home.

'Erections. What a laugh. My ancient Aunt Moragh bounced out of her coffin on the way to the cemetery. I will never forget it. You could almost hear the squawk. It was my cousin Shawn driving the pick-up when the suspension went. Now he was a bit simple – or at least that is, he never talked so you couldn't tell. But he took her dying so hard that he was swinging the wheel with one hand and crying into the other and he drove regardless, with his ass dragging in the dirt. I swear I saw Moragh rise to her feet like she was on hinges, like she was a loose plank in the floor coming up to hit you in the face. And she yelled out "Shawn! You come back here!" I was only six, but I wouldn't deny it, no matter how much they said I was a liar.'

There was a thin white man in her bed, and when he got up to go to the toilet he disappeared through the doorframe like the line of light from a closing door. They were no longer drunk. He stayed, because he didn't know what else to do. He was fragile, like a man let out of prison, who bumps into a stranger on the street and feels a lifetime's friendship. He stared, and she felt all the stories she had inside her looking for him like home.

'So Todd tells me about this woman that he is in love with. I mean that's OK, but why do men have to take all their clothes off before they can tell you about the woman they love? So there we were, sitting in the U of T canteen and I'm saying "Todd, please, it's OK, I'll survive, please put your clothes back on."'

'All the same, I could have spent the rest of my life with him, having bad sex. Honestly. He made love like I was a walrus, something huge and strange. Spent half an hour kind of paddling his hand on my left buttock which must be the least interesting, the most mistaken part of my body. Then sort of dodged in, like I was an alley on the way to school. I didn't know whether he had come, or a picture had slipped on the wall . . . True love.'

He stayed the next day and she didn't go into class. She opened a bottle of good wine to educate him and they forgot to eat. They lifted the sash of the bedroom window and were surprised by the taste of the air. He was so thin it hurt her and his laugh was huge.

'We came across this swimming pool, in the woods, in the middle of nowhere. It was empty, with blue tiles and weeds growing out through the cracks. There was a metal ladder just going nowhere in the corner. So we climbed down and it was like being underwater somehow. Like we swam through the air. Then this crazy guy, he stood on the edge and he said he was going to dive in. My God was I freaked. I could just see his head splitting on the tiles. I screamed until I fell over. Men always think I'm neurotic and I suppose it's true.'

'Are you?'

'I suppose.'

He was grateful for it, whatever it was. Compared to her body, her mind was easy to understand. There were wine stains on the sheets which he wrapped around him like Caesar. He sang, and paced the room, and looked at his naked feet, which weren't ugly anymore. The razor in her bathroom confused him and he asked about other men. So she made love to him at the sink and he looked at his face in the mirror, as if it was blind.

He wasn't so amazed by sex as by people, who did this all the time and never told. Never did anything but laugh in the wrong way. 'They do this night and day,' he said, 'and it doesn't show. Walking down the street and you think they'd look different. You think they'd recognise and smile at each other, like "I know and you know". It's like the secret everyone was in on, except me.'

The light deepened. 'What is it like for a woman?' he asked.

'How should I know?' she said. 'What is it like for a man? Sometimes, after a while, it's like your whole body is crying, like your liver even, is sad. It's more sweet than sore. In here. And here.'

'Where?'

Her touch saturated him to the bone and he had to pull away from her, in case something untold might happen. Which it did.

The next day he rang up the matinée man whose astonishment was audible from the other side of the room. He asked for clothes from his flat and looked at her and laughed as the questions kept pouring out of the phone.

The matinée man's name was Jim and he entered her place with a comic air of apology. Kevin poked his head around the jamb of the open doorframe and asked for his clothes. 'You bollocks.' They all went out for a drink.

What she noticed in the pub were his eyelids, that disappeared when he looked at her, and made him look cruel. She couldn't understand most of what they were saying and they laughed all the time. He was wearing a nylon-mix jumper, cheap denim and bad shoes.

'I thought the friend was the kind of Oh-so-interesting bastard,' said the letter, 'with that glint in his eye that cuts me right up. You know capital P. Primitive, the kind that want to see the blood on the sheet or the bride is a slut. What I mean is . . . Attractive to the Masochistic, which, as we all know, is the street I've been living on even though the rent is so high. What I need is a romantic Irish farmer who is sweet AND a bastard at the same time. So he's looking at us anyway like we've been Sinning or something equally Catholic and I just started to fight him, all the way. He says "Did you have a good time then?" and I said that "Kevin was the best fuck this side of the Atlantic." DUMB! I KNOW THAT! and Kevin laughed and so that was . . . fine. And then I said "Maybe that surprises you?" "Not at all," he says. "That's what they are all saying down Leeson Street," which is their kind of Fuck Alley. And I laughed and said "Hardly," I said, "seeing as he's never done it before . . ." and there was this silence.'

She went to the toilet, and when she came back, his friend was gone.

'Why did you pick me, if it doesn't mean anything? That's what you are saying, isn't it? You're saying I shouldn't have stayed.'

'Don't worry, you're great. You'll make some woman a great lover.'

'You should have fucked Jim. He understands these things. You both understood each other like I was an eejit.'

'I'm sorry,' she said.

He was no longer polite. He walked her back to the flat when he should have gone home.

'So. Welcome to aggressive sex,' she said. 'I enjoyed that.' He had broken her like a match.

'You're all talk.'

After a while he turned to her and felt her body from her shoulders to her hips, passing his hands slowly and with meaning over the skin. She felt herself drifting off the bed through the black space where the door should have been. It seemed to grow in the dark and swallow the room.

'When I was a kid, there was a monumental sculptors in the local graveyard and the polishing shed was covered in marble dust. The table was white, the floor was white, the coke can in the corner was white. There was an old wardrobe up against the wall with the door hanging off, all still and silent like they were made out of stone. And outside was this rock with "Monumental Enquiries" carved into it like a joke. Which just goes to show.'

After he left, she saw the shadow of flour on the carpet, where his clothes had lain, like the outline of a corpse, when the clues are still fresh.

HISTORICAL LETTERS

I.

So. I wouldn't wash the sheets after you left, like some taw-dry El Paso love affair. No one is unhappy in El Paso. There is lithium in the water supply. So it all still smells of you and at four in the morning that's a stink and at five it's a desert hum, with cicadas blooming all over the ceiling. Because you are on the road.

I am not hysterical. We have mice – just to go with all this heat and poverty and lust business, two flatmates with grown-up salaries and lives to run after. Actually, it is hot, which I hate. If I want weather I pay for it, besides, the sun only came out for you. Actually, also, there is something in the water supply.

I have prehensile toes because you made my feet grip like a baby's fist. That's not something you forget so easily.

You, on the other hand, do forget – easily and all the time. This is something I admire. You don't make up little stories to remember by. Which means that I am burdened with all the years that you passed through and neglected. I can handle them, of course, with my excellent synapses that feel no pain.

There is something about you that reminds me of the century. You talk like it was Before as well as After and you travel just to help you think – as if we were all still living in nine-teen-hundred-and-sixty-five. There's nothing special about you, Sunshine, except how gentle you are. And you talk like it was nineteen-hundred-and-seventy-four. 'Live a quiet life, be true, try to be honest. Work, don't hurt people.' You said all this while putting on your socks, which were bottlegreen, very slowly.

Sleeping with you is like watching a man in a wet suit cleaning the aquarium glass, in with the otters on the other side.

All I want to say, before you disappear into that decade of yours, all I want to say is how things became relevant, how the sugar-bowl sits well on the table, how the wood seems to agree.

But it is a gift, like snow. It is a gift the way the bowl sits so well on the table, it is a gift how it all, including you, was pushed out through a cleft in time. Pop! I can move my hand from the bowl, over a fork, to my own blue cup, and the distance between them makes me content.

2.

You may say, in you turn, that I am an aquatic kind of girl, an underwater sort of thing. Since you left I spend most of my time on my back, as it were. I can see the street in a fan of light on the bedroom ceiling. When someone walks past, they move a line of shadow like the needle on a dial. Cars make everything shiver.

I remember most of what you said and I said. I don't see the point of this landscape of yours, blank and full of frights with no clock in it. All your pain strikes me as very nineteen-hundred-and-sixty-seven. I come from the generation that never took drugs, the generation that grew up. I am a woman that was born in 1962.

And you know what that means.

Despite the fact that I was born in nineteen-hundred-and-sixty-two, I go around the house mouthing words like they were new, like the whole problem of words was as fresh as Paris. You have infected me with the fifties, une femme d'un certain âge who knows how to dress but not how to speak. Sweetheart.

Tell me. When was the Spanish Civil War? Is that where you are? Having a serious discussion about reification and blood, rubbing alcohol and the future. I bet the people you meet all have stories, perplexities, Slavic bones.

When I was ten a white horse ran into the side of the school bus and died. I saw the blood bubble out of his nose.

You should go to Berlin in nineteen-hundred-and-eighty-nine, with the wall coming down. You could put the Cabaret and the Jews back in perhaps. I am there, watching it all on TV, getting everything wrong. I am wrong about remote-control televisions, denim, history in general. I can't tell where the party is. I do not have a democratic mind, but if I watch the right movie, the horse dies every time. (Why is it always white?)

So I am supposed to sit here with my finger in my gee until you come back – from Moscow in 1937 where you discover what music really is. From New Orleans in 1926 where you are eating the heart out of artichokes. From Dublin in 1914 where you are walking, pretentiously enough, on the beach. When I just got my credit cards, the sign of a woman who does not wait around.

History is just a scum on reality as far as I am concerned. You scrape it away.

Listen.

When de Valera died, I didn't care either way, but a girl in my class was delighted, because her granny was buried half an hour before him, and all the soldiers along the road saluted as they went by.

I saw them landing on the moon, but my mother wasn't bothered. She wanted to finish drying the dishes, so she said, 'Sure I can see the moon, right here in the window.'

When I was ten a white horse ran into the side of the school bus and died. I saw the blood bubble out of his nose.

That is what I want to say. I was not washed up on the beach of your life like Venus on the tide. I know the distance between the cup and the bowl. I have seen Berlin. I have seen the moon. I will find out how to speak again and change the sheets, because it must change, I say, in order to give pleasure.

Never mind the horse.

LUCK BE A LADY

The bingo coach (VZE 26) stopped at the top of the road and Mrs Maguire (no. 18), Mrs Power (no. 9) and Mrs Hanratty (no. 27) climbed on board and took their places with the 33 other women and 0 men who made up the Tuesday run.

'If nothing happens tonight . . .' said Mrs Maguire and the way she looked at Mrs Hanratty made it seem like a question.

'I am crucified,' said Mrs Hanratty, 'by these shoes. I'll never buy plastic again.'

'You didn't,' said Mrs Power, wiping the window with unconcern.

'I know,' said Mrs Hanratty. 'There's something astray in my head. I wouldn't let the kids do it.'

Nothing in her tone of voice betrayed the fact that Mrs Hanratty knew she was the most unpopular woman in the coach. She twisted 1 foot precisely and ground her cigarette into the plastic mica floor.

When Mrs Hanratty was 7 and called Maeve, she had thrown her Clarks solid leather, solid heeled, T-bar straps under a moving car and they had survived intact. The completion of this act of rebellion took place at the age of 55, with fake patent and a heel that made her varicose veins run blue. They pulsed at the back of her knee, disappeared into the fat of her thigh, ebbed past her caesarean scars and trickled into her hardening heart, that sat forgotten behind two large breasts, each the size of her head. She still had beautiful feet.

She kept herself well. Her silver hair was rinsed and set and there was black jet hanging from her ears. She was the kind of woman who squeezed into fitting rooms with her daughters, to persuade them to buy the cream skirt, even though it would stain. She made her husband laugh once a day, on principle, and her sons were either virgins or had the excuse of a good job.

Maeve Hanratty was generous, modest and witty. Her children succeeded and failed in unassuming proportions and she took the occasional drink. She was an enjoyable woman who regretted the fact that the neighbours (except perhaps, Mrs Power) disliked her so much. 'It will pass,' she said to her husband. 'With a bit of luck, my luck will run out.'

At the age of 54 she had achieved fame in a 5-minute interview on the radio when she tried to dismiss the rumour that she was the luckiest woman in Dublin. 'You'll get me banned from the hall,' she said.

'And is it just the bingo?'

'Just the bingo.'

'No horses?'

'My father did the horses,' she said, 'I wouldn't touch them.'

'And tell me, do you always know?'

'Sure, how could I know?' she lied – and diverted 126,578 people's attention with the 3 liquidisers, 14 coal-scuttles, 7 weekends away, 6,725 paper pounds, and 111 teddy bears that she had won in the last 4 years.

'If you ever want a teddy bear!'

'Maeve . . .' she said, as she put down the phone. 'Oh Maeve.' Mrs Power had run across over the road in her dressing gown and was knocking on the kitchen door and waving through the glass. There was nothing in her face to say that Mrs (Maeve) Hanratty had made a fool of herself, that she had exposed her illness to the world. Somehow no one seemed surprised that she had numbered and remembered all those lovely things. She was supposed to count her blessings.

There were other statistics she could have used, not out of anger, but because she was so ashamed. She could have said 'Do you know something – I have had sexual intercourse 1,332 times my life. Is that a lot? 65% of the occasions took place in the first 8 years of my marriage, and I was pregnant for 45 months out of those 96. Is that a lot? I have been married for 33 years and a bit, that's 12,140 days, which means an average of once every 9.09 days. I stopped at 1,332 for no reason except that I am scared beyond reason of the number 1,333. Perhaps this is sad.' It was not, of course, the kind of thing she told anyone, not even her priest, although she felt a slight sin in all that counting. Mrs Hanratty knew how many seconds she had been alive. That was why she was lucky with numbers.

It was not that they had a colour or a smell, but numbers had a feel like people had when you sense them in a room. Mrs Hanratty thought that if she had been in Auschwitz she would have known who would survive and who would die just by looking at their forearms. It was a gift that hurt and she tried to stop winning teddy bears, but things kept on adding up too well and she was driven out of the house in a sweat to the monotonous comfort of the bingo call and another bloody coal-scuttle.

She was 11th out of the coach, which was nice. The car parked in front had 779 on its number plate. It was going to be a big night.

She played Patience when she was agitated and on Monday afternoons, even if she was not. She wouldn't touch the Tarot. The cards held the memory of wet days by the sea, with sand trapped in the cracks of the table that made them hiss and slide as she laid them down. Their holiday house was an old double-decker bus washed up on the edge of the beach with a concrete block where the wheels should have been and a gas stove waiting to blow up by the driver's seat. They were numberless days with clouds drifting one into the other and a million waves dying on the beach. The children hid in the sea all day or played in the ferns and Jim came up from Dublin for the weekend.

'This is being happy,' she thought, scattering the contents of the night bucket over the scutch grass or trekking to the shop. She started counting the waves in order to get to sleep.

She knew before she realised it. She knew without visitation, without a slant of light cutting into the sea. There was no awakening, no manifestation, no pause in the angle of the stairs. There may have been a smile as she took the clothes pegs out of her mouth and the wind blew the washing towards her, but it was forgotten before it happened. She just played Patience all day on the fold-down table in a derelict bus and watched the cards making sense.

By the age of 55 she had left the cards behind. She found them obvious and untrustworthy – they tried to tell you too much and in the wrong way. The Jack of Spades sat on the Queen of Hearts, the clubs hammered away in a row. Work, love, money, pain; clubs, hearts, diamonds, spades, all making promises too big to keep. The way numbers spoke to her was much more bewildering and ordinary. Even the bingo didn't excite or let her down, it soothed her. It let her know in advance.

5 roses: the same as

5 handshakes at a railway station: the same as

5 women turning to look when a bottle of milk smashes in the shop: the same as

5 children: the same as

5 odd socks in the basket

5 tomatoes on the window-sill

5 times she goes to the toilet before she can get to sleep.

and all different from

4 roses, 4 shakes of the hand, 4 women turning, 4 children, 4 odd socks, 4 tomatoes in the sun, 4 times she goes to the toilet and lies awake thinking about the 5th.

The numbers rushed by her in strings and verification came before the end of any given day. They had a party all around her, talking, splitting, reproducing, sitting by themselves in a corner of the room. She smoked them, she hung them out on the line to dry, they chattered to her out from the TV. They drummed on the table-top and laughed in their intimate, syncopated way. They were music.

She told no one and did the cards for people if they asked. It was very accurate if she was loose enough on the day, but her husband didn't like it. He didn't like the bingo either and who could blame him.

'When's it going to stop?' he would say, or 'the money's fine, I don't mind the money.'

'With a bit of luck,' she said, 'my luck will run out.'

On Wednesday nights she went with Mrs Power to the local pub, because there was no bingo. They sat in the upstairs lounge where the regulars went, away from the people who were too young to be there at all. Mr Finn took the corner stool, Mr Byrne was centre forward. In the right-hand corner Mr Slevin sat and gave his commentary on the football match that was being played out in his head. The women sat in their places around the walls. No one let on to be drunk. Pat the barman knew their orders and which team were going to get to the final. At the end of the bar, Pauline made a quiet disgrace of herself, out on her own and chatty.

'His days are numbered . . .' said a voice, and Mrs Hanratty listened to her blood quicken. 'That fella's days are *numbered*.' There was a middle-aged man standing to order like a returned Yank in a shabby suit with a fat wallet. He was drunk and proud of it.

'I've seen his kind before,' he counted out the change in his pocket carefully in 10s and 2s and 5s, and the barman scooped all the coins into one mess and scattered them into the till. Mrs Hanratty took more than her usual sip of vodka and orange.

'None of us, of course,' he commented, though the barman had moved to the other end of the counter, 'are exempt.'

It was 2 weeks before he made his way over to their table, parked his drink and would not sit until he was asked. 'I've been all over,' he told them. 'You name it, I've done it. All over,' and he started to sing something about Alaska. It had to be a lie.

'Canada,' he started. 'There's a town in the Rockies called Hope. Just like that. And a more miserable stretch of hamburger joints and shacks you've never seen. Lift your eyes 30 degrees and you have the dawn coming over the mountains and air so thin it makes you feel the world is full of . . . well what? I was going to say "lovely ladies" but look at the two I have at my side.' She could feel Mrs Power's desire to leave as big and physical as a horse standing beside her on the carpet.

He rubbed his thigh with his hand, and, as if reminded slapped the tables with 3 extended fingers. There was no 4th. 'Look at that,' he said, and Mrs Power gave a small whinny. 'There should be a story there about how I lost it, but do you know something? It was the simplest thing in the County Meath where I was as a boy. The simplest thing. A dirty cut and it swelled so bad I was lucky I kept the hand. Isn't that a good one? I worked a combine harvester on the great plains in Iowa and you wouldn't believe the fights I got into as a young fella as far away as . . . Singapore – believe *that* or not. But a dirty cut in the County Meath.' And he wrapped the 3 fingers around his glass and toasted them silently. That night, for the first time in her life, Maeve Hanratty lost count of the vodkas she drank.

She wanted him. It was as simple as that. A woman of 55, a woman with 5 children and 1 husband, who had had sexual intercourse 1,332 times in her life and was in possession of 14 coal-scuttles, wanted the 3-fingered man, because he had 3 fingers and not 4.

It was a commonplace sickness and one she did not indulge. Her daughter came in crying from the dance-hall, her husband (and not, in fact, her father) spent the bingo money on the horses. The house was full of torn betting slips and the stubs of old lipstick. Mrs Hanratty went to bingo and won and won and won.

Although she had done nothing, she said to him silently, 'Well it's your move now, I'm through with all that,' and for 3 weeks in a row he sat at the end of the bar and talked to Pauline, who laughed too much. 'If that's what he wants, he can have it,' said Mrs Hanratty, who believed in dignity, as well as numbers.

But even the numbers were letting her down. Her daily walk to the shops became a confusion of damaged registration plates, the digits swung sideways or strokes were lopped off. 6 became 0, 7 turned into 1. She added up what was left, 555,

666, 616, 707, 906, 888, the numbers for parting, for grief, for the beginning of grief, forgetting, for accidents and for the hate that comes from money.

On the next Wednesday night he was wide open and roaring. He talked about his luck, that had abandoned him one day in Ottawa when he promised everything to a widow in the timber trade. The whole bar listened and Mrs Hanratty felt their knowledge of her as keen as a son on drugs or the front of the house in a state. He went to the box of plastic plants and ransacked it for violets which were presented to her with a mock bow. How many were there? 3 perhaps, or 4 – but the bunch loosened out before her and all Mrs Hanratty could see were the purple plastic shapes and his smile.

She took to her bed with shame, while a zillion a trillion a billion a million numbers opened up before her and wouldn't be pinned down at 6 or 7 or 8. She felt how fragile the world was with so much in it and confined herself to Primes, that were out on their own except for 1.

'The great thing about bingo is that no one loses,' Mrs Power had told him about their Tuesday and Thursday nights. Mrs Hanratty felt flayed in the corner, listening to him and his pride. Her luck was leaking into the seat as he invited himself along, to keep himself away from the drink, he said. He had nothing else to do.

The number of the coach was NIE 133. Mrs Maguire, Mrs Power and Mrs Hanratty climbed on board and took their places with the 33 women and 1 man who made up this Thursday run. He sat at the back and shouted for them to come and join him, and there was hooting from the gang at the front. He came up the aisle instead and fell into the seat beside Mrs Hanratty with a bend in the road. She was squeezed over double, paddling her hand on the floor in search of 1 ear-ring which she may have lost before she got on at all.

He crossed his arms with great ceremony, and not even the violence with which the coach turned corners could convince Mrs Hanratty that he was not rubbing her hand, strangely, with his 3 fingers, around and around.

'I am a 55-year-old woman who has had sex 1,332 times in my life and I am being molested by a man I should never have spoken to in the first place.' The action of his hand was polite and undemanding and Mrs Hanratty resented beyond anger the assurance of its tone.

All the numbers were broken off the car parked outside the hall, except 0, which was fine – it was the only 1 she knew anymore. Mrs Hanratty felt the justice of it, though it made her feel so lonely. She had betrayed her own mind and her friends were strange to her. Her luck was gone.

The 3-fingered man was last out of the coach and he called her back. 'I have your ear-ring! Maeve!' She listened. She let the others walk through. She turned.

His face was a jumble of numbers as he brought his hand up in mock salute. Out of the mess she took: his 3 fingers; the arching 3 of his eyebrows, which was laughing; the tender 3 of his upper lip and the 1 of his mouth, which opened into 0 as he spoke.

'You thought you'd lost it!' and he dropped the black jet into her hand.

'I thought I had.'

He smiled and the numbers of his face scattered and disappeared. His laughter multiplied out around her like a net.

'So what are you going to win tonight then?'

'Nothing. You.'

'O.'

REVENGE

I work for a firm which manufactures rubber gloves. There are many kinds of protective gloves, from the surgical and veterinary (arm-length) to industrial, gardening and domestic. They have in common a niceness. They all imply revulsion. You might not handle a dead mouse without a pair of rubber gloves, someone else might not handle a baby. I need not tell you that shops in Soho sell nuns' outfits made of rubber, that some grown men long for the rubber under-blanket of their infancies, that rubber might save the human race. Rubber is a morally, as well as a sexually, exciting material. It provides us all with an elastic amnesty, to piss the bed, to pick up dead things, to engage in sexual practices, to not touch whomsoever we please.

I work with and sell an everyday material, I answer everyday questions about expansion ratios, tearing, petrifaction. I moved from market research to quality control. I have snapped more elastic in my day etcetera etcetera.

My husband and I are the kind of people who put small ads in the personal columns looking for other couples who may be interested in some discreet fun. This provokes a few everyday questions: How do people *do* that? What do they *say* to each other? What do they *say* to the couples who answer? To which the answers are: Easily. Very little. 'We must see each other again sometime.'

When I was a child it was carpet I loved. I should have made a career in floor-coverings. There was a brown carpet in the dining room with specks of black, that was my parents' pride and joy. 'Watch the carpet!' they would say, and I did. I spent all my time sitting on it, joining up the warm, black dots. Things mean a lot to me.

The stench of molten rubber gives me palpitations. It also

gives me eczema and a bad cough. My husband finds the smell anaphrodisiac in the extreme. Not even the products excite him, because after seven years you don't know who you are touching, or not touching, anymore.

My husband is called Malachy and I used to like him a lot. He was unfaithful to me in that casual, 'look, it didn't mean anything' kind of way. I was of course bewildered, because that is how I was brought up. I am supposed to be bewildered. I am supposed to say 'What *is* love anyway? What *is* sex?'

Once the fiction between two people snaps then anything goes, or so they say. But it wasn't my marriage I wanted to save, it was myself. My head, you see, is a balloon on a string, my insides are elastic. I have to keep the tension between what is outside and what is in, if I am not to deflate, or explode.

So it was more than a suburban solution that made me want to be unfaithful *with* my husband, rather than *against* him. It was more than a question of the mortgage. I had my needs too: a need to be held in, to be filled, a need for sensation. I wanted revenge and balance. I wanted an awfulness of my own. Of course it was also a suburban solution. Do you really want to know our sexual grief? How we lose our grip, how we feel obliged to *wear* things, how we are supposed to look as if we mean it.

Malachy and I laugh in bed, that is how we get over the problem of conviction. We laugh at breakfast too, on a good day, and sometimes we laugh again at dinner. Honest enough laughter, I would say, if the two words were in the same language, which I doubt. Here is one of the conversations that led to the ad in the personals:

'I think we're still good in bed.' (LAUGH)

'I think we're great in bed.' (LAUGH)

'I think we should advertise.' (LAUGH)

Here is another:

'You know John Jo at work? Well his wife was thirty-one yesterday. I said. "What did you give her for her birthday then?" He said, "I gave her one for every year. Beats blowing out candles." Do you believe that?' (LAUGH)

You may ask when did the joking stop and the moment of truth arrive? As if you didn't know how lonely living with someone can be.

The actual piece of paper with the print on is of very little importance. John Jo at work composed the ad for a joke during a coffee-break. My husband tried to snatch it away from him. There was a chase.

There was a similar chase a week later when Malachy brought the magazine home to me. I shrieked. I rolled it up and belted him over the head. I ran after him with a cup full of water and drenched his shirt. There was a great feeling of relief, followed by some very honest sex. I said, 'I wonder what the letters will say?' I said, 'What kind of couples *do* that kind of thing? What kind of people *answer* ads like that?' I also said 'God how vile!'

Some of the letters had photos attached. 'This is my wife.' Nothing is incomprehensible, when you know that life is sad. I answered one for a joke. I said to Malachy 'Guess who's coming to dinner?'

I started off with mackerel pâté, mackerel being a scavenger fish, and good for the heart. I followed with veal osso buco, for reasons I need not elaborate, and finished with a spiced fig pudding with rum butter. Both the eggs I cracked had double yolks, which I found poignant.

I hoovered everything in sight of course. Our bedroom is stranger-proof. It is the kind of bedroom you could die in and not worry about the undertakers. The carpet is a little more interesting than beige, the spread is an ochre brown, the pattern on the curtains is expensive and unashamed. One wall is mirrored in a sanitary kind of way; with little handles for the wardrobe doors.

'Ding Dong,' said the doorbell. Malachy let them in. I heard the sound of coats being taken and drinks offered. I took off my apron, paused at the mirror and opened the kitchen door.

Her hair was over-worked, I thought – too much perm and too much gel. Her make-up was shiny, her eyes were small.

All her intelligence was in her mouth, which gave an ironic twist as she said Hello. It was a large mouth, sexy and selfish. Malachy was holding out a gin and tonic for her in a useless kind of way.

Her husband was concentrating on the ice in his glass. His suit was a green so dark it looked black – very discreet, I thought, and out of our league, with Malachy in his cheap polo and jeans. I didn't want to look at his face, nor he at mine. In the slight crash of our glances I saw that he was worn before his time.

I think he was an alcoholic. He drank his way through the meal and was polite. There was a feeling that he was pulling back from viciousness. Malachy, on the other hand, was over-familiar. He and the wife laughed at bad jokes and their feet were confused under the table. The husband asked me about my job and I told him about the machine I have for testing rubber squares; how it pulls the rubber four different ways at high speed. I made it sound like a joke, or something. He laughed.

I realised in myself a slow, physical excitement, a kind of pornographic panic. It felt like the house was full of balloons pressing gently against the ceiling. I looked at the husband.

'Is this your first time?'

'No,' he said.

'What kind of people *do* this kind of thing?' I asked, because I honestly didn't know.

'Well they usually don't feed us so well, or even at all.' I felt guilty. 'This is much more civilised,' he said. 'A lot of them would be well on before we arrive, I'd say. As a general kind of rule.'

'I'm sorry,' I said, 'I don't really drink.'

'Listen,' he leaned forward. 'I was sitting having a G and T in someone's front room and the wife took Maria upstairs to look at the bloody grouting in the bathroom or something, when this guy comes over to me and I realise about six minutes too late that he plays for bloody Arsenal! If you see what I mean. A very ordinary looking guy.'

'You have to be careful,' he said. 'And his wife was a cracker.'

266

When I was a child I used to stare at things as though they knew something I did not. I used to put them into my mouth and chew them to find out what it was. I kept three things under my bed at night: a piece of wood, a metal door-handle and a cloth. I sucked them instead of my thumb.

We climbed the stairs after Malachy and the wife, who were laughing. Malachy was away, I couldn't touch him. He had the same look in his eye as when he came home from a hurling match when the right team won.

The husband was talking in a low, constant voice that I couldn't refuse. I remember looking at the carpet, which had once meant so much to me. Everyone seemed to know what they were doing.

I thought that we were all supposed to end up together and perform and watch and all that kind of thing. I was interested in the power it would give me over breakfast, but I wasn't looking forward to the confusion. I find it difficult enough to arrange myself around one set of limbs, which are heavy things. I wouldn't know what to do with three. Maybe we would get over the awkwardness with a laugh or two, but in my heart of hearts I didn't find the idea of being with a naked woman funny. What would we joke about? Would we be expected to do things?

What I really wanted to see was Malachy's infidelity. I wanted his paunch made public, the look on his face, his bottom in the air. *That* would be funny.

I did not expect to be led down the hall and into the spare room. I did not expect to find myself sitting on my own with an alcoholic and handsome stranger who had a vicious look in his eye. I did not expect to feel anything.

I wanted him to kiss me. He leant over and tried to take off his shoes. He said, 'God I hate that woman. Did you see her? The way she was laughing and all that bloody lip-gloss. Did you see her? She looks like she's made out of plastic. I can't get a hold of her without slipping around in some body lotion that smells like petrol and dead animals.' He had taken his shoes off and was swinging his legs onto the bed. 'She never changes you know.' He was trying to take his trousers off. 'Oh

I know she's sexy. I mean, you saw her. She is sexy. She is sexy. She is sexy. I just prefer if somebody else does it. If you don't mind.' I still wanted him to kiss me. There was the sound of laughter from the other room.

I roll off the wet patch and lie down on the floor with my cheek on the carpet, which is warm and friendly. I should go into floor-coverings.

I remember when I wet the bed as a child. First it is warm then it gets cold. I go into my parents' bedroom, with its smell, and start to cry. My mother gets up. She is half-asleep but she's not cross. She is huge. She strips the bed of the wet sheet and takes off the rubber under-blanket which falls with a thick sound to the floor. She puts a layer of newspaper on the mattress and pulls down the other sheet. She tells me to take off my wet pyjamas. I sleep in the raw between the top sheet and the rough blanket and when I turn over, all the warm newspaper under me makes a noise.

WHAT ARE CICADAS?

Cold women who drive cars like the clutch was a whisper and the gear stick a game. They roll into petrol stations, dangle their keys out the window and say 'Fill her up' to the attendant, who smells of American Dreams. They live in haciendas with the reek of battery chickens out the back, and their husbands are old. They go to Crete on their holidays, get drunk and nosedive into the waiter's white shirt saying 'I love you Stavros!' even though his name is Paul. They drive off into a countryside with more hedges than fields and are frightened by the vigour of their dreams.

But let us stay, as the car slides past, with the pump attendant; with the weeping snout of his gun, that drips a silent humiliation on the cement; with the smell of clean sharp skies, of petrol and of dung. The garage behind him is connected in tight, spinning triangles as his eyes check one corner and then the next. There is an old exhaust lying on a shelf in the wall, there is a baseball hat stiff with cobwebs, hanging in the black space over the door. There is a grave dug in the floor, where the boss stands with a storm lamp, picking at the underside of cars. Evenly spaced in the thick, white light that circles from the window are rings set in the stone, to tether cows long dead.

He has a transistor radio. He has a pen from Spain with a Señorita in the casing who slides past a toreador and a bull, until she comes to rest under the click, waiting for his thumb. He has a hat, which he only wears in his room.

He is a sensitive young man.

What are cicadas? Are they the noise that happens in the dark, with a fan turning and murder in the shadows on the wall? Or do they bloom? Do people walk through forests and pledge themselves, while the 'cicadas' trumpet their purple and reds all around?

It is a question that he asks his father, whose voice smells of dying, the way that his mother's smells of worry and of bread.

They look up the dictionary. "'Cicatrise,'" says his father, who always answers the wrong question – "'to heal; to mark with scars" – I always thought that there was only one word which encompassed opposites, namely . . . ? To cleave; to cleave apart as with a sword, or to cleave one on to the other, as in a loyal friend. If you were older we might discuss "cleavage" and whether the glass was half empty or half full. Or maybe we can have our cake and eat it after all.'

When he was a child, he asked what a signature tune was. 'A signature tune,' said his father, 'is a young swan-song – just like you. Would you look at him.'

He searched in the mirror for a clue. But his eyes just looked like his own eyes, there was no word for them, like 'happy' or 'sad'.

'Why don't cabbages have nerves?'

'A good question.' His father believed in the good question, though the answer was a free-for-all.

If he was asked where his grief began, or what he was grieving for, he would look surprised. Grief was this house, the leaking petrol pump, the way his mother smiled. He moved through grief. It was not his own.

He read poetry in secret and thought his mind was about to break. Sunset fell like a rope to his neck. The Señorita slid at her own pace past the man and the bull and nothing he could do would make her change.

'Come and do the hedges on Wednesday afternoon,' said a woman, as he handed her keys back through the window. Then she swept off through the hedges with the exhaust like an insult. The car had been full of expensive smells, plastic and perfume, hairspray, the sun on the dashboard. The lines around her eyes were shiny and soft with cream. Her skin reminded him of the rice-paper around expensive sweets, when you wet it in your mouth.

He rehearsed in his room until he was ready, then came and did the work. He hated her for her laugh at the door. 'It's only money,' she said, 'it won't bite.'

In years to come he would claim an ideal childhood, full of fresh air and dignity, the smell of cooking, rosehips and devil's bread in the ditch. On a Saturday night his sisters would fight by the mirror by the door and talk him into a rage, for the fun.

'The place was full of secrets. You wouldn't believe the secrets, the lack of shame that people had. Children that were slow, or uncles that never took their hands out of their trousers, sitting in their own dirt, money under the bed, forgetting how to talk anymore. It wasn't that they didn't care, filth was only filth after all. It was the way they took it as their own. There was no modesty behind a closed door, no difference, no meaning.'

To tell the truth, he did not go back for the money, although he knew the difference between a pound note and nothing at all. His pride drove him back, and the words of the man under the hat in his room. 'Give her what she wants.'

There was a small girl playing football on the grass, just to annoy. They knew each other from school. 'Your father is a disgrace,' she said in a grown-up voice. 'A disgrace, in that old jacket.' Then she checked the house for her mother and ran away. The woman sat knitting in the sun and watched him through the afternoon. Her back was straight and hands fast. She kept the window open, as if the smell of chicken slurry was fresh air.

She touched him most by her silence. The kitchen was clean and foreign, the hill behind it waiting to be cleared of thorns and muck. It was the kind of house that was never finished, that the fields did not want. It sat on a concrete ledge, like a Christmas cake floating out to sea.

He liked the precision of things, the logic of their place, the way the cups made an effort as they sat on the shelf. There were some strays, here and there, an Infant of Prague forgotten on the back of the cooker, a deflated football wedged behind the fridge. The cistern from an old toilet was balanced against the back wall, although the bowl was gone.

Waiting for his cup of tea, he forgot what it was he had come for. She was ordinary at the sink, ordinary and sad as she took out the sugar and the milk. When she sat down in her chair at the far side of the room, she was old and looked impatient of the noise his spoon made against the cup.

She asked after his mother, and turned on the radio and said he made a good job of cutting the lawn with the grass still damp. They listened to the tail-end of the news and she took a tin down from the cupboard. 'I suppose I can trust you,' she said grimly as she opened it up and a swirl of pound notes was seen, like something naked and soft. There was music on the radio.

He fought for the pictures in his room, of a man with a hat, who casually takes her by the wrist and opens out the flat of her palm, as if he understood it. He thought of the taste of rice-paper melting on his tongue, of the things she might wear under her dress. He struggled for the order of things that might happen if he held his breath. She gave him an indifferent smile. He did not understand.

'Women,' said his father, 'torture us with contradiction, but just because they enjoy it, doesn't mean that it's not true.'

There was a soft scratching at the door, and the two of them froze as though caught, with the money trapped in the woman's hand. When it opened he saw an old, fat crone who would not cross the threshold. Her shape was all one, he couldn't tell where one bit ended and the next began. There was a used tissue caught in the palm of her hand. She had a shy face. 'Monica, is the creamery cart come?' 'Yes,' said the woman in a loud voice. 'It's a tanker, not a cart.' 'Oh no,' said the old woman, 'I'm fine, don't worry about me.' She closed the door on herself without turning away.

Her name was Monica. She smiled at him, in complicity and shame. 'Deaf as a post,' she said, and the room dilated with the possibilities in her voice. She was embarrassed by the money in her hand. She looked at the bob of panic in his throat.

'There was a woman lived up the way from us, the kind that had all the young fellas in a knot. You could tell she wanted something, though probably not from you. She was ambitious, that was the word. It wasn't just sex that gave her that look – like she knew more than you ever could. That she might tell you, if she thought you were up to it. She had an old husband in the house with her, and a mother, senile, deaf, who pottered around and got in the way. And one day the old woman died.

'My father came in from the removal, rubbing his hands. He was a mild kind of man. "Sic transit," he said. "Sic, sic, sic." He took off the old coat with a kind of ceremony. I remember him taking the rosary beads out of his pocket and putting them beside the liquidiser, which was their place. I remember how ashamed I was of him, the patches on his coat and the beads and the useless Latin. When he sat down he said "How the mighty," and I felt like hitting him.

'When someone died, this woman Maureen would wash the body, which was no big deal. She might take any basin they had in the house and a cloth – maybe the one they used for the dishes. I don't know if she got paid, maybe it was just her place.

'"The secrets of the dead," said Da, "and the house smelling of fresh paint. Oh but that's not all." He told me one of those country stories that I never want to hear; stories that take their time, and have a taste to them. Stories that wait for the tea to draw and are held over when he can't find the biscuits. "Do you know her?" he said, and I said I did. "A fine woman all the same, with a lovely pair of eyes in her head. As I remember." He remembered the mother too of course and what kind of eyes she had in her head, as opposed to anywhere else.

'It was the son-in-law broke the news that the old woman had died, and when Maureen came to lay out the corpse, she found the man in the kitchen reading a newspaper and the wife saying nothing, not even crying. She offered her condolences, and got no sign or reply. There was no priest in the house. So Maureen just quietly ducked her head down, filled a basin at the sink, tiptoed her way across the lino with the water threatening to spill. When she got to the door of the old woman's room the wife suddenly lifted her head and said "You'll have a cup of tea, Maureen, before you start."

'The corpse was on the bed, newly dead, but rotting all the same. The sheets hadn't been changed for a year so you couldn't tell what colour they should have been. She had . . . lost control of her functions but they just left her to it, so her skin was the same shade as the sheets. Maureen cut layers and layers of skirts and tights and muck off her and when she got to the feet, she nearly cried. Her nails had grown so long without cutting, they had curled in under the soles and left scars.

'"Those Gorman women," said my father, with relish. "So which of them came first, the chicken or her egg?" and he laughed at me like a dirty old codger on the side of the road.'

After he left the house, the sun was so strong, it seemed to kill all sound. He met her daughter on the road and tackled her for the football, then kicked it slowly into the ditch.

'When I lost my virginity, everything was the same, and everything was changed. I stopped reading poetry, for one thing. It wasn't that it was telling lies – it just seemed to be talking to someone else.

'Now I can't stop screwing around. What can I say? I hate it, but it still doesn't seem to matter. I keep my life in order. My dry-cleaning bill is huge. I have money.

'My father knew one woman all his life. He dressed like a tramp. Seriously. What could he know? He knew about dignity and the weather and words. It was all so easy. I hate him for landing me in it like this – with no proper question and six answers to something else.'

Mr Snip Snip Snip

The cinema projectionist in Frank's home town was often drunk. When he was thrown out by his wife he slept the night in the projection booth and ate the stale Mars Bars and crisps from the counter in the foyer. He threw up once over a roll of film and had to spend the day cleaning and untangling it. Frank's first experience of 'The Dam Busters' was splattered with small, mucky explosions and the sound-track was a mess.

Even so, everyone went to the pictures, and the boys at the front shouted at the couples snogging in the back row. Frank was not enchanted by the plush red seats, nor by their sexual possibilities, though their smell still sometimes hit him unawares. He felt nothing but the dread of the picture to come, the size of it on the screen, the colours, and the way that it jerked from place to place. The projectionist sometimes put the reels on in the wrong order and the beginning of the picture came halfway through. Most exciting of all was the time that the drunken projectionist fell asleep, and the film, passing close to the bulb, had gone on fire. This was the terror that provoked Frank into a job in television.

The air in the editing room had been around the building four times. It seemed to settle there and go cold. Frank sits in a hardback chair in front of the console and a producer sits at his back. What the producer does is his own business. Some of them click their fingers at a cut, or catch their breath or say 'There!' Some of them make faces behind his back, field phone-calls, pace up and down the room. Some of them go away. In front of them are three monitors, and Frank sits all day and staples the picture from one monitor onto the picture of another, without any seams showing. He is the magic of television.

Frank doesn't work on celluloid, he works with tapes that slot in and happen in the machines like they were happening in his head. He can mix or fade, he can freeze the picture at any selected moment, at a laugh, or a fumble. He can make figures move slowly, as if they are pushing their way through honey, or scatter them along the street like Charlie Chaplin. The moment is as long as he likes. Ninety seconds of a finished programme can cover a minute or three years. He is a master of time. No wonder then, that he likes the job.

At three o'clock in the morning the urge to subvert got very strong. He could feed in the word 'FRAUD' behind Charlie Haughey, for a micro-second that would hit the heart of the nation. He could put a dog whistle on the other track, so that all the dogs in the country would bark at the same time. He could slow down an interview the fraction it took to make someone slur like a drunk. Of course he resisted this need, because he was responsible, and part of the broadcasting machine. (Frank's sister beat him up when he was five, for drawing over the walls with her lipstick, and the pain ticked at the edge of his mind when he was very tired, and subversion was at his fingertips.)

Frank sometimes wondered where it all went, the stuff he threw away; smiles, swear-words, faces that slid out of focus. There is a parallel universe, he thought, in 'Star Trek', made up of all the out-takes; the fluffs, blunders and bad (worse) acting that never made it to the final cut. A world where Captain Kirk says 'shit' and Spock's ears become detached. Perhaps the story is better over there. He thought of a universe made up of all the different silences that are nipped, tucked and disposed of. The silence of a hospital at night, the silence when a woman forgets what to say, the silence of a politician. They have to go somewhere. It is a terrible crime, Frank thought, to throw away a silence.

It was the sheer waste that depressed him; the waste of a movement. The woman in the interview raises her arm to smooth an eyebrow and the editor throws away a feast of under-arm hair. He had that gesture, there in his hand, and he threw it away.

When the signal is beamed all the way to Alpha Centauri, the aliens will never see a hairy woman. They will wait for centuries for that one signal, the one they expect and recognise as a call to come and save the world. Who is to say otherwise? Beautiful hairy aliens who never throw anything away except what is deliberately made. Spontaneous Aliens who talk in semaphore and discover everything by accident, in the dustbins of science – which is why they are so advanced.

Frank was dreaming of aliens. He was dreaming of better pay and probably of under-arms. He was dreaming about someone's laugh that he threw out that day. He was dreaming of the split-second where a man wavered and Frank cut him dead.

Over his monitors, Frank had pasted a sign 'The mills of the gods grind slowly, but they grind exceedingly small.'

Soon after he started the job, Frank began to pick up the pictures on the side of the road and string them together in his head. His car stops at the lights beside some road-workers. They talk over the pneumatic drill in glances and a toss of the head. The age of the men is surprising, they have pot bellies and cement dust has settled in the creases of their clothes. Everything is coated with the road; there is cement caked under their fingernails, and their boots are encrusted with tar – in three weeks' time they will be altogether solid. Frank turns the dust, the wheelbarrow full of flaming tar, the traffic cones, and the way the drill turns everything mute, into a beer commercial, where the world is tinted blue. He catches the looks between the men to the rhythm of the song 'Heart of Stone'. It is a good piece, but short. Someone changes the station on a remote control as the traffic lights go green.

It got worse. Frank dreamt of the slice of time between shots, so thin, it couldn't be said to exist at all. He edits and re-edits the film of his father in his sleep. The story of his father is a loose montage that also involves clay and calloused hands, a boot on the side of a spade, a figure moving over the brow of a hill. Sometimes the music is sentimental, sometimes unsettling. Most often he uses the sound of a distant wireless where a quiz show is being played out, and the sound gets closer when his father walks into the room.

The Sunday dinner table is composed of glances from one child to another, and warning looks from his mother. The camera goes under the table, where one small foot in a long grey schoolboy sock kicks out at another. He sees his father's mouth chewing, he sees his knife and fork cutting the meat with delicate violence. The sound-track is silent, except for the scrape of cutlery.

Frank twitches in his sleep. He is running along a mile of tape where his family are caught like ants in amber. Sometimes he feels as though he will fall into the picture, as though the dinner table is under a stretch of water, or glass. Every few seconds he leaps over the gap between one shot and the next, and the gaps become wider.

His father at the table lifts his fork and points it at the camera. Frank leaps away to the salt-cellar, then drives over to his mother's face, jerks back to his father's hand. His father is talking. Frank cuts out the word 'slut' and, before he can stitch it up, falls headlong into the thin, deep hole that he has made. 'You were dreaming.' Moira wakes him with a smile.

Moira makes it easier for him. Every time she moves, she throws it away. She has an abandoned grace. She hardly notices him there on the other side of the table, and he picks up the casual pieces as her hand drops into her lap.

'I don't know.' It is a sigh. She doesn't know that she has spoken. Her hand scratches the top of her leg and Frank drives into work thinking about sex that is entirely random, the way people graze each other in their sleep.

It would be nice to have a child, to go into work wrecked after a night of two-hourly feeds and claim it was the pints. It would be nice to say that no matter how frantic the work got, no matter how much the world was cut up into shots and the producer at his back paced the room, there was something of his that had its own slow time. He would do a gardening programme that looked at a rose growing for half an hour, or use a single shot of waves on a beach that went on for as long as the tape was in the camera. No tricks. He would take the memory of his father's cigarette smoke, coming from a hand that had fallen by the side of the chair, and he would stay with it until the cigarette burned down and was dropped on the floor. Force himself to look. Don't cut away.

Moira is hard to find these days. She spends a lot of time in various attitudes around the house. The evening is like a locked-off shot on the sitting room as she fades from the arm-chair and appears at the table, then fades again and is standing at the window, one hand holding a cigarette at an angle and the other cupped around an elbow that should be wearing evening gloves. When they talk she looks at the carpet as though she sees something growing there. There is a small eddy in her eyes, a slight shift of the current that strays from where she is looking. Moira was always aimless, casual, troubled. It was a look that mothers have and it made his lovemaking hopeful and direct, like a man posting a letter that would change everything.

On Sunday morning Frank surprises himself by getting up early and cleaning the house. He washes the kitchen floor, runs a cloth along the skirting-boards, cleans out the toilet and talks to Moira over the sound of the hoover with a nod of the head. On Monday she wakes up to find him standing by the window with no clothes on, scratching his stomach and staring. He goes to the supermarket on his own and buys some trout and almonds which he makes for her that night, with a salad full of vegetables that he never knew existed until he was twenty-one. He kisses her back while she sleeps and puts his hand over the Y of her legs, to keep her safe.

In unguarded moments while he is at work, Moira flicks into the corner of his eye. There is no pattern to it. She has taken to reading children's books. She has eaten her way through Dr Doolittle and enthuses about Dab Dab the duck.

'What is the difference,' she asks him, 'between doing something and not doing something? When I was a kid, hell would open up if you stepped on the crack in the path and the devil would kiss you – but he never did.'

'You sound disappointed.'

She rubs the corner of her mouth hard with the tip of a finger, as though her lipstick was beginning to smear.

'I want to go somewhere.'

'Anywhere you like.'

'Bolivia?'

'Sure.'

For some reason everyone is using Spanish music in their programmes that week. It makes the cutting very fast and the colours as sharp as an ad for washing powder. He passes a small girl in her communion dress in the street and there are flamenco flounces down the back of her white skin.

'How about Barcelona? We can afford that.' But she just laughs.

It came together in all the things she threw away. As he sat working at his console, the pictures knitted one into the other. Moira glancing at the phone. Moira rubbing at her thigh, as though there was a burr caught between her leg and her jeans. She comes in through the hall door, with the keys between her teeth and they drop to the floor. She wakes in the morning surprised and her mouth seems caught on the pillow.

It is all in the fraction of the second before he cuts away.

They are sitting in the dining room, in an endless two-shot.

'I love you,' Moira says; she leans over to put her hand on his arm but stops. 'I love you more than anything. Anything. It happened by accident. I don't understand the why. I stepped on the crack in the path by accident and nothing happened. It didn't open up. I didn't fall into hell.'

Reaction shot Frank. The film goes on fire.

'Frank, I can't tell the difference between things. I can't tell the difference between what I want to do, what I mean to do, and something that just happens.'

'What was his name?'

She opens her mouth to speak. He cuts away to the hand that holds the cigarette and before he can stitch it up, falls headlong into the thin, deep hole that he has made.

Seascape

He stood like a young seminarian at the water's edge, refusing to see the bodies that were strewn all around him. His eyes rested on the cool line of the horizon, and sweat gathered in the white creases of his face. His only concessions to the sun were the jumper he had removed, which never left his hand, and the thick boots that stood waiting in the sand behind him. He seemed to be standing quite still, but in fact was edging his feet forward, inch by inch. After a while, a thin film of water pulled at his bare toes, and he leapt back. The jump was awkward, and when he turned to walk back up the beach, he had the loping, twisted stride of an old tramp. He belonged to the street, and not to the sea, because his eyes had that puzzled, childish look, and his mouth was hard.

A woman rose from the sea behind him, the water running from her shoulders and hair.

'Daniel!' He stooped to pick up his boots, without turning around, so she ran up the slope after him, her body scattering a wet trail on the sand. The swimsuit she wore was azure blue, with a triangle of viridian at the neck, and her wet blonde hair had a greenish sheen in the strong light.

'Daniel,' she said again, catching up with him, 'are you coming in?'

'Nope.' He still didn't turn around.

'You grunter! You pig!' She shook herself at him like a wet dog and he pulled away from the drops. When she was done, he caught her by the arms and pushed her into the sand, then laughed and walked on. There was a moment's shock before she screamed and scrabbled up again, then charged after him up the beach. The old boots banged together in his hand as he evaded her, but when he reached the towels he turned around and let himself be caught. She pushed him down and sat on his chest.

'You need the wash, you old pig. I should throw you in like a drowned cat.'

'I can't swim.'

'You can't swim? Sure everyone can swim. I'll teach you.'

'Of course I can swim.'

'Liar.' She swung off him.

'You are a liar,' she said, picking up the towel, which was yellow like her hair. 'You're always lying to me.'

He lay on his back, his eyes slits in the glare of the sun. He seemed to be watching the sky. She flicked her body with the towel to get rid of the grit that had lodged in the creases, but he still didn't turn around. The laces of the boots were tangled in his hand and there were sweat marks and the marks of her wet body on his thick, old shirt.

'You like it,' he said and rolled on his belly to watch her. She covered herself with the towel to block his gaze.

'And anyway . . . I don't,' and he rolled back again with a small grunt.

He pursed his mouth. 'Pour us a cup of tea, will you?' It was an old joke.

'Pour it yourself, you bad bastard. You're not in your mother's house now.'

She sat there, for what seemed like a long time, and watched him sprawled damply on the sand. She did not stretch out, ignoring the freak weather with the confidence of one who already had the perfect tan. The colours of her swimsuit brightened in the sun.

After a while, she became aware of someone staring. It was a small child, naked as a cherub. He turned away from her when she looked up, and put his hands up to his face, but continued to watch her through his fingers.

'Hello.' She smiled at him and he ducked away at the sound of her voice.

'Look,' he said, suddenly bold, and with one hand still to his face, he pissed delicately on to the sand.

'Lovely,' she said, at a loss – trying not to give the child a complex.

'No, it's not,' he said, 'it's very bold,' and he ran off as his

288

mother lumbered up after him; 'Come back here and I'll give you a belt!'

'That's the woman for you,' she told Daniel, as she caught the struggling child and trapped his legs in a pair of pants.

'A good, pink-skinned Irish ma with strap marks.'

Daniel lay still.

'Strap marks and stretch marks and Dunne's nighties. A fine hoult for you in the bed at night.' Daniel grunted assent.

'Well, take the old shirt off at least. You look like a maggot under a rock.'

'I look,' he said carefully, 'like something the tide washed up.'

Affairs, she thought, should stay in the place where they were conceived, they do not transplant well. He lay on the sand as though it were the gutter, while she turned her patch of towel into a little piece of the Riviera. Her face was drawn with effort.

'All I want', she finally said, with deliberation and a fake smoothness, 'is an intelligent life. You *know* what I mean.' He turned to face her and his eyes were both puzzled and wary.

'No, I don't,' he said, and then as a small concession, 'it was far from intelligence that I was reared.'

'Well, start now,' she said, 'do my back.' He lifted his head and looked along the beach.

'I will not.'

'Pig.'

She flicked out the towel then lay down on it, with her back to him. After a moment's pause he made his way across to her on his belly.

'Here,' he said, taking the plastic bottle of sun oil from its dugout in the sand. 'What do I do with this?' He spilt some on his fingertips and slapped it on her back, then moved over the skin like a farmer with a new lamb.

'You're done,' and quietly he lifted the hair from the nape of her neck. He stroked the side of her face, until her breathing eased, his eyes still out to sea.

'Did you see the body in the water?'

'Which one?' Her voice was muffled by her arms.

'With the clothes on.'

'No.'

'Floating on its face.'

'No.' Her voice had an edge to it.

'It was badly swelled. The gas brings them up, you know, after nine days.'

'No, I did not see it.'

'Pity.' His hand left her face, and he lay down the length of her. After a while, he seemed to sleep.

The afternoon wore on, and still neither of them moved. There was something obscene about the two forms lying so close together, one fully dressed and curved around the naked limbs of the other. She looked like a tropical fish in a dirty pond, with a bad old pike to protect her. Everyone around them was busy being amazed by the good weather, playing and shouting and soaking up the sun, but these two were not sun-bathing or flirting. They were probably not even asleep.

The heat grew less intense, and as a slight breeze pulled at her hair, she stirred and slipped away from the curve of his body. She sat up and stared around her, as though surprised by what she saw, and then she reached for her bag and started to search around in it. She produced a bundle of postcards and a pen, and shuffled through them to find the right one. It was a picture of a cat in a window, reaching for the blind above her, with the sign 'Guinness is good for you' posted on the wall outside.

Dear Fiona, (she wrote) the weather is glorious. The lump is being lumpish, haven't seduced him into the sea as yet. Will you check the cat for me? Should never have trusted her with that couple downstairs. We miss ickle pussums, we does, and you too.

She tore it up and took out a fresh one; this had a picture of a donkey and a red-headed girl with a turf creel in her arms.

Dear Fiona, is he psychotic or what? The nights are, as always, amazing, but the weather doesn't seem to suit his sensitive skin. Besides, he keeps on sneaking downstairs to make dubious phone calls. I don't care about An Other Woman . . .

maybe, but I keep fantasizing that he's got a kid salted away somewhere. If you see Timmy, say I'm fine, i.e. give him a crack in the gob and tell him I'm sorry. All is . . .

She had run out of space and was writing where the address should go. The breeze had brought up the hairs on her arms, and she paused for a moment to examine them. Then she started to write on the front of the card, over the donkey's face:

I have lovely arms. Not that it makes any difference.

And she abandoned everything where it was and ran off down the strand, into the sea.

She could swim for hours. The water was beautiful, despite the cold, and she aimed straight for the horizon. She felt like diving down, wriggling out of the swimsuit and swimming on and on. The foolish picture of its limp blue and green washed up on the beach drifted into her mind. They might even accuse Daniel of the crime.

She took a breath, grabbed her knees to her chest and bobbed face down on the surface of the water. Slowly, as she ran out of breath, her muscles eased. She blew what was left in her lungs out in an explosion of bubbles, then shot up into the air and took breath. No. She would not be angry. Anger did not suit her. She would carry around instead the chic pain of an independent woman – the woman who did not whinge or demand, or get fat on children.

'I like independent women,' he had said once.

'Bloody sure you do,' she answered. 'They're not allowed to complain.'

The shadows had grown harsher and longer by the time she got out of the water, her hands numb and her legs stiff with the cold. She made her way up the slope heavily, shaking her fingers in front of her. Long before she reached their place, she saw that Daniel had gone. The postcard she had written and left was torn up like the first, the pieces scattered and half-buried in the sand. Among them was his discarded shirt, and a pair of trousers lay broken-limbed and empty on her yellow towel. She yanked at the towel to clear it of debris and the bundle of postcards flew up into the air. Moving slowly, and shivering with the cold she went to each one in turn and picked it up. Daniel had written on the face of them all.

The first was a pictue of a Charolais cow on the cliffs of Moher. The sky was a hazy mauve, and the cow, which was right on the edge of the cliff, stared seductively at the viewer. Across the line of the sky he had written, 'A Rathmines Madonna Dreams of The Intelligent Life.' The next was a glossy reproduction of the beach in front of her, the colours artificially bright. Along the curve of the strand were the words, 'Yes, the nights are amazing, but as yet, I have no child.' She stared at it for a long time, and looked around to see where Daniel could be, before picking up the next one. It had an oul fella sitting in a pub, the light bounding off the polished surface of the bar counter and a fresh, new pint in the shaft of the sun. There was a crudely drawn balloon coming out of the old man's mouth with the words: 'What is the difference between a pair of arms?' Finally, there was the beach again, though this time there were footprints drawn along the strand, enormously out of proportion, and a figure in the sea with HELP! coming from it. The caption read, 'O Mary mo chree, I am afraid that the water will claim me back again.'

'All washed up.' The voice came from directly above her, and she gave a start. When she looked up he was there, perfectly dry. He was wearing a pair of navy high-waisted swimming trunks. His body was white as wax and his front was sticky with hair. She was ashamed to look at this body and so looked at his face.

'Oh all right,' she said, and wanted to turn off the sun like a lamp, so they could make love on the beach.

Felix

Felix, my secret, my angel boy, my dark felicity. Felix: the sibilant hiss of the final x a teasing breath on the tip of the tongue. He was the elixir of my middle years, he was the sharp helix spiralling through my body, the fixer, the healer, the one who feels. But when he was in my arms he was simply breath, an exhalation.

Did he have a precursor? He did, to be sure. There might have been no Felix at all had I not loved, one summer, a certain boy-child in my Tir na nÓg by the sea. Felix was as young as I was that year, the year I first fell asleep, and when he whispered me awake, my life became fierce and terrible. (Look at that tangle of thorns.)

Believe me, I write for no one but myself. Mine is not the kind of crime to be spoken out loud. This, then, is the last, or the penultimate, motion of these fingers that burned alive on the cool desert of his skin. You can always count on a suicide for a clichéd prose style.

I was born in 1935 in Killogue, a small town in the west of Ireland. My father was a small, introverted man of uncertain stock, who ran the pub that faced out on to the town square. My mother died of creeping paralysis in my seventh year, and nothing remains of her in my mind save the image of a woman sitting in the parlour in a perpetual Sunday dress, her throat caught in a stained circle of ancient diamanté and a charm bracelet at her wrist. When they laid her out, again in the same room, with the glass-fronted china cabinet pushed precariously against the back wall, I noticed that her 'jewels' had been removed. This sensible, pious figure seemed to have nothing to do with the woman I remembered, and I was suddenly aware that she must have undressed like that every night, unless she wore the diamanté to bed.

My father grew more nervous after my mother's death, his silences grew longer and were punctuated by sudden rushes of speech, always about the harvest or the Inland Revenue, the goings on 'beyant'. He began to sleep over the bar at night, bringing a small iron bed into what had once been a storeroom, and leaving the bedroom that they had shared intact. He became a crusader for the gombeen class, claiming that there was no such thing as good staff to be found. The days were spent in a silent frenzy of suspicion, watching every boy who was brought in to serve behind the bar, until the explosion burst loose and the boy was sacked – for not charging his friends, or shortchanging the regulars, or simply for sloppy work, licking the knife that was used to cut the sandwiches. Meanwhile, I sat outside, squatting on the kerb that faced the square, where I could see over the brow of the hill to the sea beyond. The strand was hidden by a dip in the road, and it looked as though the water came right up to the crest of the hill and joined it in one clean blue line. I ran towards it like a plane taking off, hoping to dive straight in, always disappointed to discover the street below, the untidy line of houses, the sea wall, and then the beach with its load of mothers wrapped up against the cold, children playing in the sand, and the breakers rolling in beyond.

I was nominally attached to a good woman who lived in a rundown house between the hill and the strand; who washed my clothes, fed me and let me go – perhaps because of some old debt she owed my father, perhaps for a small fee. As far as I can remember, I was a brave child. (It is not the loss of innocence that I regret, but the loss of that courage.) I swam in the deep, underwater world of childhood, my limbs playing in the shattered light of the sea. I loved the cold shock, diving off the cliffs, my body growing numb as I prised free the starfish that hid in the crevices, or teased the nervous mouths of translucent sea anemones. I chatted easily and dangerously with the visitors to the town, with a friendliness that came as second nature to the daughter of a publican. Old men with whis-

key breath would lift me on to the bar counter, tip the wink
to my father for a bag of crisps and call me 'princess.'

It was the summer of my eleventh year. I was grown wild
– more reckless in the sea, more brash with the locals and coy
with the tourists, who filled the town with their white, bared
flesh. My father picked on a young boy called Diarmuid to
help behind the bar, some distant relative from Galway with
(I can't continue this for much longer) . . . with the black hair
and fine, blunt cheekbones of a Connemara man. Daddy gave
over the storeroom to house the boy and slept again in his old
room, treading carefully and with a sense of unfamiliarity over
the wooden boards. His presence there was light, but unsettling. He brought back the ghost of my mother with him.

I must stop. 'Ghost,' 'flesh,' 'fine, blunt cheekbones,' these
words are all strangers to me. I am trying to construct a childhood, so I can pick my way through it for dues. 'Felix came
because' . . . because in the summer of my eleventh year, my
father hired a boy called Diarmuid. Any other boy would have
done, any other childhood. The secret must be in the style. If
I must choose some way of lying to myself, I thought, this
might be the most appropriate. Take on the cadences of an old
roué in a velvet smoking jacket, cashmere socks, and a degree
of barefaced and thoughtful dignity that is not permitted to the
rest of mankind. But look at me. I am a woman of fifty-one
years of age, in a suburb of Dublin; not exactly sitting with
rollers in my hair, but certainly subject to the daily humiliation of coffee-morning conversation and the grocer's indifference. I buy winter coats in Clery's sale. I have a husband.
Every year we drive to the same guesthouse in Miltown
Malbay. There has been no tragedy in my life, you might say,
apart from the ordinary tragedies of life and death that Ireland
absorbs, respects and buries, without altering its stride. In my
clean, semi-detached house there are only a few sordid clues;
my daughter's empty bedroom, a doll without a head, one
broken arrow from a boy's bow, that sits like so much junk
at the back of the coal house. Where is the poetry in that?

I have always been struck by the incongruous picture of an old woman with a pen in her hand. Is it not slightly obscene, Ms Lessing, to show your life around like that? Of course your neighbours are rich, they respect you, they are proud to have you living nearby. They don't watch you in the street and say, 'Why write about orgasms, when you look like that?'

Middle-aged women write notes to the milkman, not suicide notes. When they die, they do so quietly, out of consideration for their relatives and friends. And then there is the subject of perversion. Old women are never perverts. They may be 'dotty' or 'strange', poor things, they may, and often do, 'suffer from depression', but they emphatically do not feel up boys in public parks. Their lust is a form of maimed vanity, if it exists at all. It is not the great sweeping torment of the poet. It is not love. The only thing we suffer from is the menopause ('Let me tell you something, Iris dear, the change of life is a blessing . . . when he stops . . . you know, wanting things in the middle of the night.' I want I want I want). I want I want I want. I am not an hysteric. I am a woman of ten and a half stone with a very superior brain. I do not know what the word 'maternal' was ever supposed to mean.

So it is back to the smoking jacket and the man with refined hands who translates Baudelaire for a hobby; the man with a bubble of hot poison in his loins and a super-voluptuous flame permanently aglow in his subtle spine, poor fella, may he rest in peace, God bless him. It is back to the summer I fell asleep (in fact a bout of glandular fever) and Diarmuid, who is no lamia, but a man I met in the street the other day, short, fat, his 'Connemara bones' laced with a filigree of hot purple veins. Incidentally, I too have read my Poe and Proust, my Keats and Thomas Mann. Who cares? None of them chased things that were real. My boy-child *was* real – does that mean that I am not a poet? Oh, but I am. I am a poet not quite in curlers, because I make the poets' claim that '*Form . . . ja wesentlich bestrebt ist, das Moralische unter ihr stolzes und unumschranktes Szepter zu beugen.*' You see. In a woman who dresses from Clery's sale, such tactics can only be childish.

★　★　★

The summer when I was eleven was hot, salty and golden. I would come out of the sharp light of the street and into the pub, lean my cheek against the worn dark wood of the bar, and watch Diarmuid. The wood was soaked with the smell of every old hand that had worn it smooth, and Diarmuid smelt of old men too, his clothes saturated with smoke and spilt porter. But under the clothes he smelt alive. My father did not object to my proximity to the boy – he was too busy scrutinizing him for signs of another kind of fall and with it, the excuse to put him back on the train, back to the rocky fields and sour crop of the family farm. But Diarmuid kept his small hands clean. He spoke like an old man to the customers, neither overly familiar nor reserved. He wiped the counter constantly in wide, smooth circles and he rinsed the cloth out every hour. His small body was steady and sure, with the singular grace of a young boy whose limbs have not yet betrayed him into awkwardness. But he knew that he was being watched, and when my father turned away from him, disgusted by his virtue, I would catch the flicking eye and the wild incomprehension of a horse at the start. We never spoke.

It seems to me now, with plenty of adult, if somewhat perfunctory sex behind me, that I did not know what I was feeling then, or even that I was feeling at all. I now know what it is to ache, and how to free that ache by some mechanical means – I am speaking, I suppose, of my husband, of whom it must be said, I became very fond. And you will excuse my tone, I remain prissy about mere sex, though I would go from the coffee-morning euphemism that was conjugation with my husband, straight to the mordant touch and cool, shy eyes of Felix, who recreates in me, and refines beyond endurance, that first passion. Perhaps passion is the wrong word. The sight of Diarmuid made my limbs feel large, as though I were sick. My whole body emptied itself out of my eyes when I looked at him. Objects became strange, and made me clumsy. At night the sheets felt as though they were touching me, and not the other way around.

So one afternoon, with the place deserted, I slid under the flap that guarded the space behind the counter, and I pressed my hot, flat body wordlessly against his. It was a matter of instinct only. The brittle, swollen feeling in my skin broke and melted away. It was several days before we learned how to kiss.

I took some tins from the shelf, poured a can full of new milk into a bottle that had once contained stout, and corked it firmly. I took my blue cotton frock and the red Sunday dress, wrapped the food in them and secured the bundle with my father's best funeral tie. We found our separate ways in the dark to the flat rock that lies fallen at the end of the headland to the north of Killogue. The feelings of the week before seemed very strange as we stood and watched each other. I laid my cardigan in the shelter of the slab of rock and lay down on it. After a silence that went on forever Diarmuid lay down with me.

What do you want? 'The sceptre of his passion'? 'My deep, throbbing heart'? Descriptions of the sexual act always pain me. I am reminded of a book published by a vanity press in the United States, where the hero puts – no, *slides* his hand into 'the cleft of readiness' and finds 'the nub of responsiveness.' And, in fact, that description will do as well as any other. We fooled around, like children. There was no technical consummation, though some pain. We didn't have a clue, you could say. That was all.

Why bother? We all have had our small, fumbling initiations on dirty sofas or canal walks. Why bother to remember, when it is our business to look for the better things in life, and our duty to forget. ('A bunch of baby carrots please, and a pound of potatoes, isn't it a nice day, thank God,' the last words spoken by this atheist, pervert and hopeless cook.) Sentiment is all very well (wedding cake), even large emotions – so long as they are mature (sound of baby's first cry, the look of love in paralysed husband's grateful eyes). But what about passion? Passion is the wrong word. I are speaking of the feeling that hits like a blow to the belly in ordinary places. See that woman in a headscarf stop dead on the footpath, her mouth shaping to form a word. But before she remembers what it is, the image is tucked away, the shopping bag is changed from one hand to the other, and she walks on. What kind of images collect in an old woman's head?

My moment of passion was a cold one. I woke up just before the dawn, a white light spreading over the bay turning the sea to a frosted blue, and a shivering in my body that scarcely left me intact. Every organ was outlined with a damp pain and I could sense every muscle and bone. I couldn't feel the ground, or the clothes on my back. I was floating inside my numb skin like the jelly of an oyster, and my shell seemed to have sprouted some extra limbs. They were Diarmuid's. He lay in my arms asleep, and a perfect, empty, blue freedom was all around. The sun had not yet risen. I was already feverish.

School settled over me like a blanket when you are sick. Up at seven, silence till eight, Mass, breakfast, class. I didn't want to speak and there was no room for friends. Instead, I showed off to the nuns as though they were the old men in my father's bar; my hand was permanently up in the air, my poems were read out at assembly.

I was allowed special access to books, and my religion essays were scattered with references to St John of the Cross, Julian of Norwich, even Kierkegaard. You may not think that it is possible, but yes, it is possible to be so clever at sixteen, and then to ignore it. And I was the cleverest of them all. The other girls whispered about escape into town, while I read under the sheets. I thought about Diarmuid, but not for long, there was no relief in it. I decided to become a nun, decided to become a writer, decided finally, to become nothing at all. I lost my faith, in the best male tradition, but did not consider its loss significant. There was something about the nuns that made individual lives seem inconsequential, and I admired them for it. What I wrote, I burned and forgot.

Daddy died the summer I left school – he had only held out for the sake of the fees – and so I was free to turn down my university scholarship, despite Sr Polycarpe's pleading, and three novenas from my English, biology and maths teachers respectively. I took a flat on the Pembroke Road and a secretarial job. I also took a boy from the office home with me one night and woke up to find that he had fallen in love. We got over the embarrassment with a small wedding, me in a blue suit and pill-box hat, a light veil of netting at the front. When we went to France on our honeymoon, I pretended not to speak French. This is why, I suppose, I am plagued with travel sickness and we spend our holidays now on the Irish coast.

My husband is a good man, and I love him, though not in the usual way. By this I mean that he is kindly, not that he is dull – I have learned to find interest in the expected. I should write about my daughter too, I suppose, except that this confessional mode agitates and bores me. Something, somewhere, marked my life out like this. I make up childhoods to try and explain. Nevertheless, I do not change. I gave birth to a daughter and I did not change.

One morning (a writer's lie this, like all other 'realizations'), one morning, it could be said, I looked in the mirror and found that I was middle aged.

Do you understand? I looked in the mirror and found that I was middle aged. The relief was overwhelming. My anonymity was crystallized, my life since Diarmuid was staring me in the face, tepid and blank. Everything had dropped away – *I could do anything now*. What interests me, I thought, is not life, the incidents that fill it, not images or moments, but this central greyness. I saw that I was ready. It was into this greyness that Felix would drop, like a hard little apple into the ripe ground.

Felix was only a boy that I loved. Will you believe that I did not harm him, that I made him happy? And not only with sweeties. I knew his mother, a proud, vulgar woman, and had shared my pregnancy with her, putting to rest her useless fears about breech births and extra chromosomes. I even (the irony of it!) placed my hand on her tight belly in the seventh month, a gesture that in our semi-detached world belongs to the husband alone. There was the little nugget of Felix, wrapped up in the silt of her body. I sometimes wonder whether I corrupted him then with that touch, whether my voluptas was sent through his transparent limbs, turning them

302

into the clean, radiant flesh that was to possess me before he was fully grown.

In the meantime, I was the woman up the road and my daughter was his friend. They played doctors and nurses on the front porch, I suppose. Recently I dug over their dolls' graveyard. I took some pleasure in their growing, though grazed knees and the simple, sloppy cruelty of children hold little charm for me. Felix was quiet – even then, you could not tell his arrogance, his animal calm, from the shyness of other small boys. In retrospect, he was probably beautiful, and I kissed him sometimes, as children need to be kissed. (Was I a bad mother? Oh no.) When I regret all those wasted caresses, I comfort myself with the fact that I could not have known. Looking at myself as I was, I can only see what those two children saw, a solid, transparent shape that wasn't quite flesh, but 'mother' – the creature that was wrapped about them like certainty.

When gradually things began to change between them, I did not notice that either, and would have found it tedious if I had. My daughter started slamming doors and stealing lipsticks. One afternoon she came home crying and hid up in her bedroom. I was attacking the hall with the vacuum cleaner, hoping that the noise would disturb the concentration her self-pity seemed to require, when the knock came at the door. There was Felix on the doorstep, a grown boy, with an indifferently guilty look on his face, and his overlarge hands thrust into his pockets. Little Miss Madam opened her bedroom door and shouted down the stairs, 'You've spoilt everything!'

What a charming scene! I looked at Felix (he smelt of gutting rats and climbing trees) and he looked back at me and laughed with an innocent, evil sense of complicity. That same cold dawn broke over my body and I had to shut the door.

Please believe me, I waited for months. I did not touch him, but carried instead a deep, hard pain in the bowl of my pelvis. I became clumsy again, everything I reached for fell to the floor and the kitchen was a mess of fragments. All that I saw opened up the ache, and I wanted the whole world inside me, with Felix at its centre, like a small, hard pip. The loss of dignity was wonderful, ghastly. I mimicked my daughter at the bathroom mirror, and haunted the fitting rooms of increasingly expensive shops. I put sex back into my appearance; brittle enough, but real. His sharp boy's eyes, meanwhile, became blank again. Perhaps he was waiting too, though it seemed that when he looked at me, he saw nothing at all. I only had to touch him to become real.

He came to the house one day when she was out. I sat him in the kitchen on the promise of her return. I made a cup of tea and the impudent child held the silence and looked bored, while one knee knocked and rubbed against the table leg. I set down the mug of tea and the Eden-red apple on the table before him and then . . . I leaned over and touched him, in a way that he found surprising.

Small, dirty, strange. Felix's eyes focused on me and it was like falling down a tunnel. He put his hand on my arm, to stop me, or to urge me on, and the pain I carried inside me like a dead child dropped quietly, burning as it went.

This was just the first time. There was a second, a third, a fourteenth. I might describe them – I have the words for it – but your prurience does not interest me; neither does your disbelief.

Our subterfuges became increasingly intricate, snatching an hour here or there while I pushed my daughter out to hockey practice, piano lessons, even horse riding. Lucky girl. Meanwhile Felix and I pressed out the sour honey of the deepest ecstasy that man or beast has ever known. And while she bounced along on rattle-backed, expensive old nags, while my husband fretted over mislaid returns and his secretary's odour, I wrapped Felix, insensate with pleasure, in the fleshy pulp of my body where he ripened, the hard, sweet gall inside the cactus plant.

Then, of course, she found the letter:

Dear auntie Iris,
Mammy is sick and I can't come today.
    Love
      Felix.
PS Larry Dunne was talking about sex again today enough to make you puke. He says he has been putting it into Lucy

down the road but I just had to laugh because he obviously hasn't seen any of that and was just blowing. I nearly said about you but I didn't. Don't worry.

I never throw hysterics. So how could I have reared such an hysterical child? She gave up the riding lessons, the hockey, the piano, and became a large, uncultured lout. She rang him night and day, she wept in his bedroom. She lived at our throats and by the time she left, he had turned into a large, normal young man. He went to discos, he wanted to get into the bank. I met his mother on the street one day; she boasted of his many girl-friends, and complained that they never lasted long. I can imagine why.

   I could have killed myself then. I allowed myself to fanta-size cancers and car accidents. I might have killed myself even before Felix, but I didn't have a life before, so it was ridicu-lous to think of throwing it away. Felix made everything pos-sible, including dying, and it is for this that I am grateful, more than for anything else. I lived, of course. For a while I thought of finding a replacement, combing housing estates like a queen bee, waiting for the look of recognition. There was one sup-porting lead in a school play, but that blank gleam in his eye was only stage fright.

   Recently I discovered their dolls' graveyard; decapitated plastic, split by my spade. There was clay in the artificial hair and I thought about – I longed for – the clay that would clog my own.

   So. Adieu Adieu Adieu. Self-indulgent, I know, but what do you want me to become? My husband's nurse? (Oh, the grateful took in his paralysed eyes.) And then one of the army of widows, with headscarf and shopping bag, who stop in the middle of the street, shake their heads and say 'Someone must have walked over my grave.' Felix.

   Felix sitting on my headstone, with an apple in his fist, like he sat at the bottom of the bed, laughing, puzzled, amazed at every inch of me. Felix at that particular point of refinement where wonder, cruelty and hair-trigger skin make even the imaginary and the ridiculous real. He could look at offal, at grass, at the streaks his fingers made on my thigh with the same indifferent glee.

It is easier to die when you have seen your own flesh; as I saw my own flesh for the first time, some five years ago. It was, at that moment, on the very cusp of decay. But decay, I have since discovered, takes far too long. I don't want to drift away, I want to splatter.

I met him in the local shop one day at the height of it all.

'How's your mamma, Felix, and haven't you grown?' and he turned to his friends.

'Stupid old bat,' he said. Making up was very sweet, and his tears tasted hot as needles.

ACKNOWLEDGMENTS

'Luck Be a Lady' first appeared in the Summer Fiction series in *The Irish Times,* July 1990; 'The Portable Virgin' was first published in *Revenge* (Virago, 1990), edited by Kate Saunders. Both of these stories, along with 'The House of the Architect's Love Story,' 'Men and Angels,' '(She Owns) Every Thing,' 'Indifference,' 'Historical Letters,' 'Revenge,' 'What Are Cicadas?' and 'Mr Snip Snip Snip,' first appeared in *The Portable Virgin* (Secker & Warburg, 1991). 'Seascape' and 'Felix' were first published in *First Fictions: Introduction 10* (Faber and Faber, 1989).

Thanks to Mary and Bernard Loughlin, the Tyrone Guthrie Centre, Annaghmakerrig, where many of these earlier stories were written.

The rest of the stories in this collection were first published in *Taking Pictures* (Jonathan Cape, 2008). 'Pale Hands I Loved, Besides the Shalimar' first appeared in *The Paris Review;* 'Pillow' was first published in *Picador New Writing: 11* (Picador, 2002), edited by Colm Tóibín and Andrew O'Hagan; 'In the Bed Department, 'Nathalie,' 'Taking Pictures,' and 'Della' first appeared in *The New Yorker;* 'Little Sister' first appeared in *Granta;* 'The Bad Sex Weekend' first appeared in *The Dublin Weekend;* 'Honey' first appeared in *The Irish Times* – it was written for, and won, the Davy Byrnes Irish Writing Award in the Bloomsday centenary; 'Green' first appeared in *The Literary Review* (Radio 4); 'Shaft' first appeared in *Granta 85* (Radio 4); 'Yesterday's Weather' was first published in *Irish Stories 06;* 'What You Want' first appeared in *Prospect,* March 2008 (Radio 3); 'Here's To Love' first appeared in *The Guardian*'s Christmas edition, December 2007; 'Caravan' first appeared in *The Guardian,* October 2007; 'Until The Girl Died' first appeared on RTE Radio; 'Cruise' first appeared on Radio 4.

Thanks to Bill Buford and Deborah Treisman, Brigid Hughes, Ian Jack and Matt Weiland, David Marcus, Brendan Barrington, Colm Tóibín and Andrew O'Hagan, who published and commented on the original texts. Thanks also to Caroline Walsh, Tobias Hill, and A. L. Kennedy, who adjudicated the Davy Byrne Award, and to Duncan Minshull, Heather Larmour, Kevin Reynolds, and Kathryn Brennan, who commissioned and directed the work for radio. 'Until the Girl Died' was written for the voice of actress Eleanor Methven.

Thanks to Mary Chamberlain who braved my punctuation for the final copy-edit, and to Lucy Luck who worked to place these stories as they were written. Thanks, as ever, to Gill Coleridge and Melanie Jackson, and to my editors Robin Robertson and Amy Hundley.